A SCALLOP SHORES NOVEL

Always My Hero

Jennifer DeCuir

Published by
Crimson Romance
an imprint of F+W Media, Inc.
10151 Carver Road, Suite 200
Blue Ash, OH 45242. U.S.A.
www.crimsonromance.com

ISBN 10: 1-4405-9045-1
ISBN 13: 978-1-4405-9045-0
eISBN 10: 1-4405-9046-X
eISBN 13: 978-1-4405-9046-7

To my readers,
Thank you so much for taking a chance on my Scallop Shores series.
This town is near and dear to my heart, as it is based on my own
hometown. Every time I write a new book, it's like revisiting fond
memories. So grab a drink, sit down, and enjoy your visit to a very
special town. Welcome to Scallop Shores. We hope you come back soon.

Chapter 1

New Year's Eve. It was the perfect date for a wedding. It was all about new beginnings. Ten … nine … eight … Out with the old. Seven … six … five … Starting the next chapter of their lives. Four … three … looking toward the future—together. Two … one …

"Happy New Year!" Bree had edged toward the outskirts of the dance floor while everyone counted down but not quickly enough. A large hand snaked around her waist and pulled her up against a very hard chest. She recognized the cologne she'd been secretly sniffing throughout the night. Feeling her blush right down to her toes, she looked up at the man holding her against him.

"Oh no you don't. I see you sneaking away. They paired us up for a reason. It's only right that we ring in the New Year with a kiss." Foster Duncan, groomsman and the head chef of this restaurant hosting their friends' wedding reception, grinned down at her. She doubted any woman in their right mind could say no when he flashed those sexy dimples.

"You know full well that we're the only two people in the wedding party without significant others." Rising to her toes, she gave him a quick peck then slipped out of his arms.

Yeah, she was crazy for turning down a proper kiss with probably the most handsome man in the room. Her heart tripped in her chest as she considered changing her mind. He was right there. She just had to walk back into his arms. Pausing, she chewed at her bottom lip. Nope. Couldn't do it.

He gave her a long, considering look from under his sinfully dark brows. Bree stood her ground, resisting the urge to run for cover in the ladies' room. After a moment, Foster raised his champagne flute, downed the contents and gave her a little wave, drifting into the crowd. She was such a ninny!

"I know I've already told you this, but you really do look lovely tonight." Bree's mother, Lyssa, murmured as she approached from behind. Then she kissed her oldest child on the temple.

Distracted, Bree patted her normally plain brown hair. She was amazed to find not a single curl out of place nearly twelve hours after the town hairdresser, Kayla, of Kayla's Kut and Kurl, had transformed her into a Grecian goddess. The soft velvet gown of cranberry did wonders for her coloring. She stood up taller. She almost felt beautiful.

"Your brothers have reached their limits. I need to get them home." Her mom gestured to a table in the corner where three little boys had pushed their plates of wedding cake to the center of the table so they could rest their heads on the white linen. They had been so excited to be invited to such a grown up event.

"Of course. I'll help you get them home and tucked in. Let me get my purse and say goodbye to Cady and Burke."

"No, dear. I won't hear of it. You stay and enjoy yourself. This is their special moment and you are a big part of that."

Lyssa pulled her daughter in for a hug, hanging on a second longer than necessary. Gripping Bree by the shoulders, she studied her, almost as though she were looking for something.

"Mom?"

"It's a new year, sweetheart. Anything can happen if you want it bad enough."

"Mmm hmm, like my own happily ever after?"

"And why not? You are an amazing woman, Bree Adams. You deserve to find your own happiness. Put yourself first, for once in your life. Stop thinking about what might have been." Her mother gave her one of those looks that only a mother could.

Bree kissed her mother goodbye, watching as the woman collected her three sleepy boys and herded them toward the restaurant exit. If she only knew the whole truth. Oh, she'd put herself first once, when she was young and foolish. The tragic results of which she'd used to punish herself every day for the last thirteen years. It was exhausting, and it really had to stop. The only man she'd ever imagined a happy ever after with had moved on a long time ago. It was time she did as well.

"It's my wedding day, Bree—dance with me!"

Breathtaking in a simple sheath of white silk with just a touch of lace at the edges, Cady grasped Bree's hands and twirled her around. They laughed until they were out of breath. Seeking out an empty table, they sank onto the tulle-wrapped chairs. Cady slipped her feet out of her three-inch heels, wiggling her toes before propping them up on another chair. Bree grinned, toeing off her own cranberry-dyed shoes and jockeying for room on the same chair.

"I know I gave my mom a hard time about all this froo-froo stuff," Cady picked at a stiff satin bow on the back of her chair, "but it really is gorgeous. Mother knows best, huh?"

"It was so nice of Foster's parents to close down for a night so we could have your wedding here."

Bree looked around at the restaurant she had frequented with her own mom since she was a little girl. The Lobster Pot was the best place in Scallop Shores to get great seafood. The views were phenomenal. But for tonight the casual atmosphere was transformed beneath rented linens, tiny white lights and fancy flower arrangements. It would be fun to come back on a normal visit and remember the restaurant decked out as it was now for Cady's wedding.

The friends leaned back, giggling as they watched a mixed-age group struggling their way through the Macarena.

"What's your New Year's resolution, Bree? I don't know mine. I have everything I could possibly want."

"Oh, I can't say it out loud."

"No, honey. You're thinking of a wish on a star. If you tell someone what that is, it won't come true." Cady gave her foot a little kick. "Tell me."

"I want what you have. I want my own happily ever after. I want my forever to start now." She blinked. That had been a lot easier to say out loud than she'd thought. Maybe all that champagne had loosened her tongue.

"Atta girl. Go get it!"

"Oh, Mrs. Sanders? Your presence is requested upstairs. There is a bubbling hot tub with our names on it. And a huge four-poster bed that I might let you nap in … after."

Burke had undone the collar and the first couple of buttons of his starched tux shirt, his bow tie hanging rakishly from his neck. He reached a hand down and pulled his wife to her feet, winking at Bree.

"I'm sorry, Bree. Time to fulfill my wifely duties." Cady chuckled as she slipped back into her shoes.

She watched the two of them go, eyes locked, hands linked, hip to hip. To Burke and Cady, the still-crowded restaurant ceased to exist. Bree knew by the way they were looking at each other that they had already begun to make love. Her sigh was long and deep.

Standing up, Bree stepped back into her heels. She retrieved her wrap from her seat at the head table and slid it across her shoulders. Time for some air and a little quiet reflection. She smiled and nodded at the wedding guests who called to her as she made her way to the restaurant's entertaining deck.

Stepping through the door, she marveled at the thousands of tiny white lights strung up along the railing. Whether they were leftover from Christmas or placed specifically for the wedding, it didn't matter. The effect was still magical. In the summer months, live bands would play on the small stage set up in the corner of the deck. The view was stunning, the crowds coming for the great food and staying for the spectacular sunsets over the Atlantic Ocean.

She'd expected to be alone on this frigid winter evening, so she was surprised to find one of the Adirondack chairs occupied. Foster had propped his feet up on the deck railing. The jacket to his stylish black tux was MIA, the sleeves of his white dress shirt rolled up, dark hair dusting his forearms. Taking a long pull of the beer he seemed to have traded for the champagne he'd been drinking earlier, he offered her a slow grin as she approached.

"It was a beautiful wedding." She lowered herself into the chair beside him.

"They're happy together."

Butterflies swarming in her belly, Bree knew what she had to do. She gripped the arms of the Adirondack and hoped it was too dark to see her white knuckles.

"So everyone has been asking what my New Year's resolution is." She felt like she was babbling. Foster still hadn't given her his full attention.

"May I?" She held a hand out for his beer.

He turned to her, his eyes narrowed slightly. He was trying to figure her out. She gripped the bottle of beer and pulled it easily from his grasp. Taking a big swallow, she swiped the back of her hand across her lips before handing it back to Foster. Now or never.

"Anyway, I resolve to take more chances this year. To put myself first and go after my own happiness." Her jaw jutted out just the tiniest bit.

"I thought books made you happy." His voice threaded with challenge, she knew she now had his undivided attention.

"Of course books make me happy. But they aren't everything. I need more." Being the town librarian shouldn't define her. Only perhaps it had begun to. Her mouth had become dry as dust, but she didn't want to ask for another sip of his beer.

Foster waited. He wasn't going to make this easy for her. Nor should he. Bree pinned on a brittle smile. She could do this.

"I thought maybe we could go out some time, you and me."

"Maybe?" Those dimples. That grin, teasing.

"Definitely. On a date."

"I've got to say, I'm used to being the one asking."

A hot flush flooded her with embarrassment. He thought her too forward. This was a disaster. Her breath hitching in her chest, she gave him a small smile and started to rise. Foster reached out a hand and clasped her wrist.

"You didn't let me finish. I was only going to say that you beat me to it."

"I … you were going to ask me?"

"I meant to, a long time ago. I should have. It's just … you've always got your head stuck in a book. Like you're trying to keep people at arm's length."

That was exactly what she'd been trying to do. And now that she realized how successful she'd been, she was ashamed.

"Well, this is a new year and I'm trying out a new me. And the new me says no more hiding behind books."

"Nice to meet you, New Bree. Welcome to Scallop Shores. I think you're going to like it here."

The butterflies in her stomach had changed their pattern. No longer nervous, they were excited to start a new phase of her life. She was through punishing herself for the past. It was time to look to the future.

• • •

"I would have thought you'd have packed a lot more? Where are all your things? You only brought enough for a quick visit."

Anne Pettridge, Ryan's mother, puttered about her small kitchen, fixing a quick meal of sandwiches and soup. Her worried eyes flitted from Ryan to her grandson, Wesley, and back again. Ryan stretched his long legs out beneath the battered kitchen table and looked around the room he hadn't seen in over ten years. Same wallpaper covered in little teakettles. Same yellow appliances that were probably older than he was. Same hand carved wooden clock on the wall, in the shape of an owl.

"I keep telling you, Ma, we're only here to help you and Dad get back on your feet. My work gave me a leave of absence to help out after Dad's stroke. Wes can finish out the school year here, but come summer, we'll go back home."

Her pinched expression said without words how *this* was his home. He was welcome to stay as long as he wanted. He'd come home to run the family business, a hardware store, handed down for several generations. It was his to do with as he pleased.

Wesley sat quietly at his end of the table, only eight years old and working his way through the fifth Harry Potter book for the second time. He gave his grandmother a shy smile as she set the grilled cheese sandwich and tomato soup down in front of him. All but strangers they were, and Ryan only had himself to blame.

"So grown up. He looks just like you did at this age, sweetheart." She brushed a lock of hair away from Wesley's blue, plastic-rimmed glasses.

He supposed he could see some similarities. Wesley had the same strong chin, the same stubborn cowlick at the back of his head, the same feet that seemed too huge for his skinny body. But he had his mother's bright blue eyes and golden hair. The rest of him? Wesley was definitely his own person. Ryan's smile was tight as he watched his son tune out his surroundings, preferring the world he could escape to in his books.

When Ryan was his age, he was rarely without some sort of ball in his hands. Or he was knee deep in chores, paying for whatever damage he'd caused by tossing one of those balls around.

"By the time you were his age, you'd broken how many windows? And my reproduction Tiffany lamp in the family room.' Anne laughed, even if her sigh sounded a bit wistful.

Note to self, he thought. *Buy Ma a new Tiffany lamp for Christmas.*

"Hey, I worked off my debt. That entire weekend I had to clear out the garage? Or the time I had to stain the deck while Dad put up that hammock on the lawn and drank lemonade?"

"You broke windows?" Blinking owlishly, Wesley stared with wide eyes from his dad to his grandmother. "Why would you do that?"

"Well, not on purpose, buddy. It was all in fun. Tossing a baseball around." Ryan shrugged.

"I believe my lamp was destroyed with a basketball."

"Yeah, that's right. It was winter. Couldn't play out on the snow covered driveway."

As one, they all looked out the window at the new fallen snow. He'd taken Wesley up to Big Bear a few times, but snow was still a pretty rare sight for a kid born and raised in sunny Southern California.

"How about we bundle up and go build us a snowman?" He leaned over and ruffled his son's hair.

"Nah. I'm good. If I keep at it, I can finish this book by tonight." Wesley returned his attention to the book cracked open beside his plate and bowl.

"It's the funniest thing, but you know who he reminds me of?" Anne tapped a finger to her temple.

Don't say it. Please don't say it.

"Bree Adams. Remember her? Always more interested in reading back when you two were in high school. Guess it makes sense that she ended up running the children's library here in town."

"No, that can't be right. Bree was going to be a teacher. I remember she was going to a teaching college up north."

"Haven't you kept in touch with her, sweetheart? She only went there for a semester. Then her stepfather was diagnosed with cancer. She came home to help her mom with the boys. I don't know how she ended up getting her degree, but she's been here pretty much all along."

Keeping in touch with Bree would have meant reopening a painful wound every time they talked. For his own sanity, Ryan had made it a point to tune out whenever his mother had tried to fill him in on town gossip during their weekly phone conversations while he was in California.

"Have you kept in touch with anyone in town? You really ought to take a drive around. I know a lot of folks who would be happy to see you."

Ryan bit the inside of his cheek, trying to keep the grimace off his face. His mom didn't get it. She'd never understood why he didn't come back home to visit, flying his parents out to California instead. He took a giant bite of his sandwich, giving himself time to brood as he chewed.

Scallop Shores was a tight community. They banded together when needed. They helped each other out. They celebrated victories as a town. When he'd taken the Wildcat football team to the state championships, it might as well have been a national holiday. Businesses closed down so that the townsfolk could attend the game up in Augusta. And when they'd won, Ryan had been lauded a hometown hero.

When he'd been accepted on a football scholarship to UCLA, he couldn't go anywhere without a slap on the back, well wishes, and lots of "We're so proud of you, son." He had to admit that it was a pretty heady feeling. That last summer before college was the best of his life.

And then he'd failed them. In one day, one freak accident, he'd blown his chances of a career in pro football. Oh, the people of Scallop Shores were too polite to say anything. They had put him up on a pedestal, and there he would stay. Instead of coming home a champ, he was coming home a chump. Well, an accountant, but really, for someone who was supposed to be the town football hero, what was the difference?

"I'll take Wes around tomorrow, show him my old stomping grounds."

Wesley, the one thing in his adult life that he was supremely proud of. Maybe folks would be so distracted by his son that no one would want to rehash his glory days.

Chapter 2

It couldn't have been more than fifteen degrees as Bree and Foster shuffled down the deserted business district in Port Kitt. Her breath came out in great plumes of icy vapor and she could no longer feel her nose. She'd dressed for a dinner date, not the outdoors, and pantyhose did nothing for the winter chill. Her feet and legs were screaming at her.

They had eaten at Molly Malone's, and as it was still early in the evening, decided to do a little window shopping. Hugging her arms around her middle, Bree stamped her feet while they paused in front of an art studio to study the portrait in the window.

"Here, let me help."

Foster pulled off one of his gloves and one of her mittens. Wrapping her hand in his, he stuffed them both inside his coat pocket. It was a sweet gesture and she smiled up at him shyly. He returned the smile, those deep divots in his cheeks popping out in stark relief against his smooth skin. Bree waited. His thumb pressed a rhythmic circle into her palm. She should be feeling a bit breathless by now, right? Maybe it was just the bitter January night.

"Thanks, but I really think it's just too cold to be out and about tonight. How about we head back to my place for some hot cocoa?"

"Sounds good to me." He gave her hand a squeeze.

Too late, Bree worried that she might be giving Foster the wrong message. She hoped he understood cocoa meant cocoa. It wasn't code for "please spend the night and see how I look wearing your shirt as I cook breakfast in the morning."

On the way back to her place, she silently applauded the genius who invented heated car seats. Oh, happy bottom! She'd assumed that Foster's parents were pretty well off, having such a successful restaurant in the harbor. But these luxurious leather seats and the satellite radio station tuned to soft jazz, not to mention the seat warmers and other fancy gadgets in this pricey hybrid, told her Foster wasn't doing too bad for himself, either.

They were both silent during the twenty minute drive, and though that could have been construed as a little awkward, Bree was relieved to have a moment to herself to reflect. She leaned her head back against the headrest and tried to think positively.

She had been a busy beaver that week following the wedding, and should be patting herself on the back. It looked like fate was giving her a little nudge out of the starting gate. Just for kicks, she had stopped to check out the community bulletin board on her way in for her morning coffee at Cady's Dream on Monday.

The first step toward a happy ever after was to get out of her mother's house and start living her own life, in her own place. Ever since her stepfather had died, Bree had been more of a second parent to her little brothers than a sister. She told herself she was needed. But it was really an excuse to keep from dealing with her own issues. Sam, Perry, and Theo kept her so busy she barely had time to dwell on the pain she was hiding.

There was an ad for a duplex not too far from the library. Fully furnished and for less than she was paying her mother for the room she'd lived in since she was born. She checked it out on her lunch break and had signed the lease and received the keys by the end of the day.

Rather than get all melancholy over her daughter's decision to move out of the house, Lyssa was thrilled for her. Perhaps a little too thrilled, when she boxed up all of Bree's clothes, knickknacks, and personal belongings while she was at work the next day. They each took turns dropping a few boxes off at a time, during the day. Bree had the utilities switched over and spent her first night in her new place Thursday evening.

It was a lot quieter than she was used to. No little brothers running around like maniacs, body slamming each other off the walls and using every surface of the house as their own private jungle gym. The first night in her new place, she couldn't sit still. Pouring herself a glass of wine, she walked from room to room, touching a couch cushion, the toaster oven, a roll top desk in the study, the carved wooden bedpost … "Mine," she said with every caress. It was a great feeling.

Bree had been looking forward to her date with Foster on Saturday night. She was still riding the high she'd gotten from having the nerve to ask. She honestly couldn't remember the last time she'd been on a date and was abysmally aware that her wardrobe showed that. Just one more thing to add to her to-do list of what she'd need as she started her new life. Shopping for clothes and shoes was not her idea of a good time, but this was a year for changes. She'd find a way to make it fun.

He'd brought her flowers, held the door for her, and been incredibly attentive all evening. But as the night wore on, Bree waited for that connection, the spark that told her he was "the one." She wanted to eagerly await the good night kiss on her doorstep. She wanted to feel … something. But the only time her heart started racing was from nerves and embarrassment, not heat and passion.

Foster was a great guy and she hoped he found the perfect woman to make him happy. All the same, she was disappointed, frustrated, and a little scared that she would have to put herself out there again in order to find her Mr. Right. Worried she hadn't given the guy enough of a chance, she glanced over at him.

He flashed her those wicked dimples and she smiled back at him. Without saying a word, he reached over the console and squeezed her knee. Nope. Nothing. Oh dear Lord, what if she was broken? If a sexy guy like Foster couldn't get her hot and bothered, who could?

"Looks like you have a new neighbor." Foster pointed as he pulled into the snowy driveway.

"Who on Earth would choose to haul stuff around at this hour?" Bree didn't wait for Foster to come around to her side. She opened the car door and headed for the stranger whose face was hidden behind a huge box.

"Excuse me. Can we help you?" Bree slipped her mittens off and stuffed them in her coat pockets, so she could get a better grip on the cardboard boxes.

She reached out and placed her hands on the box her new neighbor was carrying up to the porch. Her chilled fingers made contact with the stranger's, the electric current of awareness causing her to gasp. She hadn't felt that kind of reaction since ...

"I'm almost done here. But if you really want to help, there are a couple of boxes left on the tailgate." He shifted the box to the side to peer around the edge. "I appreciate the ... Bree? Bree Adams?"

Even with a ski cap covering his hair and a thick wool scarf muffling his words, she recognized those soulful brown eyes, that gravelly voice. No, no, no. Not him. Anyone but him. Not here. This was her new sanctuary. Her new start. No old mistakes allowed. Realizing she still had her hands around the box he was carrying, Bree let go and took a few steps back.

Too late, she remembered the snowy edges to the driveway and the fact that she wore heels and hose. She squealed as snow filled her shoes, the icy sensation startling her so much that she lost her balance, her arms pinwheeling uncontrollably. She landed on her butt with a less-than-ladylike grunt, hoping she hadn't flashed her white granny panties in the process.

"Whoa, sweetheart, are you all right?" Foster reached down and pulled her upright, brushing the snow from her wool coat and skirt.

Putting an arm around her and pulling her against his side, he acknowledged Bree's new neighbor.

"Hey, there's a familiar face. Ryan Pettridge, hometown hero. Good to see you again. Dude, I am so sorry about your dad."

Bree's face heated. She'd completely forgotten that his father had suffered a stroke. Of course he'd come home. He was probably going to run the hardware store for his parents now.

"Thanks. He's a stubborn cuss, my old man. I'm sure he's going to be just fine. But yeah, I'm helping out for now." He gave Bree a long look. "You okay? I didn't mean to surprise you like that."

"Oh, don't mind me. I'm just a klutz. Let's help you get those boxes inside." She shifted her gaze to his left shoulder, a safe spot to focus on. Those eyes of his only caused her to go weak in the knees.

"No way. You two should head on home. I'm not even staying tonight. Got another load tomorrow. It was good seeing both you again."

Before she could correct his assumption that she and Foster were a couple and explain that she lived in the other half of the duplex alone, Ryan had already turned around and scuffed up the stairs to his front door. Her toes on fire, she lurched toward her apartment.

"Talk about a blast from the past, huh? I remember now. You're the reason Ryan was able to get that scholarship to UCLA. You tutored his lazy butt in English."

"And math and history."

"The guy owes you big time, then." Foster held the door open for her, kicking the snow off his shoes before he stepped in after her, shedding his coat and shoes and heading into the living room before she could feign a headache and get out of the rest of the date. Cocoa it was, then.

Bree took her time hanging up her coat in the hall closet, turning Foster's last sentence over and over in her head. The way she saw it, she owed Ryan. She owed him more than she could ever repay in a lifetime. Because of her, Ryan would never get to know the child they had conceived together.

• • •

The shatter of glass as a waitress accidentally tipped her tray and sent several beer mugs sliding to the floor shook Ryan out of his reverie. He peered through the cigarette haze toward the bar, where his buddy, Luke, was buying the next round. It was pretty crowded for a Sunday night. Or that was his assumption, seeing as Ryan hadn't been out to a bar on a Sunday night, or any other night, since before Wesley was born.

"Glad you could make it out tonight." Luke handed him a Sam Adams and sat down at the water-ring stained table.

"My mother put you up to this, didn't she?"

"I was going to look you up. No joke."

"Christ, did she actually go down to the station?" Ryan grimaced, already knowing the answer.

"She brought chocolate chip cookies. Your mom has every firefighter in Scallop Shores wrapped around her finger." Luke smiled, unashamed.

"Man, I don't know if I can get used to...that scruff." He ran a hand over his own chin to signify the ginger beard his old friend from high school now sported.

"Hey, comes in handy this time of year." Luke grinned.

"A big hit with the ladies, too, no doubt."

"Huh. Wouldn't know. I'm too busy to deal with the female set."

While his friend looked a lot different, it was clear Luke was still painfully shy around women. Shelving the topic, so as not to embarrass the guy, Ryan took a swig of beer and people watched for a few moments.

"Can you believe that the last time I was in town, I couldn't even drink legally? This is the first time I've actually seen the inside of Smitty's."

"You've been hiding out a long time."

"I have not been hiding." Ryan turned his head to the side and muttered, " … much."

"Well, you're back now. We ought to get the guys together for hockey out on Perkins pond."

"Who still lives in town?"

The idea of reconnecting with his former teammates, aside from Luke, should have felt good. Except that his mind automatically wondered whether the guys would judge him for abandoning football, the town, and all his friends for so long. He deserved to be judged. He'd been a weenie. Still, there had been a time when they were as close as brothers and Ryan had to admit that he missed out on seeing what they'd done with their lives.

"Jamie teaches high school science. Ironic, huh? Kid voted Most-Likely-To-Blow-Up-The-Chem-Lab now has his own classroom. Doyle works for the town manager. I want to give him shit over the fact that they make him wear a tie, when he looks more like he belongs in a biker gang, with all those crazy tats of his. But he'd probably kick my ass.

"Scott lives the next town over. We call him the 'Sperminator'. Would you believe he has two sets of twins? Freaky, huh? 'Course he's also a little whipped, so we'd have to ask his wife for permission in order to snag him for a game.

"Chase is on the police force. He and Amanda had a little boy last year. Oh and then there's Foster. You probably remember he went off to some fancy-schmancy culinary school? Could have worked in any of the ritzier restaurants in the country, but he manages his parents' restaurant now."

Foster. Yeah, he'd run into that particular teammate last night. His new neighbor. Ryan shoved a hand through his hair and tried to keep the scowl off his face.

It wasn't like he had anyone to blame but himself. He'd left town. He'd chosen Haley because it was the right thing to do. Bree had every right to move on with her life, to find a husband and settle down. And if he had any say in who she ended up with, he had to admit Foster Duncan would have been on the short list. He was a standup guy. And a damned lucky one, at that.

"You see Bree yet?"

Ryan slammed his knee on the underside of the table. This, in turn, jostled the beer bottles and had both men scrambling to grab their own before they tipped over. Luke raised the bottle to his lips and watched his friend, a curious smile playing at the corners of his mouth.

"I'm gonna take that as a yes."

"She was just a friend. Just my tutor."

"Uh huh. You keep telling yourself that." Luke took another sip and continued to watch him.

"I don't know what you're getting at." He'd been so careful not to let anyone know exactly how he'd felt about Bree. He had a girlfriend, for crying out loud! Only a dick would have flaunted that in front of her.

"Ever heard the expression 'wear your heart on your sleeve'? That was you, buddy."

"No, that's bullshit. If Haley knew I liked Bree, she would have said something. She would have been pissed."

"Perhaps. She would have made Bree's life a living hell in high school. But look at it this way, she knew she'd won. She had what she wanted and screw everyone else." Luke's shrug looked almost like an apology.

"Tell me how you really feel," Ryan drawled.

It wasn't like his friend was making up stories. Haley was the classic Mean Girl in high school. But she'd had her good points too. She'd been his biggest supporter. When his coach had insisted he hire a tutor or lose all chance of his free ride to UCLA, Haley had done the legwork and brought him Bree. She wanted the best for him and she went out of her way to help him get it.

"I'm sorry you guys didn't work out. Really I am. Haley wasn't my favorite person in the world, but she made you happy."

Or so he'd led everyone to believe. Ryan sighed, raising his arms above his head in a lazy stretch.

"Hey, I wish her well, you know?"

"You two still talk? She ever make it as an actress out there in LaLa land, like she wanted? I haven't seen her on the big screen and I don't really watch much TV. She keep tabs on her little boy?"

"Haven't heard from her in years. Once she signed those papers, Wes and I ceased to exist." He shrugged. No big deal. "Let's just say motherhood isn't Haley's strong suit."

"That's gotta be rough on Wes. A boy needs his mother."

"We're doing just fine on our own." More like they were doing a good job faking it for the rest of the world.

"I'm sure he'll make lots of friends, now that you're home. I think one of Bree's little brothers is in Wesley's school."

Bree again. There were reminders of her everywhere.

"See, the thing is, I'm not planning to stay in Scallop Shores. I didn't come home to take over the store for my dad." Ryan squirmed in his chair. "I'm going to try to convince them to sell it."

A silence fell over the little table and Ryan could only assume it was as awkward for Luke as it was for him. He flagged down a waitress and ordered another round of Sam Adams, adding in nachos since he'd forgotten to eat dinner.

"I thought you got your own place?"

"Yeah, but the lease is month to month. Dad's got all these visiting nurses popping in. They have a hospital bed set up in the living room. Ma turned my bedroom into a sewing room. Wes and I have been sleeping on a futon. I think she's happy to have us close … but not too close, you know what I mean?"

"How's he doing, your dad?" Luke nodded as the waitress set a beer in front of each of them and slid a plate of loaded nachos toward the center of the table.

"The idea is to get him moving again. He lost all mobility on one side. Even his speech was affected. It kills me that I can't understand him when he tries to talk. I think Wes is scared of him."

"I'm sorry, Ry. Your dad was always such a tough son of a gun."

"We'll get him up and out of bed again. Hopefully able to go fishing and hunting with his buddies. But he'll never be able to run that hardware store again," he continued, feeling as though an explanation was in order. "I'm doing this for them. Sell the store. Get top dollar and set my parents up for a sweet retirement."

"You think they'll go for it?"

"I think Dad's stroke was a wakeup call and they need to realize that instead of thinking day to day, they need to plan for the future. And the future isn't going to involve handing the hardware store down to me just because it's what they want."

"And what do you want?"

"I just told you. I want to sell the hardware store." Ryan shook his head and pulled at a cheesy tortilla chip, dislodging an olive and some Pico de Gallo.

"That's what you want for your parents. What do you want for you? Got someone special waiting for you back in sunny California?"

"Well, no. No girlfriend. Just a job. Waiting for me, that is. They've given me a six-month hiatus. I was lucky that they'd hold my position that long."

Okay, it was hard to make a job as an accountant at a worker's comp insurance company sound exciting. Because it wasn't. But it paid the bills and put food on the table. He couldn't really ask for more than that, right? He had a son to raise. He no longer had time to chase foolish dreams.

"So you want to get back to your job. Crunch some numbers. Sit at a desk."

"Yeah, that's exactly what I want. Not all of us can be firefighters, policemen, and gourmet chefs. Some of us are happy playing with numbers and making sure everything adds up."

He wasn't fooling either of them. So what if he didn't know what he wanted? He had the rest of his life to figure that out. He had some regrets. Didn't everyone? But he also had Wesley and he was going to do right by his son. As soon as he could figure out a way to connect with the boy who felt more like a stranger than his own flesh and blood.

Chapter 3

Standing in front of her closet in her rubber ducky pajamas, tooth-brush hanging out of her mouth, Bree contemplated her choices. Long boring black peasant skirt with equally boring black cardigan, or long boring brown peasant skirt with washed out yellow cardigan. She worked with kids all day. They'd probably think it a hoot if she were to show up in her jammies.

She almost choked on her toothbrush when someone knocked on the front door. Who would be looking for her at this hour? The sun was barely up. Hurrying out of her bedroom and down the hall, Bree yanked open the door. Then wished she hadn't.

"Hey, is Foster up yet? I'm hoping he has an extra shovel. I figure if we work together we can get this stuff cleared in no time." Ryan stamped his feet on her welcome mat, blowing on his bare knuckles as he awkwardly looked anywhere but at her.

Foster? Bree frowned, blinking. She wasn't doing so well keeping up with a conversation before her morning cup of coffee.

"I know, it's stupid, right? My family owns the town hardware store. You'd think I would have a ton of shovels lying around. I meant to snag one out of my parents' garage, but I forgot."

"He's not ... " *Note to self. Don't try to talk when you have a toothbrush in your mouth.* With a disgusted shake of her head, Bree tossed the toothbrush] on the entryway table and swallowed the foamy paste left in her mouth.

She realized she hadn't finished her sentence. What had she been about to say? *He's not here. He's not awake yet.* This truly was a pointless charade she was keeping up. It wasn't like it benefitted anyone.

Foster didn't live here. For that matter, she wasn't quite sure where he lived. It had to be close to the center of town, because she saw him run by the library nearly every morning during decent weather, his faithful yellow lab looking blissfully pleased to join him. Bree frowned. She'd never even asked him what his beautiful dog's name was.

"It's all right. Don't bother him. I'll get Wes to help me. Do you have a shovel we can borrow?"

"Wes?" Bree peered around Ryan, who took up her whole doorway with his six foot two inch frame. The guy was almost as wide as he was tall, when she counted in his massive shoulder span.

Her eyes widened. She must have missed the weather report yesterday. Several inches of new snowfall blanketed the ground. Though the sky was a steely gray, it seemed to be done for the time being. Not enough for life in Scallop Shores to grind to a halt, just enough to make a big mess.

"My little guy. He's eight." The pride in his voice was unmistakable.

Turning around quickly, so he couldn't see how this news affected her, Bree stuck her upper half into the hall closet. Pretending to search for the shovel, she sucked in a few shuddering breaths. Ryan had a son. Correction. Ryan and Haley had a son. It shouldn't have hurt as bad as it did. But a phantom pain gripped her by the uterus and shook it hard enough that she saw stars.

"I see it, Bree. To your right."

Ryan reached around her, brushing against her side and nearly tearing a sob from her aching throat at the contact. He grasped the handle of the plastic snow shovel and jiggled it to show she'd have to get out of the way for him to remove it from the crowded closet. Bree practically climbed into the narrow enclosure to avoid any chance that they'd touch again.

"Thanks. I'll get the cars cleared off as soon as I shovel out the driveway."

"Oh, you don't have to go to the trouble. I was planning to walk to work. It's just a couple of blocks." She stumbled from the closet, shutting the door.

"Well, Foster will need the car to get down into the harbor, right?"

For crying out loud, Foster again!

"No, he won't. Ryan, Foster doesn't live here. He probably won't be here ever again." Wincing, she fervently wished she could take back that last part.

"Hey, I'm sorry. Was it me? Oh, God, did you tell him about . . you know?" He looked miserable, resting a hand on her shoulder and squeezing.

"Seriously, Ryan? Could you be any more full of yourself?" Bree jerked out of his grasp, slamming the door that was letting in the freezing cold before hugging herself tightly.

"Just listen, all right? You saw Foster and me on a date. Our first date. And our last. Not that it's any of your business, but we just didn't hit it off. If you jumped to the wrong conclusion, that's not my fault." Okay, yeah it was. Kinda.

"I'm sorry. You're right. I shouldn't have brought up the past."

Amen to that! She bumped her shoulder against Ryan's, her smile contrite.

"You aren't full of yourself. I'm just really cranky and overdue for my first cup of coffee."

"Hey, I'm going to get started on the driveway. Wes is all by himself over there. Would it be all right if he came in and hung out while I clear off the snow? He doesn't need to get all soaked before his first day of school. Just turn on some cartoons or something. Do eight year olds still watch cartoons?"

"You're asking me? He's your kid." Panic zinged through her body at the thought of meeting Ryan's son. But now she was curious.

"I admit, it sounds weird. We just don't know each other as well as we could." He coughed into his fist, shuffling his feet awkwardly.

"Ah. Custody issues?"

She'd heard through the town grapevine that Ryan and Haley divorced, but must have blocked out the part about their having a child together. Wesley would have only been an infant at the time. Bree remembered feeling a little giddy, hoping Ryan would come back to Scallop Shores to lick his wounds. But the weeks of waiting turned into months and she eventually gave up. That had been years ago.

"What? No. Haley signed over her rights in the divorce. A baby didn't fit her lifestyle."

Typical. Bree would never have pictured the former head cheerleader and aspiring actress as the nurturing type. Still. She felt sad for the little boy growing up without a mother.

"Bring him over. I'll throw on some clothes and meet you in the living room."

"Thanks, Bree."

Ryan let himself out and Bree raced back to her room to throw on the drab brown and yellow ensemble. At least she wouldn't look like she was going to a funeral. She jogged into the bathroom, flipped her hair upside down and brushed it vigorously. Maybe she could give it a little fake bounce. Swiping on a neutral lipstick and blush, she hurried back out to the living room before her guests arrived.

"Bree, I'd like you to meet my son, Wesley." Ryan gave the little boy a push forward.

"As you wish." She giggled. "I'm sorry, an obscure book reference. I wouldn't expect you to understand that."

"*The Princess Bride* by William Goldman. I read it a few months ago. Except my name isn't spelled with a 't' in the middle, like his was. Think Wesley Crusher from *Star Trek, Next Generation* instead." Wesley pushed his glasses to sit further up on the bridge of his nose.

Bree cocked her head to the side, her smile widening as she touched her own glasses, having forgotten to put in her contacts in her rush to get dressed. It would appear they had a thing or two in common. The kid was a bookworm *and* a Trekkie.

If only she could get over the fact that he looked so much like his father. Not his coloring. That was all Haley. But still, there was no denying he was Ryan's son. God, it hurt to look at him and know what she'd lost.

"How about I make you some hot chocolate? I might even have some leftover candy canes from Christmas somewhere around here."

"Can I, Dad?"

"What the heck, sugar him up! Let his new teacher deal with it." Ryan chuckled as he ducked back out the door.

Bree watched as the eager expression on Wesley's face fell away, replaced by nervousness once they were alone together. She led the way into the kitchen and waved the boy over to the small table in the corner while she looked for the canister of cocoa. Poor kid. First day at a new school was rough enough, but being from Southern California, he probably couldn't see how they'd even still have school with all the snow on the ground.

"I bet you wish you could just stay outside and play all day, huh?"

"Nah. I'd rather get back to my book. Dad wouldn't even let me bring it here. Said I had to socialize."

"Oh, I hear you. To be able to curl up with a good book, tune out the real world, and dive on in to one that you have a hand in creating. That's way easier than taking a chance that the kids at your new school are going to like you."

She turned away to hide her grin when Wesley's jaw dropped. He clearly wasn't used to an adult being able to see inside his sensitive soul. Of course she understood him. She had *been* him.

By the time Ryan came back in from shoveling, Bree and Wesley were deep in a discussion about which would be better to visit, Narnia or Hogwarts. She looked up from her second cup of coffee to find her new neighbor studying them from the doorway. He looked like he was scared to join in the conversation, for fear he'd say the wrong thing.

"You need to warm up. Pick your poison—cocoa or coffee?" She stood up from the table and motioned for him to take a seat.

"I wouldn't say no to a cup of coffee, if it's not too much trouble." He smoothed a hand over the light scruff on his cheeks as he sat down in her vacated chair. Rubbing his hands together briskly, he sent her a warm smile that she felt down to the tips of her toes.

One would have thought the man's parents had spent a fortune on braces for him to end up with a winning grin like that. But Ryan never had to experience the awkwardness of braces as a teenager. He'd been blessed with naturally perfect, white teeth. Perfect teeth. Perfect body. Perfect everything. She turned away to fix that cup of coffee before she embarrassed herself.

"Dad, Bree works in the children's library. How cool is that? Can we stop by after school? Since I'm almost done with the Harry Potter series, she has a bunch of suggestions for me. And I'll need my own library card, of course."

"I don't see why not, bud." Ryan caught her eye over the top of his son's head, as she set his steaming mug in front of him. The tender look on his face reminded her of stolen moments from long ago.

She tried to ignore the thrill from being on the receiving end of his smile. He was distracting her. She was supposed to be looking for her happily ever after. Now she was pining for a man who'd already walked away from her once. Besides, if he learned her secret, he'd walk away from her for good.

. . .

The snowy weather would make the hardware store a busy destination today, but Ryan was grateful to have it to himself for the moment. He tossed the tangled key ring on the counter near the cash register and slumped onto the stool his dad kept out of sight.

He reached for his cup of dark roast. Though he'd already had one cup at home and another at Bree's place, habit had him steering his dad's pickup toward Logan's Bakery.

The bakery, which had been there as long as he could remember, had been replaced with a comic book store, of all things. Thank God the kid behind the counter was able to point him toward a new coffee shop, Cady's Dream. Though Ryan felt like a dumbass when he realized it was only two storefronts down from the family hardware store.

Scallop Shores remained largely unchanged since the last time he'd been home, probably going on ten years or so. Sure, if he drove around long enough, he'd find new housing developments and maybe a few new businesses. But it felt good to know that he could count on things being the same.

Something about seeing that old Civil War monument in the center of town took him back. He smiled to himself, remembering the time he and his teammates had dressed the statue in a Wildcats jersey after they'd won the homecoming game against the Rangers. The stone dude had rocked the look.

The bell jangled over the door as he walked into the hardware store for the first time in a decade. He'd hated having to put in his hours back then. How he'd wanted a job where he didn't have to work for his old man. Now he'd gladly clock in, if it meant his father was working alongside him. No matter how cluttered and stuffed the shelves were, without Bo Pettridge, the store just seemed a little too empty.

Time to get this day started. He perused the shelves beneath the front counter for something to write on. They were stuffed with register tape and a myriad of other items to make his dad's life easier—if he could find what he was looking for in all the junk. Ryan grabbed a notepad with a coffee stain on it and a worn stub of a pencil and settled down to make his daily to-do list. Haley had always made fun of him for planning out his day, claiming he couldn't pee unless he'd written it down so he could cross it off later.

Writing lists calmed him. Or maybe it was being able to cross off the items he'd accomplished. Probably both. At the top of the blank page he wrote: *Drop Wesley off at school.* Then he drew a thick line through it. Talk about a blast from the past. Scallop Shores Elementary was like a frickin' time capsule. The only thing that had changed was the roster of teachers. And Ryan wondered if there might have been one or two that were still there from when he was Wesley's age.

He had to give the kid props. Wesley hadn't cried or whined or bargained for another day or two before starting his new school. He'd put on a brave face, straightened his spine and even greeted his new principal with a handshake when they'd been introduced in the front office. Not that Ryan didn't have respect for authority, but he was again reminded of how different he and his son were.

That had his mind wandering back to earlier in the morning, when he'd first walked into Bree's kitchen. Ryan set down his pencil, cracked his knuckles and brooded. On the one hand, he was thrilled that Wesley had made such a strong connection to someone new in town. He hadn't seen the kid have such an animated conversation ... ever. Okay, so that was a very good thing.

But they were talking books. And he was so happy. And she got him. Bree understood Wesley and knew exactly how to draw him out of his little walled-up self. And that should be a good thing too. If it didn't make him feel so damned inadequate.

He took a sip from his paper cup and gagged at how fast the coffee had cooled. Slipping off the stool, he realized he hadn't even turned the heat on for the day. Only the front-end lights were on, too. And his dad would have his hide if he didn't put the Muzak on. *"I pay an arm and a leg for that damned thing, we're damned well gonna play it,"* the man used to rant when Ryan would forget to flip on the sleepy elevator music, when he opened the store every weekend morning while he was in high school.

Was there still such a service? He knew his dad used to pay a monthly subscription fee. Was the old man onto satellite radio, like the Sirius stations Ryan listened to on his daily commute back in California? Honestly, he couldn't remember his father ever listening to music at home, so he couldn't imagine him switching to CDs or an iPod, where he'd have to choose the music himself.

The bells over the door jingled just as Ryan was returning from the back office. A low rumble signaled the heater kicking on. He hurried up front to make sure his customer didn't need any help.

"Well, if it isn't the younger Pettridge. Your Ma told me how you'd be taking over the joint now. Hated like hell to take my business elsewhere when they were closed for a bit. How's your Pop?" Curtis Blaise lifted his worn ball cap in greeting and yanked it back down over his salt and pepper hair.

"Dad's doing well. He's frustrated that he can't do things for himself, and that's probably the best motivator he can have for getting better. If his poor nurses can stand him, we should be fine."

Curtis chuckled as he made his way down the plumbing aisle. He wouldn't need any help. This guy practically lived at the hardware store. Ryan went back to his list.

Contact a Realtor. This one was tricky. He'd been so busy getting him and Wesley settled, that he hadn't had time to sit down with his parents and broach the idea of selling the hardware store. All right, he hadn't said anything yet because he was a wimp. He knew what had to be done, what was the best thing for all of them, in the long run. But he also knew his parents had emotional ties to the store that would make it a lot harder for them to see what was best.

Another jingle, another customer. Ryan had his smile in place before he even looked up, but it took a little extra effort to keep it in place this time. Mr. Swanson, his old high school algebra teacher, waved from the door and hurried up to the register.

"What a sight for sore eyes! I knew you'd be home sooner or later. Good to see you, boy. Good to see you."

"How are you, Mr. Swanson? Still teaching?"

"Just retired last June, matter of fact. Probably be headed to points south by next winter. These old bones can't take the cold. They want a nice moist heat ... and golf." The older man laughed heartily.

Before Ryan could say anything else, another customer slipped into the hardware store. Vera Walker, a grizzled old woman and the town postmaster for as long as he could remember (on both parts), stomped up to the counter.

"Our State Champion returneth. 'Bout time you showed your face, kid. Got any shovels left? I may have accidentally run mine over with my car."

He skirted the counter and headed for a display of snow shovels, but not before Mr. Swanson slapped him on the back on his way by.

"Say, what kept you on the West Coast? You coaching football at some fancy private school out there?"

"Nope. Just crunching numbers."

"Pardon?"

"I'm an accountant."

His former teacher laughed outright at this.

"No offense, fella. It's just that your math skills were somewhat lacking when last I knew you."

"I guess I have a lot to thank Bree Adams for then. Remember, she helped me pass your class?"

"Good gracious, yes. If it weren't for her, you'd have been kicked off the team." Ryan's old teacher paid for his rock salt and ice scraper and waved jauntily on his way out.

Didn't look like he'd be keeping a low profile in town. These people didn't have enough to keep them busy so they rehashed bygones. And if he didn't want to join in, too bad. He was a part of Scallop Shores' history and if there was anything this town loved to celebrate, it was its history.

Get in, get out. They didn't need some poser sticking around and playing the role of town hero when he was really just a washed up has-been. Ryan greeted customers, reacquainted himself with his father's ancient cash register and tried not to flinch every time someone patted him on the back and reminisced about his high school accomplishments.

This wasn't supposed to be his lot in life. When Ryan had left town on a football scholarship, it was with the understanding that he was going places. He wasn't going to be like his dad, running the family hardware store just like his grandfather before him. He was going to be a star.

Walking in the door today had been like stepping back in time. Bo Pettridge had liked things just so, which meant every aisle held exactly the same tools, gadgets and doo-dads that they'd sold back when Ryan was in high school. He remembered what it had felt like to be so full of hope. That sharp thrill of excitement that came with not knowing quite what to expect from his new school or his new teammates. How long had it been since he'd looked forward to the future with such eager enthusiasm?

He didn't deserve their admiration. Why couldn't they understand that? He hadn't gone on to a dream job in the NFL, like everyone in town expected. Like he'd expected. He wasn't even coaching as a backup career. He was just an accountant. He had failed. And if they still hadn't figured that out, then maybe he could sell the hardware store and get out of town before they did.

Chapter 4

Two blocks. It was a two-block walk to the library from the duplex. Bree was a big girl. She had boots. She could trudge with the best of them. But Ryan had insisted on giving her a ride to work. And Wesley had sounded so eager to have her join them.

Of course it stood to reason that in the thirty seconds it took to scramble down from the cab of the pickup truck, she'd been spotted by no less than three coworkers. Wonderful. Fresh fodder for the gossip mill.

Frowning, she wondered what Foster would think when he heard she'd been seen driving around town with Ryan Pettridge. She'd deal with that later. She and Foster needed to talk. Or not. Did their "non-sparking" date warrant a phone call? Should she just leave it up to him? But she'd been the one to ask him out in the first place. Oh, good grief! This is why she didn't date. Etiquette she should know but didn't and entirely too much drama.

Bree stuffed her purse and insulated lunch bag into the bottom drawer of her desk. She sat down and removed her snow boots, trading them for a pair of slip-ons she kept at work. If she had a coat rack with a sweater to change into, she could be Mr. Rogers. She shuddered at the image.

"Bree, do you have a minute? We'd love you to sit in on the board meeting downstairs," Martha Bruce, the head librarian, called from the top of the stairs.

"Certainly. Can I make a pot of coffee or anything?"

Staff meetings she was used to. Board meetings were another thing. Bree wasn't involved in the budgetary concerns of running the library. She wasn't sure if she should be worried or excited. They could be offering her more responsibilities, a way of advancing her career. Or they could be calling her in to explain that, due to budgetary concerns, they were letting her go. Surely she wouldn't need to go before the *whole* board for that?

"It's already done, dear. Help yourself to a Danish while they are still there. Harold has already eaten three."

Wait. She always made the coffee for the staff meetings. Something was up. Bree wiped her palms on her skirt and hummed the *Jeopardy* theme song, her favorite relaxing tune, to herself. She gathered herself together to face the library board members.

"Good morning, Bree. Have a seat. Cheese Danish? I'm afraid the cherry ones are all gone." Board president Harold Macon swiped at his bushy mustache with a napkin.

"I ate earlier. Thanks."

Sitting in the empty chair across from Harold, she nodded a greeting to the other board members. There were six people seated around the oak conference table, not including herself. Martha busied herself at the back of the room, returning to place a cup of coffee on a saucer in front of Bree, before taking her own seat. Okay, now she knew something was going on.

"Thank you for joining us today. We know you have a lot to do. I'll get straight to the point." Harold placed his beefy palms against the surface of the table and faced the children's librarian.

"As you are more than aware of, given that you work on the upper floor of the building, our poor library needs a new roof."

Indeed, she had probably been the loudest complainer over that fact. Bree had been setting out buckets, every time it rained, for months. Try to keep a curious group of toddlers from playing in the water. Just try. Even now, after a good snowfall, once the sun came out and started melting it from the rooftops, she was scrambling to save her precious books from getting damaged.

"We're getting a new roof? That's fantastic!"

"No, Bree, we're only agreeing that we need a new roof. However there isn't enough money in the budget to afford one." Harold shrugged one shoulder, as though in apology.

"But then why … ?" They *had* called her here to fire her. She placed her palms on the conference table and swallowed hard.

"We could hold a fundraiser. When the town rallies together we can do anything. I could put together some other ideas. Maybe a dinner, a hundred dollars a seat? Foster Duncan's restaurant could cater it." Her mind filled quickly with different ways the board could raise money for the repairs. If she could just get them to see they had options, lots of options.

"What did I tell you? I knew we had the right person for the job." Martha smiled proudly from her seat beside Harold. She reached across the table and patted Bree's hand.

"We thank you for the ideas, Bree, but we've already come up with one that we hope will work well. It's quite clever and … very 'with the times,' I guess you could say. We invited you here to offer you the chance to spearhead this campaign."

"I'd be honored. Truly. Thank you so much." Breathless, she turned this way and that, making sure she'd thanked each board member personally, with a grateful smile and a nod.

"Now hold your horses. It's going to mean taking some time away from your work. Naturally, we'd find someone to cover your hours."

Bree nodded. Yes, yes. Planning took time and it was actually quite generous of the board to allow her to use work hours to complete it, instead of expecting her to fit it into her personal time. Though she had no problem with that, either. Whatever it took to raise money for a new library roof.

"And as you mentioned, you have the perfect contacts. Foster Duncan, Chase Eaton, perhaps. Oh, I'm sure you'll think of others. We'd just need … well, twelve, really. The only one we would insist on is Ryan Pettridge. We must have him on board."

"On the planning committee? Ryan?" She started to realize there was a large piece of the puzzle that she hadn't been given yet.

"What a great idea, Bree! I'm sure he'd be a huge help getting the other men to sign on." Martha clapped her hands together.

Everyone was smiling and nodding as though everything had been decided on. Bree was beginning to feel a bit like Alice in Wonderland. She looked around wildly, waiting for someone to clue her in. When everyone began to chat amongst themselves, Bree held up her hands and waved them around.

"Um, excuse me! Not to be rude or anything, but you seem to be under the impression that I have been filled in on exactly what my role in all this is."

Silence followed her outburst. Bree dropped her hands quickly into her lap, staring down at the table. This wasn't like her at all and now they were probably regretting handing over so much responsibility to a person who couldn't control her manners.

Martha's tinkling laugh rang out. "Good gracious, you're right! We never told you what you'd be doing. Harold?"

"Yes. Yes. The board came up with the idea to produce a calendar. It should be a hot seller. We could stock them in the chamber of commerce, in the beach businesses after Memorial Day, the police station, and the fire station, naturally."

"Naturally?" She still wasn't following. Or perhaps it was the crazy loud warning bells clanging inside her head that made it hard to focus on the details.

"You're such good friends with Cady Eaton that we assume you'll ask her brother to be one of the models."

"Ryan Pettridge can be any month you decide, but we insist he also be on the cover. He is our hometown hero, after all." Martha rubbed her hands together, the look on her wizened face making Bree slightly sick to her stomach.

"This calendar of male models—are we talking something that plays up their roles in the community? A police officer in uniform. A fireman in turnout gear. Something ... tasteful ...

right?" Belatedly, Bree remembered the feeling that Martha was trying to pull a fast one on her. Oh, crap!

She glanced at the closed door of the conference room, longing to be on the other side of it. Wishing she'd never been dragged into this meeting in the first place.

"We believe that wouldn't sell quite as many copies, you understand. Mind you, there are limits. This will be a family friendly calendar, after all. Uniforms would be an excellent idea. Minus their shirts." Harold coughed into his fist, his ears turning pink.

Good. Why should she be the only one uncomfortable about this idea?

"So I'm to round up twelve models, making certain they are all gorgeous and have a perfect set of abs?" She could barely get the words out, they were so embarrassing.

"That won't be too hard, will it?" Harold arched a fuzzy eyebrow that perfectly matched his fuzzy mustache.

"Of course not. I would guess, though, that if Chase Eaton is to be asked, then being single is not necessarily a prerequisite for appearing in the calendar?"

"We aren't asking you to start a dating service, Bree. Just make sure they're hot stuff." Martha winked.

Bree choked down her mortification. She may not want the job, but she sure as heck couldn't pass up this chance to show the board what she was capable of.

"Good. Good. It's settled then." Harold paused, placing his palms on the conference table as he watched her carefully. "Because if this is too difficult, we'll have to resort to other methods to obtain funds for the new roof."

Ouch. Message received.

"You've got the right person for the job. You won't be sorry. I'll give you the sexiest calendar New England has ever seen."

Bree reached for the last cheese Danish on the platter and stuffed it into her mouth before she could scream.

•••

How would Bree convince Ryan to pose for this calendar when even *she* didn't want him to do it? Living on the other side of the wall from the man was hard enough. Ever since she and Foster had come upon him moving in, her emotions had been in a constant state of flux. One minute, "*Hurray, he's back!*" then "*Good God, no, he's back!*" The less time she spent with him the better. Except that this had nothing to do with her and everything to do with a new library roof.

He'll think it's a lark. A hoot. It will give him a chance to preen and strut those peacock feathers. It's not like he'd say no. Seriously. What guy would turn down the chance to pose for a calendar that will earn him recognition from Scallop Shores and possibly several of the surrounding towns in the area?

"You want me to what? Oh, hell no!" Ryan practically shrieked when she finally made her way to the other half of the rented duplex.

"Shh! You're going to wake up Wes." Her eyes darted toward the hallway and back again to the man towering over her.

"Yeah, right. It's not like he's asleep." He gave her a disgusted look.

"But it's almost nine p.m."

"When you were his age, what did you do after lights out?" Ryan put his hands on his hips and waited.

"I don't know. I was eight." A smile touched her lips as a memory flickered to life like some old home movie. "I read under the covers with a flashlight."

"Exactly."

Except that he didn't look like an indulgent father. Ryan looked sad, frustrated.

"If it upsets you, just say so. Put your foot down. You're the father."

"I don't need parenting tips from you, thank you very much. And it doesn't upset me. It's not like he's smoking weed and squirreling away porno rags. He's reading. It's his passion."

Still stinging over the first part of that diatribe, Bree turned around so he couldn't see how badly he'd hurt her. He was absolutely right. She had no business offering parenting advice when she didn't even have any children of her own. She pressed her arms rigidly against her sides, worried that one slight jostle would shatter her entire body.

"I'm sorry." His voice was low, calmer.

"For what?" Panic squeezed her muscles to the point of aching. What did he know?

"For going off on you. For taking out my issues on you. It's been a long-ass day."

"You're right. I shouldn't be here. We'll discuss the calendar another time." Bree reached for the shawl she'd slung across the back of the kitchen chair but Ryan touched her hand.

"Don't go. I could use the company."

She looked down to where their skin just barely made contact. Years fell away and she remembered the night he'd come to say goodbye before leaving for college on the West Coast. The night she'd finally been able to show him how much he meant to her. The night her life had changed forever.

Ryan grasped her more firmly by the hand, pulling her into the living room and not letting go until they were both seated on the couch. She wanted to bolt. Quickly, before she did something she'd regret ... again. She wanted to touch his face. He'd changed. There were lines around his eyes. Worry lines. She wanted to reach out, smooth them away with her fingertips.

"Can I get you a drink? I'm mostly a beer guy, but I think this occasion calls for some whiskey."

An addled brain is exactly what she *didn't* need.

"I'd rather not, thanks."

"That's my Bree. Always the good girl." He teased her with his smile.

If he knew she was currently picturing him without his shirt—heck, without much of anything on—he wouldn't be saying that. No beer, no whiskey, no coffee even. Just get in, get out and get on with her life. The sooner the better.

Her nose tickled as she picked up traces of a spicy scent that could have been his shampoo, his deodorant, or even some new male body spray. Breathing through her nose as shallowly as possible, Bree was ashamed to admit to herself that she was sniffing him. Good God! Yeah, she needed to wrap this up quickly. She set her jaw and scooted a safe distance away on the couch.

"So, clearly the theme of this particular fundraiser was not my idea."

"Yet you were only too eager to be the one to execute it." Again with the teasing tone.

"I didn't know what I was signing up for! They tricked me."

"It wouldn't have been difficult. You always did go out of your way to help people. I see that hasn't changed." His smile turned reflective, his eyes darkening just the slightest bit. "Why pick me, though? Is it the abs? I was always able to drag your eyes out of a book whenever I took off my shirt." Then he winked. Memories from another lifetime flooded her brain.

It was late, school having ended hours ago. She had stayed to watch football practice. Oh, who was she fooling? She'd stayed to watch Ryan. Grabbing her books out of her locker, she slammed it closed, only to find the object of her fascination leaning lazily against the one on her right. He was sweaty and grass-stained and in desperate need of a shower. Yet Bree found herself swaying breathlessly toward him.

"Saw you in the stands today."

"I was here late. Figured I'd hang out for a bit."

"Cool." He placed a palm against the hard metal beside her head, leaning in almost imperceptibly.

"Anyway, I should go. My mom will be wondering where I am." Pushing her thick glasses up the bridge of her nose, she swallowed hard. She studied the length of his arm, following it up to his face.

He seemed to be watching for her gaze to reach his eyes, because he chose that exact moment to wink. The breath she'd been about to exhale froze in her lungs. Her attention quickly snapped to his mouth. He licked his lips, the action practiced, unhurried. If he didn't kiss her now, she would surely die!

And then he did. His lips were soft, the hint of a bristling mustache on his upper lip adding an exciting roughness. Only their mouths touched, and only for the briefest of moments. Before she could acknowledge that this was truly happening, he was already stepping back. He looked as stunned as she felt. Without a word, Ryan spun on his heel and jogged off, down the hall to the locker room. Bree brought a shaky hand to her lips as she watched him go.

A mixture of old hurts and sexual frustration had her snapping at him, "It wasn't my idea. In fact, if it were up to me, you wouldn't even have to do this stupid calendar." *Was it hot in here?*

She might as well have slapped him. Ryan looked ... wounded. Oh, for crying out loud! First he doesn't want to have anything to do with the project, then he's hurt when she agrees with him. There was no pleasing this man!

"It had already been decided, among the board members, that you would be the calendar cover. The piece de resistance." He only glowered at her so she elaborated. "The whole 'hometown hero' thing."

"And there it is." Ryan faced forward, slapping his hand against his thigh and biting his lip as though he had a lot more to say.

"You don't like being put into that position." She reached out a hand, barely touching his bicep with her fingertips.

"Ya think?" He leaned forward, elbows on his knees, and tunneled his fingers through his hair.

"Ryan, talk to me. I want to understand."

He used to thrive on the limelight. Back in high school he was proud of the attention. He couldn't go anywhere in town without a slap on the back, a handshake, and a hearty wave. And it wasn't just praise. Bree could remember the free sodas they'd offer Ryan at the mini mart. The two gas stations in town vying for his business with free gas and car washes. He'd loved it all.

"You know what a hometown hero is? It's someone who has made a sacrifice for their town. Someone who has given their life or a limb or something in service to their country. Something important.

"But Scallop Shores is so damned tiny that they don't have one of those. So they make do. They pick a high school kid who was pretty talented with a football. He gave them some good memories, something to be proud of all these years later. And they put him up on this pedestal. Where he doesn't belong." He spit the last words out on a snarl, his hands curled into fists in his lap.

"You said it yourself. You made them proud. If they want to honor that, what's the harm?"

"I was supposed to make them proud. I was on my way. I tried." His anguished expression focused on his worn denim-clad thighs.

Bree bit her lip, unsure of what to do. She wasn't used to grown men showing their emotions. Ryan was bitterly upset and it killed her to see him like this. If it were one of her little brothers, she would have taken him on her lap and held him close until he calmed down. But Ryan was an adult, way too big to put on her lap. Her cheeks grew hot.

"No 'tried' about it. You did make them proud, Ryan. We're a simple town. You worked hard to get us to State and we won. You deserve the accolades."

"Aw hell, that's all I did. The recognition was for what I was supposed to do. I was on my way to a career in the NFL. I was supposed to be a pro football player. Then they could have called me a celebrity. But not now. Not when I failed them."

"What are you talking about? Because you aren't a football player now? You honestly think they care, Ryan? You don't know for a fact that you would have gone pro. Sure, it would have been great. But it certainly wasn't a given."

"I got a full ride to UCLA on a football scholarship and I ended up a bean counter. And why? Because I got injured during a game? At practice? No! Because I slipped on the wet tile in the friggin' dorm bathroom and messed up my knee bad enough to end my career before it even started. I'm not the town hero. I'm the town joke."

Okay, this part she didn't know. Word got back to Scallop Shores that Ryan had gotten hurt, that he'd torn his knee and needed surgery to correct it. It had just been assumed that he'd received the injury during a game. But it didn't matter. The only person who cared about the specifics was Ryan.

The silence that followed told her he'd revealed more than he meant to. He was embarrassed. Again, she was torn between the desire to get up, give him the space to compose himself and the urge to take him in her arms and comfort him. She'd made the hard choice to let go of her own difficult past and it looked like Ryan needed to do the same thing.

"I'll do it for you. The calendar." He finally spoke, looking over at her, his warm brown eyes full of pain and regret. "Not for the town. Not for the notoriety. Just you. But I ask one thing in return."

"Name it." She didn't need to ask first. She knew she could trust him.

"Help me connect with Wes."

She blinked. "I don't understand."

"Yeah, you do. Don't pretend you don't see it. Bree, the kid is like a miniature version of you. He'd much rather be by himself, nose in a book. He has a hard time making friends. But he's happy. I don't want to change him. I just want to understand him and find some way to relate to him."

"I'm not sure how to help with that." She wrinkled her nose, her head tilted to the side.

"You two were discussing books. Series, right? Teach me about those books. Give me the Cliff's Notes version so I can have the same talks with him. Help me keep up. Help me be able to recommend something I think he'd like."

The man was a jock, through and through. He probably hadn't read a book for pleasure since ... well, probably never. But in Bree's eyes he'd just made Father of the Year. It would have been far easier to force his own interests on his son, teach the kid football, baseball, anything he felt comfortable with. But he chose to support Wesley's interests. And how could she say no to that?

Chapter 5

"So … how did your date with Foster go? Have I told you how proud I am that you took the initiative and asked him first?" Cady set a big mug of coffee in front of Bree and sat down across from her.

"It's funny you should ask. See, I don't remember telling you that I even asked him, let alone that we'd already gone out on a date." Apparently the slice of banana bread she had ordered was considered community property, because Cady was already nibbling on a corner she'd pinched off.

"Silly Bree. I see all. Okay, I am told all."

"Amanda?" She'd forgotten that Cady was best friends with Foster's sister.

"Nope. Heard it from the man himself. You shocked him. In a good way, mind you."

Bree groaned. This wasn't good. She still hadn't talked to Foster since their date several nights ago. He'd called a couple of times but, like the coward she was, she had let it go to voicemail.

"I'm guessing that means it didn't go so well." Cady's frown was sympathetic. She leaned across the table. "Was he a bad kisser? I've always pictured him as a good kisser, but I could be wrong."

"What were you doing picturing Foster and kissing, anyway?" Bree slapped at Cady's hand when the woman reached for another bite of her banana bread.

This was getting distracting. She'd come here to get some work done on the fundraiser, work out a contact list and a budget. Cady was not making that easy.

"And speaking of kissing, shouldn't you be off on your honeymoon? Generally that follows a wedding, such as you had."

"It's the middle of winter, in case you haven't noticed." Cady grinned broadly. "Burke has promised to take me to Paris in the spring."

Bree let out a long sigh. Paris. Such a romantic city. The setting for so many incredible literary classics.

"All right, already! You aren't going to bring it up on your own and I am dying to hear all about it." Cady bounced in her seat.

"The date with Foster?" Why was she still on about that?

"No, the calendar!"

"Shh!" Bree hissed across the table. "How on Earth did you hear about that one?" Cady was good, but she wasn't that good.

Her friend beamed from ear to ear. Her gaze swept the counter, where all the coffee shop regulars were busy with their own conversations. Turning back to Bree, she didn't bother to hide the mischievous glint in her eyes.

"Martha was in the other day," she began.

"She told you!"

"You didn't let me finish. She came in for some pastries for a board meeting. Said they were having trouble coming up with a fundraising idea for a new roof for the library." Cady paused to let her words sink in.

"This was *your* idea? So I suppose you were the one to suggest I be put in charge, too?"

"Hey, you were the one who had the big New Year's resolution to find your own happily ever after."

"Do I dare ask what organizing a calendar shoot of half-naked men has to do with my finding true love?"

"If you have to ask, sweetheart, it has been far too long," Cady winked.

"Oh, good lord ... " Bree threw her hands up in surrender. "What if I told you that the date with Foster was amazing and we realized we're soul mates and can't believe it took us so long to figure it out?"

"Then I'd say you were lying."

"Because Foster already told you about the date," Bree finished for her.

"Back to the drawing board, right?" Cady gestured to the notebook on the table. "So who do you have on your list so far?"

"Your brother, for one. Do you think he'd do it?" Bree hunched down into the cowl neckline of her sweater, as if she could hide from the crazy fiasco that had become her life.

"Oh, please. In a heartbeat. Next?"

"Foster. Or is that too awkward? What if he won't speak to me? I've kind of been avoiding him."

"He'll do it because you need him. And have you ever known Foster to be angry at anyone? I don't think it's physically possible. Talk to the guy. If you're on the same page about the date, great. If not, he deserves to know the truth. Who else ya got?"

"Ryan Pettridge. I asked him last night. The board wants him on the cover."

"Great idea! Love the hometown hero angle."

Bree forked up a bite of banana bread and simply nodded.

"Okay, you've got the ones you're comfortable with. Now it's time to step outside your comfort zone and ask some men you aren't as familiar with."

"We're still talking about the calendar, right?" Bree's laughter betrayed her nerves.

"Who says you can't pull double duty? You have been given an amazing opportunity here. Why waste it?"

"You mean, you arranged for this amazing opportunity. But finding someone to fall in love with is really something I need to do on my own."

"I totally understand that. But tell me the truth, when were you planning to get up the nerve to ask someone new out? Things didn't work out with Foster, but he's not the only single guy in Scallop Shores. You need to put yourself out there. And if you happen to choose some men for the calendar that you'd like to get to know better ... Again, amazing opportunity."

"I can't believe I'm doing this." Bree stood up, comfortable enough in her friend's coffee shop that she didn't think twice about heading behind the counter and refilling her own coffee mug.

"I can't believe you aren't more excited about it." Cady tagged along behind her.

"Come on, look at me. I'm a librarian. A dowdy librarian. And I am tasked with finding twelve hot guys to sell enough copies of a calendar to fund a library roof."

"You are far more beautiful than you realize, hon. But if that's what has you worried, let's do something about it."

"Like what?" Bree turned around, coffee carafe in her hand.

"A makeover. Oooh, it will be fun!"

"You mean like doing each other's nails and stuff?" She shuddered at the thought.

"I mean like taking you to Kayla's Kut and Kurl and getting you a new look. Oh, and shopping! New clothes. New shoes."

Bree gave her friend a considering look. She'd been telling herself the same thing lately. Somehow hearing Cady say it made it easier to admit. She returned the coffee to the warmer as she thought it over.

"I want highlights."

"Yes! That's perfect."

"And layers."

"See? I'm not pushing you into this at all. You've clearly been giving it some thought already."

The bell over the door sounded and the women looked up in time to see Foster stroll in.

"Excellent timing, my friend. Bree has something she wants to ask you." Cady sashayed over, hooking her arm in his and pulling him to the counter.

"Sometimes I could cheerfully punch you in the stomach," Bree glowered.

"Do you do crunches, Foster?" Cady tickled him in the ribs.

"Really. I hate you." Bree folded her arms across her chest.

"Quit hiding on the other side of the counter and come out here like a good girl." Foster held out a hand. "We need to talk."

Oh boy. Two birds, one stone. Bree took one last swig of coffee and prepared to face the music.

Foster led her to a quieter table in the corner, where they wouldn't be disturbed. She looked up to see if Cady was going to come over with coffee for her latest customer, perhaps bring a pastry that she'd shamelessly 'share'. Nope. The woman had the audacity to turn her back on Bree and focus on refilling coffee cups at the counter. No backup there.

"It didn't go quite like we were expecting, hmm?" He stretched his long legs out under the table, nudging her foot with one. Whether on purpose or not, she wasn't sure.

"I had a very nice time, Foster. Truly." Guilt may have forced her to sound a little more enthusiastic than she'd meant.

"Enough to go out with me again? I could cook." The crinkling at the corners of his eyes told her he was teasing her.

"Thank you for not insisting on a goodnight kiss. I just think that would have been incredibly awkward." She blushed, recalling the sweet hug that Foster had given her on her front porch after he'd finished his cocoa and washed both their mugs.

"Can I ask you something?" Again, his foot brushed up against hers and this time she knew it was deliberate.

"Of course."

"If we hadn't run into Ryan, if it had just been you and me with no interruptions, would you have agreed to go out with me on a second date?"

Bree's breath caught in her throat. Foster couldn't possibly know about her and Ryan. His flirty smile still in place, but she detected just a hint of resignation in his posture, in the tightness of his jaw. He already knew the answer.

"I don't know what you're talking about, with regard to Ryan," she answered breezily. "But, a second date? Probably not." She bit her bottom lip, unsure whether a pat on his hand would come across as an apology, as she intended, or a brush off. To be on the safe side, she remained still.

"Well, I hope 'new' Bree gets up the nerve to finally go after what she wants. You deserve to be happy, sweetheart."

And with that, Foster stood up from the table, leaned down and kissed her gently on the cheek. Those deliciously carved dimples flashed as he winked at her before heading up to the counter to order his coffee. She smiled. Foster Duncan wouldn't be single for long.

• • •

Guilt. He couldn't seem to get away from it today. First for dropping Wesley off with Bree for the morning while he headed over to his folks. When he reluctantly told his son that it would be better if he visited alone, it had been Wesley's idea to ask Bree if he could spend the time there. The poor kid hadn't made any friends at school this first week. The only real friend he'd made was Ryan's former tutor. Oh, who was he kidding? She'd been a hell of a lot more than that to him once. His heart was all for finding excuses to see her again. His head reminded him he'd made some really bad choices where Bree was concerned and she deserved better than the schmuck who had left her. Okay, more guilt there.

Now he'd reached his parents' house, only to discover that their driveway and porch were perfectly snow free, meaning someone else had done it for them. More than likely his mother had hired somebody local. He'd been so focused on Wesley this week, and getting the hardware store back open that he'd completely forgotten that his father couldn't clear off his own driveway or steps anymore. Worst son in the world.

To top it off, his mother seemed to feel obligated to feed him whenever he stopped by. So while Ryan took off his boots and ski jacket at the door, his mother hurried into the kitchen to fix him a snack. He'd love it if she could just sit down and relax, but that just wasn't in her nature. Knowing it would make her feel better, he waited while she put together a roast beef sandwich, potato chips, and a dill pickle on the side.

"Heard you stopped by the fire station," he mentioned between bites. "Luke says you've spoiled the whole department, baking them cookies like that."

"I refuse to apologize for pushing you to spend a little free time. Wes told me you never went out while you were living in California. He wasn't even sure you had any friends out there."

"Little traitor. It's not like he could talk. We Pettridge men are loners. That's all." There was a fine line between being a loner and being lonely, but he wasn't going to explore that just now.

"Rubbish. So what brings you by today—without my grandson?"

"Can't a son come check on his father without the third degree?" Ryan took a big bite of sandwich and blinked innocently as he chewed.

Anne shook her head, watching him speculatively as she puttered around her spotless kitchen.

"How's he doing?"

She twisted the dishtowel in her hands, lowering her voice as she glanced anxiously toward the living room doorway.

"He's frustrated. He can't speak. He can't communicate what he wants unless I ask him yes or no questions."

"Has there been any progress? Do they think this is the best situation for him?"

Ryan knew his father's doctor had recommended he go into a nursing home. His father had become extremely agitated and, in order to calm the man, the hospital agreed to let him return home. But he had to show progress. The doctors needed to know that the homecare nurses and physical therapists were worth it.

"I think so. It's really too soon to tell."

"Well, I've got some news that will brighten his day. A chance for a good laugh at my expense." Ryan winked at his mother, sweeping the crumbs off the counter onto his plate and carrying it to the kitchen sink.

"We could use a good laugh around here." Anne pounced on the dirty dish in the sink, like she'd been waiting for something to do.

"Ma, come sit down. That plate will be there when you get back."

He only wanted to have this conversation once.

The couch had been pushed to the far wall to make room for his father's hospital bed. There was just enough room to edge through between them in order to sit down. The large screen TV had been mounted right beside the big picture window overlooking the front yard and the street beyond. Ryan's dad, Bo, could watch television and still be able to see everything going on outside.

At the moment, the Patriots were playing the Bears. Ryan nodded when he saw the score. Ten, zip. Brady's team was in good shape this year.

"That Super Bowl's ours this year, Dad. Stupid Seahawks were a fluke last year."

His father grunted something unintelligible, but his head bobbed up and down, which Ryan took to mean he agreed.

"So you want to hear something utterly ridiculous? Guess who has been roped into posing for a calendar? The Sexy Men of Scallop Shores."

"Posing?" Anne asked, pointedly.

"Yep. Shirtless."

"Good heavens!" She rolled her eyes while Bo made a choking noise in his throat.

Ryan wasn't sure if he should be alarmed or not. But his dad had a twinkle in his eye. As he watched, the man lifted one shaky hand and turned it over slowly until he had one thumb sticking straight in the air. Yes!

"Oh, honey, good for you!" Anne gushed to her husband.

Bo dropped his hand on the bedspread as though disgusted. He was a grown man used to his independence. To be praised for something as little as a thumbs up must have been humiliating.

"Yeah, you'll never believe who's running the whole show, either."

"I imagine it's that little snip of a thing that runs the new coffee shop downtown. Cady?"

"Nope. Bree. The calendar is raising money for the library. A new roof."

Anne looked torn between laughing and feeling bad.

"She came up with the idea of men posing shirtless for a calendar? That doesn't sound like Bree at all."

"Wasn't her idea. But she jumped in to help."

"What a nice girl. She's always there to pitch in whenever someone in town needs her."

Ryan looked away. He'd never stopped to ask Bree if they were interrupting her plans for the morning. For all he knew, she had something to do, somewhere to be. But she'd been wearing her glasses again, and a sleepy smile. So understatedly sexy. He'd had to beat a fast retreat before he did something stupid.

"Listen, we need to talk."

He sat down on the end of the hospital bed, his back to the game. Patting the opposite side, he motioned for his mother to join him. Her lips pressed firmly together, she looked back and forth between husband and son before she finally took her spot on the bed.

"I wasn't completely honest with you when I arrived in town. I told you about the temporary leave I was able to get through work. I know you want me to stay, to run the hardware store so it stays in the family. But I left part of my agenda out." Daring a brief look at each of his parents, Ryan steeled his nerves and pressed on. "I didn't come out here to run the store for Dad. I came out here to try to sell it for you guys and then Wes and I are going back to California."

Anne gasped and Bo made a low growl in his throat.

"You need to think about the future. Both of you. Dad, you aren't going to be able to run the store again. I'm not saying that to be cruel, it's just a tough fact that we all have to face. Ma, are you going to do it? With the help you'd need to hire, it wouldn't be cost effective. I'm not trying to be cruel. I'm trying to help you.

"I want to set you up with a nest egg. Dad, you're gonna get better. Not perfect, but we'll get you out there fishing again. And you always said you wanted to take up golf. I think you ought to sell the house too. Get out of this harsh weather and move somewhere more temperate."

"You want us to move in with you?" Anne asked, confusion warring with anger on her face.

Holy crap, no! "Southern California is beautiful this time of year. But so is Florida. The Carolinas even. You've got lots of options."

"We like it right here, thank you very much." Her tone was on the waspish side as she grabbed Bo's hand. A show of solidarity?

"But you had to hire someone to clear the snow. You shouldn't have to do that."

"Oh, for heaven's sake, Ryan! You hire people to perform a service. That's their job. If we didn't hire them, they wouldn't have any work. It's how the economy works."

"But ... "

"What is so awful about living in Scallop Shores? Why can't you stay? I would understand if you had a girlfriend back home. Someone that you can't live without."

Unbidden, Bree's face floated into Ryan's subconscious. He wanted to swat it away.

"We do have a life in California. Wes thrives at his school. It's good for him."

"Scallop Shores is better. The boy needs to learn that there are more things in life than his books. He needs to experience ice hockey and camping, swimming in the cold Atlantic and making homemade flapjacks with the berries he picked himself. And family. You'd finally bring Wesley here and have him get to know his grandparents, only to yank him away again so quickly?"

He couldn't disagree with any of this. His need to leave town as quickly as possible had nothing to do with Wesley and everything to do with himself. Ryan watched his father clench his one working hand into a fist, relax it and clench it again.

It wasn't his intention to yank the man's control away. He was trying to be practical. And sometimes practical sucked. No way around it.

"I'm going to contact a Realtor. Maybe if you could see some actual numbers, find out what you could expect to get for the house and the business, that might help put things in perspective. Just think about it."

Not having anything more to add, Ryan squeezed his dad's shoulder and muttered a quick goodbye before he stood up and hurried for the hallway. His mother raced after him.

"Ryan? I know you don't want to run the hardware store. We never wanted that for you. But this job that's waiting for you? Do you really want to be an accountant? Don't be in such a rush to get back there unless it's what will make you truly happy."

"It's what I know, Ma. And here's a shocker, I'm good at it."

"I'm just asking you to consider staying. Spend a little time here. Remember what it felt like to belong."

"I've got to go pick up Wes, Ma. Tell Dad I love him. We'll stop by sometime tomorrow." Ryan shoved his feet in his boots, grabbed his jacket and flew out the door with a careless wave.

His mother was right on all counts. He had nothing waiting for him in California, beyond a job that he could really get anywhere else in the country—including Scallop Shores. And the more time he spent in town, the more he did remember, and enjoy, the closeness, the sense of community, and belonging. Which just made him all the more anxious to leave. His hometown only served to remind him that he'd done nothing with his dreams—especially the dream he had that involved the pretty town librarian.

Chapter 6

They'd made plans to meet at her place after Wesley fell asleep. His son knew he would be right next door if he needed him. But that wasn't likely. So it would be just the two of them. Ryan wiped his palms on his jeans, blew out a shaky breath, and tapped lightly at Bree's door. He didn't get where these stupid nerves were coming from. It wasn't like this was a date or anything.

She answered the door in a pretty pink sweater and long flowing black skirt. Ryan liked how she dressed now, as opposed to when they were in high school. Back then she'd opted for huge shirts that she'd had to have bought in the men's department. Shapeless outfits that, knowing Bree, were designed to hide her body rather than display it.

At least now she dressed femininely, even if she did still hide that sexy, lithe body of hers behind long skirts. The woman had legs like a dancer. It seemed a crime not to show them off.

He liked that she'd gotten contacts. Not that she hadn't looked adorable in glasses, but he'd always loved her caramel-colored eyes and was pleased that he could see them better now. Shaking his head, Ryan wondered why he was spending so much time studying the way Bree looked.

Steering him past the cozy living room that was an exact replica of the one he and Wesley shared next door, she waved him across the hall, toward the kitchen table. He stopped and blinked. It was like stepping back in time. A stack of books and homemade flash cards waited for him on the table. Just like their old tutoring sessions. He wondered if she remembered how his mother had always served them homemade cookies and a tall glass of milk.

"Are you going to make me earn my cookies?"

Bree's tutoring strategy had relied on a healthy dose of bribery. His mom would set the plate of cookies down and Bree would snatch it away, doling out cookies with each right answer. As they'd gotten to know each other and their relationship began to change, this wasn't a bribery tactic, so much as it was pure flirtation. If he knew his parents weren't paying attention, he would eat the cookie right out of her fingers.

"I thought of that just before you got here." She blushed and he could see she was remembering how he'd nibble on her fingers. "Sorry, I don't have any cookies. But I do have Kisses. You can earn those instead."

Fire shot through his body, making him rock hard in an instant. Choking down a groan, he hobbled to the table before she could see how her words had affected him.

"I beg your pardon?" he croaked out.

"Oh, for goodness' sake! Hershey Kisses? Chocolate? Not all women are as adept at baking as your mother." She set a bowl of the foil wrapped candies on the table and slid into the chair across from him.

Unsure whether her pink cheeks were from embarrassment or mutual attraction, Ryan hoped for the latter. He'd spent years trying to forget the one night they'd been together and now the more time he spent with her, the more he couldn't stop thinking about it. But that wasn't why he was here. *Focus, buddy!*

"I can't thank you enough for tutoring me … again. Wes wanted to know why I was coming over here tonight, wanted to know why he couldn't come with me. If we could just keep this between ourselves?"

"Of course. I think Wes would feel awkward if he knew the lengths you were going to in order to connect. He's a very lucky kid."

"No, I'm a lucky dad. I can't imagine my life without him in it."

A look of intense pain crossed Bree's features so swiftly that he almost second-guessed whether he'd actually seen it. Guilt clenched his gut. He knew she'd been expecting him to leave Haley after they'd admitted their feelings for one another. He'd wanted to. God, he'd wanted to. And then his son, who reminded him so much of Bree, might have actually been hers. Regrets? Yeah, he had a few thousand.

Seriously, dude! Focus already.

Bree reached for a book and began to give him an abbreviated version of the first year of Harry Potter's life at Hogwarts. She quickly explained that he couldn't hope to keep up his end of a conversation with Wesley by cheating and watching the films. She caught his eye at this point, showing him without words that she knew him better than he thought.

As he learned the characters and who held what role, Ryan was rewarded with a kiss, tossed across the table. Never mind that he would have preferred the skin-to-skin version. Spending time with Bree was a reward in itself. They got through the first book and she insisted they take a break for the night.

"How about I make coffee?"

Since he wasn't quite ready to leave her company, he nodded.

"If you've got decaf, I'd love some."

Ryan got up and wandered around while she prepared their drinks. The cheap little desk in the living room held a small laptop. She hadn't bothered to close it, so he figured he wasn't exactly snooping by checking out what was on the screen. He chuckled to himself.

"You're still trying to get on *Jeopardy*. That's awesome. When the time comes, you better tell me. I fully intend to be in the audience to watch you become the next Ken Jennings." He was proud of her, regardless.

"I don't know. I think it's time to admit I'll never be *Jeopardy* material. If I haven't made it on there by now, then I probably never will." She stepped up beside him, handing him one of the mugs she'd carried in with her.

"Promise me you won't ever give up. Your time will come."

Ryan waited to see where Bree would settle, hoping she'd choose the couch where he could sit beside her. She looked at it, then perched herself in the overstuffed chair in the corner. He didn't realize his sigh was audible until she looked up sharply and raised one brow, quizzically. Whoops.

"Can I ask you a question?" He sat down in the center of the couch, cupping his mug in his palms.

"Fire away."

"Why didn't you become a teacher? You used to talk about it all the time. It was why you began tutoring. My mom said you quit school to help your mom. But surely you could have just taken a little time off?"

Bree glanced away.

"It didn't fit in with my plans anymore. My mom needed me. My stepdad was gone. The boys needed me. I had to find a job where I could get all my training online."

"While still being able to work with kids," he added.

"A happy coincidence."

"You would have made an excellent teacher. You still could."

"I like where I am now. It's satisfying."

"Recruiting men to pose for your calendar—shirtless," Ryan teased.

"Never a dull moment, huh?" She took a sip of coffee and leaned back into the cushions.

"I've missed you, Bree."

Huh. It would appear that something as simple as decaf coffee had the power to loosen his tongue tonight.

"My turn. Can I ask you a question?"

"Don't hold back." He watched her over the rim of his mug.

"Why numbers? Why accounting? As I recall, you and numbers didn't get along."

Because it reminded him of her. He couldn't tell her that, though.

"People change, I guess. And as far as a backup career, it seemed as good as any."

"I suppose. But you didn't have to abandon sports altogether. You could have become a coach. Or gone into sports medicine. Or announcing." Oh, she was just getting warmed up. He could tell.

"After my accident, I felt like a fraud just thinking about anything sports related, you know?" He had never admitted that to anyone.

"Never too late to change your mind."

"Fair enough, Ms. Librarian. Fair enough." He drained the last of his coffee and set the mug on the coffee table. "It's late. I should let you get some sleep."

"Can I stop by the store in the next couple of days? You said you had some names of other guys that might want to help with the calendar?" She stood up from her chair, looked as though she might sit back down again and then thought better of it. Though she acted twitchy because she was anxious for him to leave or because she wished he would stay, Ryan couldn't be certain.

"I open at nine. Stop in any time after that. We'll put our heads together and come up with some detailed lists to get us started."

"Great. I'll make up for the lack of cookies tonight and bring you something from Cady's Dream. What do you like?"

Oh, there was a loaded question, if ever he'd heard one. He shook the naughty thoughts that were beginning to form from his head.

"I'm not picky. Anything you bring, I'll love."

They stood at the front door. Ryan put one hand on the doorknob but turned back to say one last goodnight.

"I meant what I said before. I've missed you."

She was so close. If he leaned in just a little ...

"I've missed you too, Ryan."

His name on her lips was all the encouragement he needed. He let go of the doorknob to cup a hand behind the back of her head. If she told him no, he'd stop. Instead, her eyelids fluttered shut and her head angled just enough to show him she had no intention of stopping him.

A low groan rumbling deep in his throat, he captured her mouth in a soul-stealing kiss. Shocked that he could still remember how she tasted after all this time, Ryan held on tight. Feelings he'd denied for thirteen years came flooding back. Love. Pain. Guilt. Regret. So much regret. He crushed her to him, wishing like hell that he could go back and make different choices. Choices that included Bree, that didn't push her away.

He felt the searing touch of her fingertips on his shoulders as a brand. Slowly they crept up to wrap around his neck, her deft fingers sliding into his hair to drive him crazy with need. Pivoting their bodies, he pushed her up against the door and released her mouth to trail hot kisses along her jaw, feasting on her sensitive neck.

His Bree.

"We should stop." Her voice was husky.

He couldn't get close enough. Her hands were grasping at his. Tangling their fingers together.

"Ryan, you need to leave."

Understanding finally reached through his sex-addled brain. Trembling, he put his hands on either side of her, pushing himself just far enough away so that they were no longer touching. His heart beat erratically. He was breathing like he'd run a marathon.

"I'm so sorry. I shouldn't ... " She placed a finger against his lips and shook her head.

"Don't ruin a perfectly wonderful moment with an apology. Please. I'll see you soon." Slipping out of his arms, Bree backed up until she was a safe distance down the hall.

He searched her expression, worried he'd scared her by coming on so strong. Her cheeks were flushed, but her eyes sparkled and her lips tilted just a bit at the edges. He realized that she had moved away not just from him, but from her own reactions. *Take it slow, Pettridge. Don't mess it up this time.* Fumbling for the doorknob, he welcomed the bite of cold that slapped him in the face as he hurried to his own place.

• • •

"The secret to having confidence is knowing you look good *under* your clothes." Cady held up a barely there red lace bra.

Bree shook her head, still amazed that she'd let herself be dragged into a Victoria's Secret, of all places. But she was with the two women from Scallop Shores that she felt the most comfortable around. Cady had been pushing her to step outside of her introvert bubble for years now, worming her way into Bree's heart along the way. She could also thank Cady for her more recent friendship with Quinn. She probably wouldn't be so close to Quinn if Cady hadn't insisted on them sharing a table at the bakery and getting to know one another when Quinn had first come back to town.

"It's like walking around with a happy little secret all day." Quinn snatched the matching panties off the display table and stretched them out between her hands, wiggling them in front of Bree.

A happy little secret. She sighed. She'd been walking around with her own happy little secret all day. She was supposed to be enjoying some girl time but it was awfully hard to concentrate when she kept replaying Ryan's kiss over and over in her head.

"Yeah. Happy. Little. Secrets." Cady drew out each word as she leaned in close to Bree's ear.

"Spill it, sister. You know you want to." Quinn nudged her shoulder as she crowded in on the other side of her.

"I don't know what you're talking about," Bree stuttered.

"Like we haven't noticed you floating around in a daze. Give us a little credit, Bree. Who's the lucky guy?"

"Oh, is it Foster? I heard you'd finally gone out with him." Quinn's eyes danced with merriment.

"Catch up, Quinn. Foster was ages ago. And Foster never put that rosy glow in her cheeks." Cady grabbed her arm and dragged her over to a bench near the changing rooms.

Bree chewed her new lipstick off her bottom lip. She wasn't used to wearing it anyway. She wasn't used to any of this. Spending quality girl time. Getting a new haircut and having her makeup done professionally. Now shopping for clothes and lingerie to complete the new look. This was all uncharted territory for her.

But she had to admit that she was having a lot of fun. And it felt good to know she could talk to her friends about Ryan. It gave her hope that maybe one day she could open up about the baby she'd lost. That particular secret was a heavy emotional burden to carry all by herself. And if she were truly moving on with her life, the next best step would be to let someone else in on what happened all those years ago.

"It's no big deal, really."

Or it shouldn't be. He was only in town for a short while. He'd made it clear that he had no intention of staying. Best not to make any more of this than it was.

"Bree, no offense, love, but no man has put a smile like that on your face in the entire time I have known you." Cady's expression was matter of fact.

"Just don't make a fuss over it. Okay?" She paused, staring them each down before continuing. "You know the duplex I rented over on Ramsdell Way? Ryan Pettridge and his son have moved into the other half."

"You slept with Ryan Pettridge?" Cady gasped.

Bree cringed. Even though they were in a Victoria's Secret in the mall two towns over from Scallop Shores, she didn't want her business broadcast for perfect strangers to overhear. When a few heads turned at this line of questioning, she clamped her mouth shut and glared at Cady. Standing up, she gathered a couple of bras, panties, and a long silk sheath and made like she was going to try them on. Hitching her head to the right, she indicated that the women should follow her into one of the dressing rooms.

"You didn't!" Quinn breathed when they were squished into the tight cubicle with the door shut.

"No, I didn't," she whispered. *At least not this time.* Bree tried not to giggle at the look of disappointment on Cady's face.

"I kissed him. Or he kissed me. He definitely started it."

"But you finished it," Quinn added.

Bree sighed. Yeah, she'd finished it all right. Though the more she thought about it, the more she wished she'd found a more satisfying way to finish it.

"So Ryan Pettridge, huh? Star quarterback. Mr. Jock. Hooking up with the bookworm. Talk about opposites attracting."

"It's not like we don't share a past." *Wait, wrong choice of words.* "He's a nice guy." She backpedaled.

Ryan had been the only person in their small high school who had ever really seemed to notice her. Okay, so she'd worked hard to fade into the background. She was just more comfortable that way. But Ryan made her feel different, pretty, even. When she was around him she didn't want to hide.

"When he gets a look at the new you, he's going to flip!" Cady reached out and let a lock of Bree's newly styled hair slip through her fingers.

"No more playing Little Miss Wallflower, all right?" Quinn admonished.

Bree stood up in the small dressing room and faced the mirror. She studied her reflection with a critical eye. The long layers added body to her normally flat hair. She gave her head a toss, smiling as she watched it all bounce back into place. And the color! The subtle streaks of blonde and red gave her own boring brown a real depth. It looked good. She looked good.

"Quinn, your sister did an amazing job. I really do love it." Bree gave her friend an impulsive hug.

"Yeah, I want that red color for myself now," Cady added. "I made an appointment on our way out."

"So now all that's left is to find a sexy wardrobe to wear under your new clothes. No more granny panties." Quinn giggled.

"But no one is going to see what I'm wearing underneath." Bree addressed her reflection, turning this way and that as she continued to get used to her new hairstyle. Though she couldn't help but wonder what a decent push up bra would do for her nearly non-existent bustline.

"Are you sure about that? What about Ryan? You've already kissed. The ultimate goal is to end up in bed, right?" Cady stood up, hovering just behind Bree's left shoulder.

"That'd be nice, but no, it's not the ultimate goal. Remember my plan—you both found your dream guys, your happily ever afters. I want mine too."

"And you can't have that with Ryan?"

"Not unless I intend to move to California with him when he goes back home. If he were to ask, that is."

Cady made a disgusted growl in her throat. "He *is* home. You just need to convince him that he has no reason to leave."

"And you'd know all about that, wouldn't you?" Bree teased. It wasn't that long ago that Cady, herself, had planned to move away from the town she'd grown up in.

"Want me to have Burke talk to him? He's pretty frickin' convincing." Cady's grin curled up at the corners and she got a faraway look in her eyes.

"I'm pretty sure he's only that convincing to the person he's sleeping with."

They all laughed out loud.

"Bree, Ryan isn't anxious to get home because he has someone waiting for him there, is he? I mean, I heard he and Haley divorced years ago, but still ... " Quinn's eyebrows drew together as she frowned in concern.

"I don't think so." But that was just it. She hadn't thought of that scenario at all.

Because Bree knew better than anyone that just because he kissed her did not mean he was single and available. She'd fallen hard for Ryan in high school and, despite the fact that he was dating the head cheerleader, Haley, she'd given herself to him. Naively, she'd been expecting their lovemaking to be a life altering enough experience that he would leave Haley for her. But it had done the opposite. Not only had he stayed with Haley, he had gone on to marry her and have a child with her.

Quinn didn't realize it, but she had just helped Bree put things in perspective. Kissing Ryan had been nice. It brought back some pleasant memories of her first time. And the amount of women who could look back on their first time with a man with only the happiest of memories were probably few and far between. But Ryan was a part of her past, and there he'd have to stay.

No more kissing. But if they were going to work so closely together for the next few weeks as he helped her on this calendar project, not to mention the time spent guiding him toward a stronger connection with Wesley, they needed to finally talk about their night together. She deserved to hear why he chose Haley, and Ryan deserved to hear how badly he'd hurt her by cutting her out of his life. He didn't need to know about the baby. He had Wesley.

"Come on, ladies. We're here to shop. Burke has been running the coffee shop all day and I plan to reward him with a naughty little fashion show later tonight." Cady winked at her friends.

One by one they filed back out into the store to focus on matching bra and underwear sets. For every demure pale pink or white set Bree found, Cady would snatch it out of her hands and replace it with something in fire engine red or lacy black. Eventually, Bree decided it was best just to give in and buy the ones Cady had chosen. She had to admit they were really sexy and part of her couldn't wait to experience that "happy little secret" that would lend her the confidence she needed to talk nine more gorgeous men into posing shirtless for her. Um, for her calendar.

Chapter 7

Bree fiddled with the veggie tray, arranging the carrots just so. Ryan had assured her that the guys wouldn't touch it, but it couldn't hurt to try. Given enough fancy dips and ranch dressing, her little brothers would try almost anything. Besides, it was colorful. Who couldn't resist all those bright oranges, yellows, reds, and greens?

Tapping her chin, she stepped back and surveyed the buffet arrangement she'd set up on Ryan's kitchen table. Seven layer dip. Check. Baked beans in the crock-pot. Check. Nachos laid out on the cookie sheet, ready to be popped into the oven. Check. Ryan had even made some surprisingly good buffalo wings. Double check.

"So what are we going to do while they watch their silly game?" Wesley slumped into a chair, grabbing a handful of potato chips and stuffing half of them in his mouth.

"We are going to watch the game with them. We're going to learn a thing or two about football." She turned and gave him a questioning look. "Unless you've already been taught the finer points of football. You and your dad must have been watching together for years."

"Nope. He doesn't watch football."

"But it's his favorite thing." She scrunched up her nose.

"So everyone keeps telling me. 'Your dad was the best football player this town ever had.' Kinda hard to picture, you know? He's just my dad. A guy who works in an office and gets really busy around tax season."

Wesley got up and grabbed a library copy of the first in the Percy Jackson series off the counter and hunkered back down in his chair. Frowning, Bree went over and snatched it out of his hands.

"Hey! You gave that to me. You can't just take it away."

"I let you borrow it and I can take it back any time I'd like." Dealing with Ryan's son was just like dealing with Sam, Perry, and Theo. Thinking of him as she would one of her little brothers made the ache in her heart over the loss of her own baby slightly less painful.

"I'll give it back after the game. But this afternoon we're going to mingle." She ruffled his hair when he tried to make a sneaky grab for the book.

"Why are we having this party anyway? Dad doesn't do parties. And you're the only girl. Doesn't that make you feel weird?"

Okay, quite honestly? She'd rather be absolutely anywhere else at the moment. But Ryan had offered to throw this little shindig as a way of getting all his old teammates together so she could ask them to pose for her calendar. She had ceased calling it the library fundraiser. This was her project and she was owning it.

"It's called 'networking' and is a little hard to explain to a second grader. But we're going to have fun, eat lots of junk food and probably use curse words." Or at least that's what she assumed went on when grown men sat around watching a sporting event on TV.

"Sweet! Do I get to swear?"

"Wait a minute—what did I just walk in on?" Ryan leaned a hip on the doorjamb and raised an inquisitive brow at Bree.

"Bree said watching football is all about having fun, eating junk food, and swearing."

"And she'd be the expert on all things football," Ryan scoffed. He grinned and added, "She came to all of my games and most of my practices, but I'll never understand why. She had that cute little nose of hers buried in a book the whole time."

He knew she'd been there?

"Hey, you told me I couldn't read during the game!" Wesley pouted.

"And I meant it. Today we're learning the rules of football. But you've got a few minutes before everyone starts arriving, so you can read until then." She handed him back his library book and smiled as he raced off.

"You really have no clue what goes on during a football game, do you?"

Ryan slipped into the room, intent on picking up where they'd left off the last time he'd been at her place. Bree looked from him to the doorway, where his son had left only moments before. She edged around to the other side of the table, maintaining distance between them.

"I thought things get rowdy? Am I wrong?"

"Depends on the game. If no one is scoring, it can be a bit dull." He continued his pursuit, like a panther on the prowl. "Have I mentioned how much I love what you've done with your hair? And your clothes?" His eyes roamed from the jeans tightly encasing her legs to the Patriots tee, the V-neck of which accentuated her new cleavage created by a push-up bra.

"Tell me why you haven't watched any football games with Wes."

That stopped him in his tracks. Ryan turned and paced toward the fridge, keeping his back to Bree.

"It's no big deal. I just don't really care for football anymore."

"Bullshit."

"Why Ms. Librarian, I am shocked!"

"Hey, I said there'd be cursing, so I may as well be the one to start. You love football. It's your passion."

"It's my nightmare. Don't worry about it. We're watching now, aren't we?"

"Why?" Bree walked up behind him, placing a small hand on his broad back.

He turned around, slipping her fingers between his own. Closing his eyes for a moment, he gave her a forced smile.

"I've seen what you're doing. These changes you're making. You're brave. I'm proud of you. And inspired. It's about damned time I made some changes of my own."

They stood silently for a moment, hands linked. It was on the tip of her tongue to ask him for that talk they needed to have. Somewhere more private. But footsteps scuffed up the porch steps followed by a loud knocking. Their guests were arriving.

Together they met Chase and Foster at the door. Right behind them was Jonah Goodwin. He and Ryan had never actually been introduced, but Bree knew him well. They'd even suffered through an incredibly awkward fake date at Quinn's behest. She gave him a hug and ushered him inside, introducing him to his host for the afternoon.

No sooner had the door shut than a quiet tapping announced another guest. Bree waved the rest of the men into the living room and answered it herself. Lucas Bretton. She smiled at the boy-turned-man who quite possibly topped her in terms of shyness. He held out a plate.

"My mom wouldn't let me show up empty-handed. It's some pasta salad type thing." Lucas shrugged down further into his coat.

"Well, you be sure and thank your mom for me. I am sure everyone will love it." Bree patted him on the arm, taking the dish from him and showing him where he could stash his jacket.

"Wes, buddy, come out and meet some of my old friends," Ryan hollered down the hallway.

"Hey, mind who you're calling old!" Chase called from Ryan's recliner, where he'd quickly scored the best seat in the house.

"I heard you're a daddy now. How are those reflexes, Pops?" A beer can sailed through the air and Chase caught it easily.

Bree shook her head. She wasn't sure she could deal with this much testosterone in one room. It was going to be a long afternoon.

The Patriots were playing the Broncos to determine which team would make it to the Super Bowl this year. She may not know much about football, but Bree realized this was the second biggest game of the year. Every man in that crowded living room was pumped—including Ryan.

She played the good little hostess, refreshing drinks, letting in the last few guests and passing the bowls of chips, pretzels, and popcorn among the men. She asked a question here and there, but Ryan made good on his promise to teach her and Wesley about the rules of the game. Filing it all away, she found herself getting caught up in the action on screen. And by the way he jumped around whenever the Patriots scored a touchdown, so was Wesley.

"Are you two finally dating now or what?" Doyle (she couldn't remember his last name) passed her an empty beer can in exchange for a new one.

"I don't know what you're talking about," she stuttered.

"You mean why Bree is the only woman in attendance today?" Foster's grin was huge. Technically, he didn't even need to be here. He'd already signed on to help her out. But he'd let her know there was no way he was going to miss her asking his old teammates for help. "Bree has a little project she'd like your help on."

Still puzzled over Doyle's question, she turned to see how Ryan had reacted. The man was pretending as though he hadn't heard a word. At the moment he was digging through the seven-layer dip like he was expecting to find treasure at the bottom of the bowl. Coward.

It was halftime and everyone was getting up to stretch and take turns using the bathroom. Unfortunately, Foster had managed to bring the group focus to Bree, who blinked owlishly. All right then. It looked like she had the stage.

"Okay, so you all probably know I'm the children's librarian at the public library. I've been tasked to raise funds for a new roof." Being men, they were hardwired to solve problems. Everyone began offering suggestions at once. Bree held up her hands and waited until they had quieted down.

"We already have an idea on how to raise the money. That isn't why we asked you all here. But thanks." She took a deep breath and launched into the speech she had practiced over and over as she'd paced her apartment the night before.

"Now this wasn't my idea, just so you know." All eyes were on her and Bree could feel the heat radiating from her warm cheeks. What was that saying, when in a situation like this? 'Picture them all in their underwear?' But wasn't that what she was kind of asking them to do? Instead, she pictured her own underwear. The lacy red, barely there thong that was the most daring thing she'd picked up on her shopping trip with the girls. Her happy little secret that was supposed to instill confidence. Well, she needed to channel a little of that confidence right now.

"The committee decided the best way to raise money for the new roof would be to put together a calendar of, um, hot men. And they figure they can sell more calendars if those men weren't wearing their shirts. Ryan was gracious enough to help me put together a list of possible calendar models and, congratulations, you made the cut." She clapped her hands and mentally patted herself on the back for getting through that moment.

Hoots and laughter filled the room. Foster gave her a cheeky grin and a wink. No bygones there. Again she looked to Ryan for support, and this time she got it. He stood up, put two fingers in his mouth and let loose a piercing whistle. The men fell silent.

"Listen up. Bree needs our help and we're gonna do it. Pretend you've got some manners and treat this lady with the respect she deserves. Before you leave today you will each give her your contact information and your schedule. Let her know when you'd be most available for a photo shoot."

Bree almost expected to hear them all shout "break" after he was done talking. But they didn't. Each man nodded his acquiescence while puffing out his chest to show he was more than up to the task. She couldn't help but chuckle a little. Ryan had fallen back into the role of quarterback quite easily. She wondered if he even realized it.

Eight men for her calendar down. Four more to go. Since this was essentially Cady's idea, her friend could help her come up with the last few. Bree had a feeling Cady was just dying to be asked.

•••

More snow. Though he'd been excited to see it when they'd first arrived back in Scallop Shores, Ryan now admitted the novelty had worn off. All it meant was more shoveling, more clearing off the cars and navigating treacherous roads.

But it was Monday and that was the one day of the week that Pettridge Hardware was closed for business. Folks knew how to reach his parents if they were desperate enough. If he got a call from his mom, he'd meet someone there. He'd originally planned to meet the Realtor and discuss how much they could expect to list the store for, but that could wait one more day.

His cell phone had rung at butt early o'clock with a message from the school announcing a snow day. That meant he and Wesley would be cooped up with nothing to do but talk and hang out. It disgusted him that the very idea made him a little queasy. Not that things weren't getting easier. Bree had coached him through the sixth book of the Harry Potter series and Ryan was almost to the point where he wanted to read the books for himself.

Ryan loved his kid more than life itself. He realized now that he'd done Wesley a disservice by turning his back on his own passions just because of one stupid accident. Football was a huge part of who he was. And if he were to truly connect with his son, he needed to introduce him to the game. There was plenty of room in his young life for books and sports.

But it was hard to think about football when they were snowed in for the day. So he sat at the table with his trusty to-do list, reminding himself to check the contents of the pantry in hopes of finding hot chocolate and microwave popcorn. Next he wrote "Netflix movies." Ryan wondered if the first couple of Harry Potter films would be appropriate for an eight year old. After all, Wesley had gotten through the entire book series without a single nightmare.

Wesley stumbled out into the kitchen, hair rumpled from sleep, slightly too-small pajamas askew. He blinked at the overhead light as he slid into a chair at the table while fumbling with his glasses.

"Snow day. No school."

"No school? Why?"

Ryan chuckled. For a So Cal kid, the concept of canceling school due to an act of nature was completely foreign. He ruffled Wesley's hair and went in search of a quick breakfast for the both of them.

A knock at the door had them both looking up, curious. There was only one person it could be at this hour, given that the driveway was currently impassable. Ryan headed down the hall to let Bree in.

"Happy first snow day! Well, for Wes anyway. How are we celebrating?" She sailed in, heading straight for the kitchen.

"I was thinking we would gorge ourselves on hot chocolate and popcorn while watching Harry Potter on Netflix." He followed right behind her.

"Perfect end to a snow day. But what are we doing outside?"

Father and son looked at her blankly.

"Oh, come on, Ryan. Where did all the kids meet on a snow day? Lots of snow. Lots of hills."

"The golf course! God, I haven't thought of that place in years. But we don't have any tubes or sleds."

"My little brothers still have theirs. And I think it's high time we introduce Wes to my youngest brother, Theo. He's only a couple of years older than you."

Sledding at the golf course. Ryan had to admit that sounded like a great idea. He grinned around a bite of Pop Tart. Holding one out in front of him, he offered it to Bree.

"Oh, come on, guys! If you're going to be hiking up and down hills all day, you need your protein."

Sashaying toward the fridge in her deliciously tight jeans, Bree took out a carton of eggs, some ham and veggies and proceeded to make them the most mouth-watering omelets Ryan had ever tasted. The woman could take over his kitchen any time she wanted.

Leaving the dishes for when they returned, the threesome bundled up and headed outside to tackle the driveway and clear off the pickup truck. Bree's mom was happy to get a cooped-up Theo off her hands for the day and helped them load an assortment of snow tubes, toboggans, and plastic sleds into the back of the truck.

Though it was still early, half the town was parked along the edges of the golf course. Ryan squeezed into a spot up against a snow bank. Bree and the boys had to slide out on his side.

Prepared for an awkward silence in the truck, Ryan had been pleasantly surprised to find that Wesley and Theo hit it off quickly. Apparently Harry Potter was a universal topic and the boys were soon bonding over Quidditch matches and favorite death scenes. Bree didn't interrupt, her eyes straight ahead and a satisfied smirk on her face. Okay, he was grateful.

It turned out that Theo was a popular kid, and with Ryan's permission, he dragged Wesley off to join a group of boys racing down one of the steeper slopes. Bree trudged along beside him, her cheeks and the tip of her nose the same rosy pink as the matching knit hat and scarf she wore. Impulsively, he grabbed her mittened hand and squeezed.

"I remember one year we were all out here after freezing rain coated the snow in a layer of ice. Do you remember that?" He glanced over as he positioned an inflatable toboggan at the top of a lesser-crowded hill.

"Oh my gosh, yes! We were all getting scratched and bloodied on that snow. It was crazy."

"Crazy fun!"

"Well, yeah." Her grin was shy.

"Come on." He sat down on the back end of the toboggan and gestured for her to sit in the cradle of his thighs. "You know we fly a lot faster if we weigh it down together."

"It's been a long time since I've gone flying down these hills, but I do recall some spectacular face plants." Bree shook her head, even while giggling.

"Do it. Do it," Ryan chanted.

She sat down on the sled, drawing her legs up to cross them in front of her. Ryan pulled her tight against his chest with one arm and pushed them off with the other.

Together they careened down the hill, laughing and shrieking the whole way. Someone had built a mogul about two-thirds of the way down and though they both tried to lean toward the right to avoid it, the toboggan hit the edge and was airborne for a few seconds before dumping the hapless couple into the snow.

Ryan was still holding on tight, so when they landed he was on his back with Bree somehow twisted to land on top of him, face to face. He could have let go and allowed her to scramble free. But they lay there, frozen puffs of breath mingling in front of their faces. His attention was drawn to her mouth as she chewed on her bottom lip. Leaning forward, he decided he needed to sample it for himself.

"We need to talk." Pushing a mitten against his chest, Bree rolled off him and hurried after their toboggan, which had continued on a few feet down the hill without them.

Uh oh. All he'd wanted was a kiss. She'd sure welcomed his advances the last time. He blew out a frustrated sigh and followed after her, grabbing the toboggan rope from her and pulling the sled up the hill behind him.

They reached a spot at the very top where they had the best vantage point of the golf course. Ryan spotted Wesley on his way back up the busiest hill. The smile on his son's face was huge and he was chatting nonstop with Theo and another little boy. Satisfied that he wasn't needed at the moment, he set the toboggan down off the trodden path and away from the hill's edge. Then he waited for Bree to sit down beside him.

"What's wrong?" He tried to get a read on her facial expression.

"Nothing is wrong. Everything is very right. Very good. And that's ... bad." She dropped her face into her mittens, pressing them against her eyes as she groaned.

Ryan watched Bree struggle to put her thoughts into words. She looked determined. Sitting up straighter, she tightened her jaw, thrust out her chin. She swallowed a few times and cast him a wary look from beneath her lashes.

"Why not me?"

He blinked, repeating the question over silently in his head until it finally parsed. "*We need to talk.*" Oh God. This was a conversation he'd been putting off his entire adult life. But she was absolutely right. He had never explained to Bree why, after such a perfect night, he had still chosen Haley.

"You must think I'm the biggest jerk. An idiot who can't make up his frickin' mind. One minute I'm telling you that you're the love of my life and the next I'm back with my girlfriend—and marrying her."

"I believed you, when you told me you loved me. And I still believe that you really thought you did. So, yeah, I'm a little confused." She didn't look confused. She looked defeated. And he'd done this to her.

"Oh, Bree. I did love you." *I still do*, he almost added. "If I'd been single ... that night ... I would have stayed with you in a heartbeat. I wanted a future with you. You were my soul mate."

"You chose Haley," she whispered.

"I thought I was doing the right thing. I'd cheated on my girlfriend. I never thought I was that kind of guy. I hated myself for the longest time. What my actions did to you. What they'd do to her if she ever found out." He remembered Haley becoming extra clingy in those weeks right after the bonfire. He'd chalked it up to nerves about moving all the way across the country, a new school, having to leave all her friends behind. He was all she had out there and he couldn't just abandon her.

"I thought I had to pay for what I did. I thought I was doing you a favor. You didn't deserve someone who would cheat on his girlfriend, even if it was for his true love. I didn't deserve someone who was willing to give me everything and yet asked nothing in return."

"We shouldn't have made love. If you truly loved me, you would have told Haley the truth, broken things off with her and then we could have had an honest relationship." A single tear leaked out of one eye to track slowly down her cheek.

"Except we were stupid kids. I mean, we were kids. I was the stupid one."

"No, I was stupid too. I was just as much to blame. I knew you weren't available. But I was so blindly happy. All my dreams were coming true. You made me believe that anything was possible. It didn't take much to persuade me. I was yours." She swiped at her face with a mitten, turning her head so he wouldn't see her cry anymore.

"It's just us now. Like it should have been back then. I know I don't deserve a second chance, but I'm wishing like hell that you'll give me one."

"Ryan, you aren't staying, remember? You said you're headed back to California as soon as you sell the hardware store. Unless something has changed since the last time we spoke?" She'd turned back to face him, hope and disappointment warring for dominance in her beautiful eyes.

The back of his neck felt prickly as he fought off a wave of embarrassment. Caught up in the moment, he *had* forgotten that theirs was only a temporary relationship. Bree's smile was resigned as she realized she had slapped him with a dose of reality.

"It was supposed to be us, you and me together for the rest of our lives. I screwed that up for us. I'm so sorry." He reached out for her hand, put it on his knee and covered it with one of his own.

"Life doesn't always happen the way we want. But you have Wes. He's something good that came out of that union. So don't you dare regret the choices you made."

She paused, like she had something else she wanted to add, but then thought better of it. Pulling gently on her hand, she tugged it out of his grasp. Giving him a tremulous smile, she got to her feet and announced she was going back for one of the single sleds.

He'd pushed too hard, too fast. But he was glad she'd forced the issue out into the open. Ryan had been surprised to find that Bree willingly shouldered some of the responsibility for their night together. He had made so many mistakes because of that night.

Asking for a second chance had not even been on his radar before today. But now that the words were out of his mouth, he couldn't stop thinking about it. Would she come back to California with him and Wesley? Would he be willing to stay in Scallop Shores for her? One thing was for certain, he had a lot to think about.

Chapter 8

Skirting the bucket parked below the biggest leak in the roof, Bree put away the books she had chosen for story time for the three-year-old crowd. She gathered up the puppets and the felt board. Grinning, she gave the cap on the bubble solution an extra twist before replacing it in her desk drawer. It was hard to sit still for so long when you were three. They deserved the little dance party she threw at the end of story time.

It was getting close to lunchtime and Bree was meeting Cady at the coffee shop to drive around and visit the last few potential recruits for the calendar. She stopped off in the stacks to pick up a book she and Wesley had been discussing the other day.

On impulse, she also grabbed a copy of *Harry Potter and the Sorcerer's Stone* for Ryan. She'd told him he couldn't expect to connect with Wesley by watching the abbreviated movie-versions of the books, but she was still doing him a disservice by offering him the Cliff Notes version in her lessons. It was high time he give the series a try. And from there, she had a few more she thought they both would enjoy.

She put the books for both Wesley and Ryan in her large tote bag that held all her notes for the fundraiser. She'd been up late the night before, inputting schedules for everyone who had gotten back to her so far, including the photographer, who had put his own project on hold to work on the calendar. Bree had tried to insist that they could wait, or work around his own schedule, but she seemed to have had him at 'shirtless male models'.

Waving to Martha and promising to be in touch via text, Bree headed down the library steps to the rock salt crusted sidewalk. She'd try to sneak in a few minutes of work at Cady's Dream, before they left to meet with another potential model. Her spreadsheet of calendar details was filling up exponentially.

Calves bared to the biting chill of the late January air, Bree burrowed further into her wool coat. Her old peasant skirts had covered her to the ankle and swirled when she walked. These new pencil skirts, though stylish, took a bit to get used to in the maneuvering department. Sitting on the floor with the children during story time was…interesting, to say the least.

The new skinny jeans that Cady had insisted she buy were her secret favorite. Not a single man at Ryan's football party had passed up an opportunity to look their fill. While she wasn't used to the attention, she would be lying if she said she didn't enjoy it. And if Ryan's attention, in particular, caused her stomach to do backflips, who was she to argue?

Ryan. Bree was proud of herself for gathering her nerve and confronting him with the question that had bothered her ever since he'd taken her heart with him to California. Though the answer she received was not one she'd expected, nor was his request for a second chance.

All of the changes she'd made, all of the progress. It was supposed to have been a means of moving forward, getting on with her life and leaving the past behind. She wanted her happy ever after, just like her friends. The more time she spent with Ryan and Wesley, the more she understood that no one else would do. Her love for Ryan Pettridge was her past, her present, and would continue to be her future. But would he stay in Scallop Shores for her?

They couldn't hope to have any kind of honest relationship unless she was willing to tell him the whole truth about that night. About the baby they had made and she had eventually lost. And Bree had vowed never to burden Ryan with the kind of pain she'd carried alone all these years. Oh, it would have been so easy to tell him yesterday. The opportunity had been right there. But she wasn't ready. She wasn't sure she'd ever be ready.

"Hey there. Grab a seat. Have you eaten?" Cady waved from behind the cash register as Bree stepped into the coffee shop.

"Aren't we headed out?" Maybe she had time to match models to background ideas, tab number three of her ever-expanding spreadsheet.

"Yeah, but I'm waiting for my slave labor to arrive to finish out my shift. And I repeat, have you eaten?" Hands on her hips, Cady lifted a perfectly shaped brow.

"Not since early this morning. But don't worry about it. I'll have seconds for dinner, okay, Mother?" She stuck out her tongue.

"Sit. Eat."

The timing was eerie as Cady swept around the counter with a flourish, depositing a toasted ham and cheese panini on a table near the window. She pulled the chair out for her friend and refused to budge until Bree was settled. The smell of the wheat toast and the thickly sliced Vermont cheddar had her mouth watering and, to her embarrassment, her stomach rumbling.

"Uh huh. Exactly what I thought. Bree, I swear you need a keeper."

"And I suppose you know just the man?"

"Man? Who said the keeper had to be a man?" Cady turned her back, but not before Bree caught the twinkle in her eye.

The bell over the door to the coffee shop cut their conversation short. Burke Sanders, Cady's new husband, walked in, not stopping until he had scooped his wife up in a fiery kiss that had the shop regulars hooting their approval. A light bulb went off in Bree's head and she let out a startled laugh.

"Hey Burke, before you don that gorgeous pink apron, would you join me for a minute?" She patted the chair beside her.

"Omigosh, why did I not even think of him?" Cady looked from her husband to Bree and back again.

"Quiet, missy. You get him all to yourself most of the time. Now is my turn to borrow him."

Burke looked decidedly uncomfortable with the direction this conversation was taking. Sitting down beside Bree, he reached out and snatched a potato chip from her plate. The look on his face was unrepentant and she narrowed her eyes. Fine, let's see how cocky he felt when stripped down to his abs in an embarrassing photo shoot.

"I need your body. Well, at least I think I do. Kind of hard to tell beneath that jacket." She didn't normally talk like this, but the man was starting to blush.

"Oh yeah, you want his body. Trust me." Cady licked her lips and widened her eyes.

"Call 911. I think someone has kidnapped Bree and left an imposter in her place." Burke pushed his chair back from the table and gave his wife a hard look. "And you? What the hell? I'm not into threesomes."

At that the women could no longer contain their mirth. Cady laughed so hard she snorted, which made her laugh even more. Eyes streaming and stomach cramping from her own laughter, Bree tried not to fall out of her chair as Burke eyed them both like they were a couple of escaped lunatics.

Once she could finally breathe again, she explained the fundraiser and why, exactly, she needed Burke's body. He'd drawn in on himself and she knew he wanted to tell her no. Interesting. While the ex-football players in Ryan's living room had preened and postured, Burke looked very ill at ease. Who knew Cady's man was such a shy guy?

"I don't really have a choice in this, do I?"

"You know it's the right thing to do." Her lips curled up at the corners as she reminded him, with only a look, of all the things she did to help him win Cady over.

"Fine. But I get to choose the background and it's not going to be lewd or lascivious."

"I promise it will be tasteful and aboveboard. Or as much as that can be when one is half-clothed." Bree stood up and carried her half-eaten sandwich to the small kitchen behind the counter.

As Burke wrapped a Cady's Dream apron around his waist, both women snuck up and left a different colored lipstick kiss on each cheek.

"Oh, that would be perfect! The lipstick is just the right touch. Minus the shirt, I'm thinking. How about you?" Bree turned to Cady for her opinion.

"Just the apron. And if you want to sell extra copies, a view from the back too."

"Out! Both of you, get out of here before I change my mind."

They took Cady's pickup truck to their first stop. Bree had actually never been out to her friend Shannon's place before. While Shannon and her triplets had been frequent visitors to story time at the library, they weren't as close as Cady and Bree were. Shannon and the children used to live in the caretaker's cottage next door, but once she married Dean Patterson, she moved into the ex-boy band singer's stunning showplace overlooking the harbor.

It was the middle of the week and Dean should have been at the elementary school, where he was now the music teacher. They had planned to drop by his classroom during a free period but Shannon had texted to let her know he was home with a cold. Armed with a container of Cady's homemade chicken noodle soup, the friends rang the doorbell.

Dean answered the door in a pair of navy blue sweatpants and nothing else. His blond hair was adorably rumpled and his poor nose was red and chapped. Eyeing them blearily, he stepped back to let them in. Before he could say a word, he was wracked with a nasty coughing fit.

Pressing the back of her hand against his forehead, Bree tsked. They shouldn't have come.

"You poor baby. Shannon told us you weren't feeling well. We should have rescheduled. Since we're already here, why don't we get you settled on the couch with some of Cady's amazing chicken soup? Then we'll get out of your hair. You can give me a call when you feel better."

"It's just a stupid cold. I'll be fine. Though I won't say no to a little spoiling, since Shannon isn't here to make me feel better." He was going for cheerful, Bree was sure, but the poor guy looked purely miserable.

She directed Cady to heat up some of the soup and ushered Dean through the marble foyer and back to his little nest on the couch. She lifted the trash can, overflowing with used tissues, and carried it into the kitchen.

"I feel terrible imposing on him like this. He should be asleep."

"But did you see those abs? Sign that man up! Do it while he's under the influence of cold meds and doesn't know enough to say no."

"You are positively evil."

"Come on, Bree. The abs?"

Cady was right. Dean Patterson did have spectacular chest muscles. She would be doing the women of Scallop Shores a favor by making sure he was part of the calendar. A summer month, she was thinking. Something on the beach. With a surfboard? It'd suit his coloring.

They returned to the ailing ex-boy band singer, fawning over him since his wife couldn't be there to take care of him herself. Bree brought him a fresh box of tissues from the hall bathroom. Cady set him up with a tray of soup, crackers, and some mint tea.

Before she could lose her nerve, Bree plunged in, telling Dean about the library roof and the board's unorthodox method of raising the funds needed for repairs. Between coughing jags and pauses to blow his nose, he nodded his understanding.

"Well, it's not like I'm any stranger to photo shoots. I could probably help the other guys out too. It's actually kinda hard having people you don't know look at you like a piece of meat. If you aren't used to it, it can be pretty intimidating."

Lowering her gaze to her toes, lest he believe she'd been taking another peek at his chest, she blushed. Because she hadn't peeked. Okay, maybe just a bit. Good grief. This calendar was going to kill her. Twelve hot men with no shirts on. Bulging biceps. Rippling abs. Soulful brown eyes and a touch of stubble. Somehow twelve men had morphed into one in particular. And he looked suspiciously like the one who lived right next door to her.

"Bree? I was saying we should thank Dean for his time and let him get some rest."

"Huh? Yes, thank you so much for helping me out, Dean. For helping us out. The library. The fundraiser." Yeah. Time to leave.

Her cheeks felt flushed and she was fairly certain that if she used the thermometer on the coffee table beside Dean, she'd find her temperature a few degrees higher than normal. Ignoring the smirk on Cady's face, Bree covered Dean with a light blanket (something she should have done from the beginning, in retrospect) and led the way to the front door.

"The Board thinks Ryan is the coup de grace for this calendar, and I do have to admit I'm more than a tad biased, but having Dean attached to this project is going to be a huge hit," Bree ruminated, once they were back on the road.

"I wonder how many women in town had Five of Hearts posters hanging over their beds when they were teenagers." The soft smile on Cady's face was nostalgic.

"Uh huh. Don't you mean, how many *other* women?" Bree giggled.

"I still can't believe I served that man coffee for months and never realized he was a freakin' celebrity!"

"And now I get to see him pose without his shirt. Have I thanked you, yet, for giving Martha such a fabulous idea?"

The two friends laughed as they drove back into town.

. . .

"Just so we're clear, we aren't committing to anything by putting the store up for sale, right? It's just a trial run, to see what the market is like. My parents are on the fence right now." More like he needed to do a little more in the way of convincing them that this was for the best.

Ryan followed the Realtor down the aisles, trying to look over the man's shoulder as he stopped to jot down notes. He'd meant to do this days ago but had got caught up in helping Bree plan her calendar shoot. He wasn't procrastinating … much.

"You're looking to sell the hardware store because your father will no longer be able to run it, is that right?"

"Well, yes. But I'd have to get a damned good price for it, for them. This is their nest egg. Their future."

"And there is absolutely no chance you'd want to run it for them?" Toby Horace had lived next door to Ryan's folks for as long as he could remember. He was the only Realtor in town that his father would entrust to put his store on the market.

Until the other day, he wouldn't have even given it a thought. Now, after asking Bree for another chance, the idea of selling the hardware store and rushing back to his lonely condo in California held surprisingly little appeal. Sure, he could say it was in Wesley's best interest, but was it?

At his parents' house last night for dinner, his mother had told him the visiting nurses reported a marked improvement in his dad's health since he and Wesley had come home. He was happier, less irritable over things he couldn't control. He would never be able to run his business again, but if his old man could have a quality of life that let him enjoy himself and just relax, Ryan would be happy.

"Nah. I'm a numbers guy, it turns out. Who knew, huh?"

"So I've heard." The man set aside his clipboard for a moment. "Your dad spoke very highly of you, you know."

"About what?" Ryan turned to face the shelf nearest him, making sure everything was tidy and pulled forward, even though it was already neat as a pin.

"His son, the accountant. Making a life for yourself on the other side of the country."

"It's not exactly glamorous. Certainly not compared to a career in the NFL."

"I don't think he cares one way or the other if you ended up in football, son. But you struck out on your own. You went to UCLA. You got a degree. Did a sight more than your pop ever did."

"Dad never went to college? I didn't realize."

"His father owned this store before he did. Sure, he took a few business courses here and there, but mostly learned the ropes right at his dad's elbow."

Ryan paused. He'd had his eye on a career in football from the time he was about ten years old. It wasn't something that he had ever discussed with his father. It was just a given. And his dad had been behind him one hundred percent. They never talked about him taking over the hardware store one day.

Then after his accident he'd been too ashamed to come back to Scallop Shores, to face the people that he'd let down. Thinking back, Ryan realized it was his own father he'd let down the most. In selfishly putting his own dreams first, he didn't even think about what his father might want for him, or of the legacy that the man would have to let go because he had no one to pass it down to.

"Maybe this was a mistake. I can't sell his store on him." He shook his head, running a hand jerkily through his hair.

"Hey, let's not be hasty, son. Give it a test run. You know you don't want to run it. You know he can't. At least get some money for it and give your old man the retirement he deserves, huh?"

He jotted a few more notes down and clipped his pen back on the sturdy board he'd been writing on.

"Give me a few weeks, see what I can come up with. If we don't get a nibble, then we'll try to come up with some other ideas. I'll be in touch." The Realtor pulled at the brim of his hat and nodded as he headed for the door.

Ryan ground his palms into his eyes. What he wouldn't give for a decent night's sleep! He eyed the ancient coffee maker in the office, debating whether or not it was worth the energy to make a pot. He didn't normally need a caffeine fix at this time of day, but a little jolt sure would do wonders.

The bus would be dropping Wesley off any time now. Where had the day gone? Yeah, if he was going to help the kid with his homework, he needed a shot of something. Slapping at his cheeks he stumbled down the aisle and into his dad's office to start a pot.

His old man was proud of him. For being an accountant. Go figure. He supposed running the hardware store would be somewhat gratifying if he got to do his own books. That is, if he never got an offer, or one worth accepting.

"Dad, Dad! Guess what? I got invited to join the chess team at school. It meets on Tuesdays and Allen said his mom could drop me off here on their way home."

Wesley blew in like a hurricane, tossing his backpack just inside the door of the store as he charged past the empty counter.

"Whoa, take a breath, little man. What's this about a chess club? And who is Allen?"

"It was so cold out that they let people stay in from recess if they wanted today. So I hung out at the school library. There was a group of kids playing chess and they asked me if I wanted to play. They're really nice. And Allen is in my class."

For a moment, the only sound in the room was the drip of coffee filling the small carafe. Wesley watched him, expectantly. His eyes were shining with excitement. Ryan swallowed down the urge to shout out in victory.

His kid had made a friend. By the sound of it, a whole group of friends. Forget that it was chess, another activity that he never would have considered when he was his son's age. The boy was stepping out of his walled off shell.

"Let's sign you up then."

"Sweet! I have the permission slip in my bag." The kid's huge grin was contagious.

Wesley ran off to retrieve his backpack, which had Ryan sighing in relief. He had been about to reach out to pull his son in for a hug, and he was fairly certain he wouldn't have stopped until there were some touchy-feely words thrown in and maybe a tear or two. Chalking it up to being overtired, he doctored a mug of coffee with some powdered creamer and half a packet of sweetener and took a big sip.

"Bree's here, Dad. She's walking up the sidewalk."

Aw shit. The source of his sleep deprivation, and while he was having a particularly emotional day to boot. Ryan pasted on a smile and carried his mug with him to the counter in the center of the store just as Bree pushed open the door and breezed in. A sweet floral scent teased his nostrils and he stifled a groan.

"Hey, Wes, how was school?" She put an arm around the boy's slight shoulders and gave him a quick hug.

"Awesome. I'm joining Chess Club. Dad said I could."

"That's great!" She looked over the boy's head at Ryan, the smile on her face showing just how huge she realized this was.

The things just her smile could do to a man.

Wesley continued to chatter on about school as he gathered his homework materials without being asked. Ryan had set up a second stool behind the counter for him to work, just as he'd done when he was the same age. Sucking down another fortifying sip of coffee, he finally addressed Bree.

"So what brings you in today? Any more luck with filling slots for the calendar?"

"I got two more, thank you very much. I'm hoping I'll fill the last two tomorrow. Come with me?"

Anywhere.

She reached into a tote bag and pulled out a book. Sliding it across the counter, she stopped when it reached him. Ryan looked at Bree then at Wesley, before finally looking down at the book. Ah, *Harry Potter and the Sorcerer's Stone.*

"For me?"

Nodding, she waited for his reaction. He picked up the book, leafed through the pages.

"I suppose there are enough pictures that I can muddle through. Or would that be 'muggle' through?"

Bree clutched at her chest like she was having a heart attack. "Wes, your dad just made a Harry Potter joke!"

"It's a miracle!" his son chortled.

"Maybe I'll give it a try tonight, when I'm having trouble sleeping." He didn't mean that to come out as snotty as it had.

"You've been having trouble sleeping?" Instead of looking offended, her eyes held a touch of concern.

That would change in a heartbeat if she knew the reason he couldn't sleep was because she had been dancing through his thoughts wearing nothing but the thick eyeglasses she'd worn back in high school. Old memories blended with new ones he'd like to make. The combination was distracting, to say the least.

"Well, then I'm glad I stopped by. I'm inviting you both over for dinner. I put on a crock-pot of chili before I left today and it's going to be amazing. I'm even making some cornbread muffins to go with it. How hard can it be to screw those up? It's the box stuff."

"I've never had chili. Will I like it?" Wesley frowned.

"You'll love it." She winked. "Especially when it comes with ice cream sundaes after."

"Way to negate the warm, cozy meal thing you had going there," Ryan grinned.

"Maybe you won't get any ice cream then, Mister." She stuck out the tip of her pert little tongue.

If Wesley wasn't there to chaperone, Ryan would have tasted that delicious looking tongue with his own.

Bree leaned over the counter and rested a hand on top of the one holding his cup of coffee. Her warm breath tickled his ear as she spoke.

"Perhaps you'd have better luck sleeping at night if you laid off the coffee in the late afternoon." She patted his hand and flounced out the door.

Flounced. There was no other way to describe it. The Bree he'd known in high school did not flirt. She had no clue how attractive she was. That's what drew him to her to begin with. This new Bree was far different, and Ryan was falling even harder and faster than he did back in high school. He watched the sway of her hips as she stepped off the sidewalk and marched toward her car. He was starting to want Bree Adams more than he'd wanted a career in football. And that was saying a lot.

Chapter 9

The sound of laughter and conversation floated to her from the living room. A man and his son bonding. It felt good to know she had some small role in that, even if she knew they would have found their way to each other eventually. After all, it was the high school quarterback who drew a lonely bookworm out of her shell and convinced her that she was worthy of someone's time and attention.

Bree slipped an oven mitt onto her hand and pulled the cornbread muffins out to set on top of the stove. Golden on the top. Cady would be proud. She reached into the cupboard beside the sink and snagged some ceramic bowls for the chili.

Calling the two in for dinner, her smile was a little dreamy, a little hopeful. Sure, Ryan still planned to sell the hardware store and move back to California. But a lot had happened since he'd come back to Scallop Shores. Part of that being her newly gained sense of confidence.

When he'd left the first time, she hadn't the courage to fight for him, to convince him that she was the one that could make him happy. She wasn't certain she had the courage now, but Bree knew in her heart she had to try. Fate had given them a second chance and she owed it to both of them to try.

"Bree, it smells great in here."

Ryan stepped up as though he meant to kiss her. Like it was the most natural thing in the world to do. He stopped just shy of doing so, the look on his face slightly stunned. She imagined she wore the mirror image on her own features as they stood facing each other awkwardly.

"Yeah, I can't wait to try it." Wesley seemed to have missed the exchange, having gone straight to the sink to wash up before sitting down at the table to wait for the adults.

"Thank you," she mumbled, holding her breath until Ryan moved away.

Bree filled a basket with muffins and set it in the center of the table with a plastic tub of margarine. She poured a glass of milk for everyone then spooned out bowlfuls of chili. Setting her napkin in her lap, she watched them take their first bites.

Martha Stewart she wasn't, but every woman should have one dish that they could make in their sleep and feel good about. This was hers. With her mother working full time and three little brothers to feed, Bree had gotten a lot of practice with her chili recipe.

"This hits the spot. I love it." Ryan's compliment came out on a low rumble that she could feel to the tips of her toes.

"It's not too spicy. I thought it would be like the Texas chili cook-offs I hear about," Wesley spoke between eager bites.

"Oh, I'm afraid I'm not as adventurous as that. Maybe we can experiment next time, amp up the spice and see what we can handle, hmm?" She grinned at the little boy.

"Can I help make it?"

"Absolutely."

"And maybe we can make the cornbread muffins from scratch," Wesley added.

"Well, let's not go crazy there." One thing that had never rubbed off from hanging out with Cady was her baking skills. The less time spent baking, the better.

For a meal that had spent the better part of a day simmering in the crock-pot, it was gobbled up in less than ten minutes flat. But Bree couldn't have been more pleased. Sitting across the table from Ryan, she watched his easy smile as he listened intently to

Wesley describe a classmate's visit to The Wizarding World of Harry Potter in Orlando.

Her mom would probably find it quite ironic that she chose to move out of her childhood home in order to have her own space. A place where she didn't have to cook for anyone else or care for children that weren't her own. And yet she found herself doing just that for Ryan and Wesley. Volunteering it even.

Okay, so over-volunteering was something she'd intended to work on this year. But Bree decided Ryan was officially exempt from that. She enjoyed spending time with Wesley. Even more so when they were all together ... almost like a family.

"I believe I promised someone an ice cream sundae if he ate all his dinner," she sang out during a lull in the conversation.

"I did eat it. I did!"

"But in order to earn it, you and I need to clear off the table rinse the plates and load the dishwasher for Bree." Ryan nodded at his son's empty bowl and milk glass.

She gave the man points for teaching his son manners. Pushing her chair back from the table, she allowed them to take her bowl away. Clearly they had an established routine at home because they worked together seamlessly, never getting in each other's way.

Once the table had been cleared and wiped down, Bree got out some smaller plastic bowls and spoons. She had some chocolate syrup, sprinkles, and even a jar of maraschino cherries she'd picked up on impulse at Dade's Grocery last week. She hoped they liked Cookie Dough ice cream. It was her favorite.

After dessert, Bree suggested a board game. It wasn't terribly late and she was suddenly reluctant to spend the rest of her evening in a quiet apartment with just a book to keep her company. She wasn't sure if Wesley was old enough to catch on to Monopoly and she immediately ruled out Trivial Pursuit. But it turned out he kicked butt at Clue—which he did, three times before Ryan finally told him it was time to get ready for bed.

Bree returned the board game to the hall closet while Ryan and Wesley gathered their coats and put on their shoes. She'd really enjoyed herself and she hoped they had too. Joining them at the door, her mind was already racing ahead, trying to come up with another reason to have them both over again. Was that pushy? Perhaps she should wait and see if Ryan invited her over for dinner next.

"Hey, buddy, here's the key. Let yourself in, change into your PJs and brush your teeth. I'll let you have thirty minutes of reading time before lights out, okay?"

"Aren't you coming home?"

"Right behind ya. I just wanted to talk to Bree for a minute."

Wesley started to brush past the adults then turned back and wrapped his arms around Bree. He was so slight, but he had a tight grip. Looking at Ryan over the top of the boy's head, her eyes misted. She hadn't thought, or expected to mean so much to him. Though it was little wonder, as he'd come to mean just as much to her.

"Thank you for dinner and the game," he mumbled against her stomach before hurrying off to the apartment next door.

"You lock your door when you leave, even just to come over here?" She teased Ryan once they were alone.

"Old habits. Scallop Shores is so different from our condo in California. I've missed this laid back lifestyle. It killed me having to coach Wes to be suspicious of strangers, to assume that people meant him harm and wouldn't think twice about stealing his stuff." He shot one last protective glance toward his own apartment before gently shutting the door. They were alone again, in her crowded entry hall.

She didn't want to get her hopes up. But his words gave her pause. Did he not want to go back to his old life? Would he stay and make a life here? Could they finally be together?

"Wes seems to be settling in quite nicely here." She ventured.

"He's making friends, Bree." He grabbed her hands and gripped them tightly, his eyes a bit too bright. "This is so big."

"He didn't have many friends in California?"

"He was always a loner. And because it meant I didn't have to interact with other parents on awkward play dates, I was cool with it. I never realized he was lonely. Not until I saw the excitement on his face after school today. He actually wants to be a part of something. He's seeking out friends and companionship."

Ryan let go of her hands, gripping her shoulders instead, pulling her to him in a spontaneous hug that had them both laughing from pure joy.

"And it's all because of you. You gave him the attention he needed, you listened to him and knew exactly what to say."

"Oh, I wouldn't—" Her words were cut off with a kiss.

His hands cupped her cheeks, fingers fanning out into her hair. His lips were gentle but insistent, encouraging her to let go, open up. She did, gasping as his tongue swept into her mouth, conquering, exploring. She leaned into him, her legs suddenly wobbly.

As quickly as he'd initiated the kiss, Ryan stepped away. His dark eyes were so full of emotion that she had a hard time breathing. He rubbed a thumb along her cheekbone, not saying a word. Bree turned into the caress, finding it difficult not to embarrass herself by climbing all over him.

"I want ... " he began.

Her breath hitched in her throat. Was he asking her ... ? Did he want to pick up where they'd left off all those long, lonely years ago?

" ... to stay. I was going to sell the hardware store. I put it on the market today, but it doesn't feel right."

"You can sell the hardware store and still stay, Ryan. Start your own accounting business from home. Find something else altogether. There are no limits."

"See? You always know just the right thing to say."

Her heart was still thudding from her hope that he was going to tell her he wanted her. But if he wanted to stay in Scallop Shores, that was a start. A very good start.

"I need to go make sure Wes brushed his teeth before bed. We've been having a little battle of wills over that particular issue lately."

He put a hand on the doorknob but stopped, resting his forehead against the wood. Turning around, he didn't bother to hide the raw need that pulled the skin tight against his cheekbones, drew his breath from his lungs in rasping shudders. An answering need filled her with the overwhelming urge to step into his arms, whisper to him to stay a little longer, appease the ache that had her clenching her thighs together so hard they shook. But now was not the time. She gave her head a little shake and stepped back instead of forward.

"Soon, Bree. Soon." His eyes fluttered shut for a moment before he opened them again and fixed her with a look that had her gripping the wall to keep upright.

Then he was gone.

•••

"You have a lot in common with Sam," Bree told Ryan on the way to recruit the last two models for her calendar.

She'd asked him to come along with her this morning, and given that she'd been doing most of this on her own so far, it clearly meant something for him to be there today. Though now that she'd started this particular thread of conversation, he couldn't help but wonder if his presence wasn't needed for the calendar but for another reason altogether. Both hands on the steering wheel, he studied her profile, trying to figure out what she was plotting.

Ryan had asked his mom if she wouldn't mind holding down the store for the morning. She was the one who'd trained him on the updates to the cash register and credit card system when he'd reopened the store, so she'd be fine for a few hours. He made her promise not to lift anything heavy, but Anne Pettridge could charm anyone into helping her, so he knew if she needed help she'd ask.

"Sam was on the baseball team my freshman year. I think he was a senior? Oh, man! I remember now. Wasn't it his parents that died together in their house? Carbon monoxide poisoning or something."

Bree nodded. "And he hid away from Scallop Shores for years and years."

"Well, clearly he came back, so maybe he wasn't hiding. Could have been taking a break."

She snorted at this.

"Listen to yourself, Ryan. Taking a break," she muttered under her breath as she shook her head.

"Okay, so we both left town for a number of years between visits. I totally get how coming home would remind him of his parents' death and how incredibly painful that would be to dredge it all up again."

"But he did it. He came home and he stayed home. He faced his demons and he never looked back."

Now Ryan rolled his eyes. To her, everything played out like it would in a book. Her favorite, he would guess, was a good love story. Because everyone always got their happy ending. Bree was a sucker for happy endings. He loved that about her.

"And the reason he came home, against all odds, was true love. Am I right?" He flashed her a grin.

"Don't tease me, Ryan Pettridge. Yes, as it happens, Sam did fall in love and his wife wanted to come back home to Scallop Shores. The only way to hang on to her was to follow her."

"I'm not teasing. Really. You just have this way of seeing the good in every situation." He turned to stare at the road, unable to meet her eyes as he continued. "You should have found your own happy ending a long time ago. You deserve it."

"It's just taking a little longer than usual, that's all. It will happen." She plucked imaginary lint off her skirt and studied the scenery passing on her side of the pickup truck.

They pulled up to a duplex not too different from their own, except this one had a wheelchair ramp where the front steps would have been. Sam was in a wheelchair? Ryan furrowed his brow as he hurried around to help Bree down from the truck.

"I haven't met Riley yet, but I've heard he can be a bit prickly. Cross your fingers we can get them both on board."

"Riley?"

"Sam's best friend. Afghanistan vet and paraplegic."

Ah. They climbed the ramp and knocked on the front door. It was opened by a woman with short, spiky red hair like fire. Ryan remembered her from high school. What was her name? It was a month. No, a season?

"Summer?" he tried.

She laughed even as Bree thumped him soundly on the shoulder.

"It's Wynter, actually—with a y. I know, it'd be easier to remember if my hair were white as snow. Come on in. Sam and Riley are expecting you."

Ignoring Bree's scowl, he stepped into the duplex. It was much more open and inviting than theirs. Looking around, he realized it was because the walls between the two apartments had been torn down to make one large residence. He liked it.

"Hiya." A tugging on his jeans alerted Ryan to an adorable toddler.

Her jet-black hair was pulled to the sides in little pigtails. Sam and Wynter's daughter? She didn't look like either one of them. He bent down to her eye level and smiled wide.

"Well, hello gorgeous. What's your name?"

"Charlotte." She gave him a shy grin and shoved her two middle fingers into her mouth, backwards. Oh, that was cute.

"Ah, the fickleness of youth. A new man steps into her life and she forgets all about her favorite uncle." The man seated in the wheelchair beside the couch could only be Riley.

Ryan ruffled the tot's head before getting up and approaching the adults. He shook hands with each man as they were introduced and then was waved toward the couch along with Bree.

"I'm Bree. You've probably seen me around town a time or two. And this is Ryan Pettridge. His parents own the hardware store. We're here to ask you probably the most bizarre favor you've ever been asked."

"Well, before you get down to business, can I get anyone a drink? I have a pot of coffee going. Or I can make tea," Wynter offered.

"I make tea." Charlotte raced off excitedly to a pint-sized toy kitchen in the corner.

"Our little hostess-in-the-making." Sam chuckled as she rushed back with a pink plastic cup and saucer, dumping it in Bree's lap before hurrying off to get one for Ryan as well.

"I wouldn't mind a cup of coffee if you have it already made. In addition to this fabulous tea. You must give me your recipe." Ryan addressed both mother and daughter, receiving a nod from one and a delighted giggle from the other.

"Cady said she'd spoken to Wynter and thought you two might be interested in posing for the library calendar?" Bree leaned forward, obviously eager to get down to the reason they were there.

"Question is, why would you want us? A messy-haired computer geek and a half-man. The photographer would have to lie down on the floor to get a good shot of me." Riley flung her a calculating look.

"So then he'd lie down on the floor," Bree agreed, affably.

"But..." Riley started again.

"I thought you were Sam's friend? So why would you sell the man short? Longer hair is in. And the scruff? Totally sexy. We'd definitely keep him in his element. Some kind of tech gadgets. Maybe just a laptop and a bear skin rug. Nice tight pair of jeans..." She tapped her chin, her eyes unfocused.

Ryan felt an unwelcome prickle of jealousy as Sam shifted uncomfortably in his recliner by the window. She found his scruff sexy? Riley hooted his amusement at the situation.

"Ooh, I like it." Wynter's eyes danced as she entered the room, setting a large tray on the coffee table with mugs of coffee, a carton of creamer, and a small crock of sugar. She handed her daughter a sippy cup of milk to keep her curious little hands away from the hot beverages.

"And Riley. You're ex-military. I bet you've got some interesting tats." Her probing gaze roved over the man's flannel covered arms and chest.

All three men coughed at Bree's assessment. Ryan sloshed a bit of his coffee over the side of his mug and hastened to wipe it up with a napkin. Where the hell was his shy little librarian now? She was going toe to ... wheel ... with the cantankerous veteran.

"You want to see my tats?" Riley leered nastily.

"The women of Scallop Shores would pay good money for a chance to put those tats up on their wall."

"What if I told you I didn't have any tattoos? I'm just a broken schmo that couldn't even—"

"Yeah. Boo hoo. You're in a wheelchair. Got it. You know what else that means? It means you have to use your arms way more than the average guy. It means you probably have the sexiest biceps in Scallop Shores. Show 'em off and I bet you'll have the ladies lining up out the door."

"I don't want the ladies lining up." He glared at her.

Bree didn't even flinch. She doctored her coffee, watched him calmly over the top of her mug and quietly took a sip before answering.

"Yes you do. You deserve a chance at love and happiness just as much as anyone else. But you aren't going to find it hiding out at home all the time."

"You sound like Wynter." Riley turned his chair to face away from the group seated around the coffee table.

"Great minds." Bree nodded at the woman and gave her a little wink.

Ryan watched the exchange like a tennis match, only this was far more entertaining. He could see the man was intrigued. She was bending him. Riley pretended to look disinterested but Ryan could see in the way his hands gripped his chair, the way he sat up just a little straighter, he was listening. He was considering.

"It's okay to be scared."

"I'm not scared!" Riley roared as he spun back to face the others, sending young Charlotte scrambling into Sam's lap with her fingers in her mouth again.

"Really? 'Cause I am," Sam admitted. "Definitely out of my comfort zone. But I'm learning that sometimes the best things are. And if we don't push ourselves, we miss out on something pretty special."

Riley slapped a hand to his forehead. Ryan took a sip of coffee as he thought over those words. Pretty profound speech for a 'techie'. He snuck a glance at Bree, who continued to look unflustered.

"Well, you aren't going to show me up, Scruffy. You're in, I'm in. But the photographer is going to have to come to me. I don't get out much."

"We will get him to wherever you need him," Sam spoke up.

"Why do I even bother to talk? I swear to God, no one listens to me." Riley threw his hands up in the air and let them slap down onto his lap.

"Thank you. Both of you. I can't tell you how much this means. We have a full calendar now. And the library is going to get a new roof." She stood up and approached Riley's wheelchair.

"So no tats, huh?" She'd placed a small hand on his upper arm, raising her eyebrows and nodding as she checked out the muscle hidden beneath his forest green plaid.

Ryan nearly laughed as he watched the gruff ex-military dude swallow hard as he stared at Bree's hand on his arm. She squealed in delight as he flexed for her. All right, enough was enough.

"We've lined up a photographer for next week, right Bree? We'll call you about when to come in." He set his coffee cup back down on the tray and stood up.

"Calm down, Pettridge. I don't have designs on your woman." Riley's eyes crinkled in merriment.

"She's not my woman," he blurted out.

"Well, in that case ... "

Bree had started to stand up, to turn away. Riley gripped her fingers before she could draw away completely. He held her hand, watching Ryan. Gauntlet thrown.

Bastard! Thrusting out his jaw, Ryan's lips peeled back in a sneer.

"Dude, she so *is* your woman. Even if you're too dumb to realize it." Riley held Bree's hand a moment longer before releasing it with a sigh. "If you ever get tired of this one, you know where to find me, sweetheart."

Mumbling a quick thank you, Ryan headed for the door before he decked the jerk. He was messing with him. But it still rankled. The guy had pissed him off just to amuse himself.

Bree hurried after him, scrambling up into the cab while he gunned the engine and turned the heater up against the frigid temperature. She didn't say a word, but her pursed lips and folded arms told him she wasn't pleased. Hey, he hadn't started it. The creep who thought he was God's gift to women had.

"He's lonely and insecure. I was showing the man a little kindness. Get over yourself." She finally turned in her seat to stare down her nose.

"You were flirting with him. You were touching him."

"And you reacted like a Neanderthal. Honestly, Ryan! I was trying to make the man feel just a little bit more confident about himself."

"Is that what you were doing with me the other night? At your front door? Giving me a little 'pep talk'?"

He knew he was being an ass, but he couldn't stop himself. Fuck the fact that they hadn't made it official. She was his. And it was high time he let her and everyone else know it.

"Don't listen to me. I'm talking like a crazy man. Just—" Words failed him at the moment so he decided to tell her how he felt in another way.

Hauling her across the bench seat, he pulled her into his arms and kissed her hard. Bree's hands slapped at his chest, flailing about until he caught them and wrapped them around his neck. Releasing her lips, he trailed soft kisses along her jawline, up into her hairline and over the shell of her ear. Her breath came out in tiny pants, encouraging him to press her closer, to show her what she did to him.

"Come back to my place. Wes is at school. We can be alone."

"Not like this, Ryan. Not now." She unhooked her arms and pushed herself up. Her hair was disheveled and her lipstick smeared. She looked sexy as hell.

"I need you, baby."

"Then it can wait until you aren't just reacting out of jealousy or some caveman need to prove your masculinity." Her smile was gentle, even as the smoldering look in her eyes told him she wanted him just as badly.

"I've got a birthday coming up." He quirked a brow.

She laughed out loud. "I was thinking of getting you something you'd be able to unwrap."

"Perfect. I knew we were on the same page." Trailing a hand up her thigh, he chuckled as she swatted it away.

"Not until your birthday, you dog!"

As Wesley used to say when he was younger, "*three more sleeps.*" Three more sleeps until he was in heaven.

Chapter 10

She could do this. She'd talked twelve hot men into posing for a calendar with their shirts off. She could walk into a bar and order a drink. She didn't have to talk to anyone until Cady and Quinn arrived. No, that was the old Bree talking. She'd challenge herself to make small talk with someone.

"Chardonnay, please." She shifted from one foot to the other while she waited for the bartender to pour her wine.

"Hey, if it ain't the sexy librarian? How you doin'?"

Bree turned around, ready with a nasty retort for the jerk making fun of her. It was one of the younger lobstermen that frequented Cady's Dream. And he was smiling. Like, friendly smiling. And his expression was almost ... appreciative? Wait, what?

The man made no attempt to hide the fact that he was checking out her ass in her skinny jeans. Well, his eyes started at the heels of her tall boots before roaming slowly up to her hair that she'd left down for the evening, but returned quickly to her ass. Huh.

"Um, good."

"Name's Norm. I'm sitting with a few buddies over in the corner there, if you'd like to join us." The bearded man with the friendly eyes pointed to a crowded table toward the back.

Bree's smile was hesitant. She searched the faces around her to see if anyone else was in on the gag. Was this a set up? She wasn't used to being picked up in a bar and her first instinct was to assume that she was being played.

Then again, this was her first time inside Smitty's. Perhaps if she'd found her way in here years ago, she wouldn't still be single. Oh, who was she kidding? She'd have never gotten up the nerve to meet her friends for drinks before now. She had barely managed to push herself through the door tonight.

"I'm sorry, I'm meeting someone, actually." Two someones, and they were women. But she left that last part out.

"Cool. Well, it was good seeing you." He winked at her before heading back to his table.

Bree paid for her drink and was relieved to see Quinn step through the door, waving as she spotted her. There was exactly one empty table left in the whole bar and they both headed for it from different directions.

"Ah, wine. Classy. I, myself, am in the mood for a mojito." Quinn lifted a hand in the air and signaled the waitress weaving her way between the tables.

"When did you get that streak? I love it!" Bree reached out and lifted a lock of Quinn's hair. The normal blonde strand was now a bright bubblegum pink. Bold. Much bolder than she could ever do. But it really looked good on Quinn.

"Kayla did it for me last weekend. Lily is begging to have one just like it but Jonah won't even consider it. He told her she has to be sixteen before she can have permanent color in her hair."

"Fuddy duddy." Bree grinned. Though she knew Jonah's little girl, from his first marriage, had him wrapped around her pinky and if she wanted something badly enough, he'd eventually give in.

"I know, right?" Quinn's drink arrived and they clinked glasses as they laughed.

"Hey, what fun am I missing? Digging the pink hair! That's the same shade we use in our advertising." Cady slipped the strap of her purse onto an empty chair and sat down to join them.

"So, I think I got hit on while I was waiting for you guys to get here." Bree frowned slightly.

"You think?" Cady pulled her chair closer to the table.

"He was nice. And he invited me to sit with his friends at their table." Bree nodded discreetly in the direction of the table in question.

"So what made you doubt his motives?" Quinn looked confused.

"I don't know. Because it's me, I guess. And he recognized me as the town librarian."

"And didn't run screaming in the other direction?" Cady shook her head. "Sweetie, you need to get used to the attention. Things like that are going to happen more and more often."

"Until word gets out … that I'm off the market." She hunched her shoulders and winced, unsure what their reaction would be to that bombshell.

"Whoa, are we still talking Ryan Pettridge? Girl, you have it bad for him." Quinn took a sip of her Mojito and shared a knowing look with Cady.

It was now or never. The reason she'd invited them to meet her for drinks tonight. They didn't understand the history between her and Ryan. No one did. Theirs had been a secret love, all those years ago. And quite short-lived as it turned out.

But now he wanted to start over—or was it again? Oh, it was so confusing! And he wanted to pick up right where they'd left off. It wasn't like she was a prude or anything. Sure, she hadn't had sex since their one and only night together. But the more time she spent with Ryan, the more she was reminded that she had a libido and it was tired of waiting.

And then right behind that, the guilt. She owed him the whole truth about what had happened that night. Ryan deserved to know that he'd fathered a child before Wesley. That his son or daughter hadn't made it past their twelfth week of gestation. But keeping news like that to herself had become such a force of habit that sharing it with him, with anyone, was almost impossible to contemplate.

So she'd called Cady and Quinn and initiated her first girls' night out. She'd made herself a promise: no more keeping this painful secret alone. No more holding it over her own head as punishment for acting on her feelings for Ryan. Tonight she'd finally get it out in the open, get some advice from the women she'd come to trust.

"Wait, I definitely need a drink for this!" Cady waved down the waitress and ordered a beer.

And I need another one. Bree asked for another Chardonnay, gulping down the last two sips remaining in her glass before plunking the empty stemware onto the startled waitress's tray.

"Damn, we should have chosen a designated driver for tonight." Cady sat back in her chair, slapping a happy tune on the table with her hands.

"This will be my only one then." Quinn sipped slowly, her gaze speculative.

"Good thing we talked you into buying out Victoria's Secret. What set are you going to wear? The black lace thong? That hot electric blue number?"

Bree took a deep breath, looking from one friend to the other as she collected her nerve. The wine had relaxed her muscles, made her tongue go a little numb. But the butterflies in her stomach were still restless as hell and she wished they'd take a little nap, just long enough for her to tell her story.

The waitress brought their drinks around and Bree left her a big tip, encouraging her to come back and check on them often. After seeing her down half of this second glass of wine before she spoke, both women now watched silently. She chewed at her lower lip, laughing nervously.

"Sorry, I'm a little out of my element tonight. The bar scene, girl talk ... trying to get up the nerve to spill some heavy shit." She gasped, surprised that a curse word could slip out of her mouth so easily. Maybe she shouldn't hit the alcohol quite so hard.

"Sweetie, you can tell us anything, you know that, right? It goes no further than this table." Cady scooted her chair closer, patting Bree's hand.

"Okay, yeah, so … Ryan Pettridge. This isn't the first time we've fallen for each other. It won't be the first time we've had sex."

"But I thought he dated the head cheerleader all through high school. Haley Carmody? He married her while they were still in college, right?" Quinn pulled her own chair closer to Bree's.

"Yes and yes. And so that you don't have to be the one to say it out loud, I slept with him the summer he left for college—while he was still dating Haley."

There was a long pause while the other two women digested this news.

"You were so shy in high school. He must have meant a lot to you for you to be so brave," Quinn breathed.

"Why did he stay with her?" Cady looked like she was starting to get defensive on Bree's behalf.

"We were very much in love and the stupidly ironic part is that he stayed with her because he felt so awful for cheating on her. And he felt that I deserved better than a man who couldn't be faithful to his girlfriend."

"Clearly he was meant to be with you, not her. They didn't even last." Cady clinked her bottle of Sam Adams against Bree's glass of Chardonnay.

"And fate has brought them together again. It's kismet." Quinn's hands fluttered over her heart, and Bree knew by the dreamy look on her face that she was sincere.

She'd done the right thing, coming to them. Taking another fortifying breath, she continued.

"There's just one thing Ryan never knew about our time together. A big thing. That I never told anyone about before tonight."

Reaching for her glass, she downed the contents in one gulp, shuddering as it burned a trail down her throat. She carefully set it back on the table as the room began to spin just a little. If she weren't so focused on purging herself of this guilt, she might have giggled over how carefree she felt, limbs pleasantly heavy. Did she still have lips? She brought a hand to her mouth just to make sure. Yep, still there. Just couldn't feel 'em.

Gone were the guessing games as Cady and Quinn waited patiently for her to tell her story. That sobered her up a bit. She blinked, hoping like hell that she could get through this without crying.

"There was a baby. I didn't tell anyone, not even my mother. But I was so happy. A little piece of Ryan, of the love we shared. I could only have him for that one special night. But this baby was mine forever." She twisted her fingers together in her lap, too scared to look up and gauge her friends' reactions so far.

"I knew he loved me. I never doubted it. He did the noble thing by staying with Haley. And since I had my own little reminder of our love, it didn't hurt quite as much."

She reached for her wine glass, only to remember it was empty. Cady made to signal for the waitress and Bree stopped her with a shake of her head. She needed to be able to remember this conversation in the morning or it was all for nothing.

"I was twelve weeks along when the bleeding started. I was away at college. They couldn't stop it."

"Oh, Bree."

Her eyelids stung as both her friends reached out, pulling her into an awkward group hug. When they drew away, tears rolled unchecked down their own cheeks. She was holding it together by a thread, her chest thick with emotion, concentrating on keeping her breathing even. Cady grasped one of her hands and Quinn the other. They sat like that for a few moments, just holding on, lending their support and sharing in her grief.

"I thought, this isn't a coincidence. God is punishing me for being with someone else's boyfriend. I pulled into myself—even more than usual. I hid behind my books. I told myself I didn't deserve friends, dates, or any kind of social life."

She gave them a tremulous smile.

"But this has gone on long enough. I made a decision at your wedding, Cady. I am through punishing myself over something I had no control over. Ryan and I have a chance to start again, to do things right this time around."

Cady pulled out her phone and started texting. Bree's eyes widened and she made a panicked grab for Cady's arm.

"What are you doing? You promised not to say anything!"

"I just asked Burke to come by and pick us all up in an hour. Screw the DD role, Quinn, this night requires fortification. Waitress!"

Bree let out a shaky laugh. The tightness in her chest began to ease. Her friends had stopped crying. The mood at the table wasn't exactly convivial, but it was getting better. She felt lighter than she had in years. The guilt she'd carried over the loss of her baby was a physical weight that had dragged her down. And now it was very nearly gone.

"He needs to know, Bree."

"One step at a time. I've spent the last thirteen years protecting Ryan from the pain I have dealt with every day. I don't want to think about how he's going to feel to know he lost a baby."

"Just so he doesn't feel betrayed that you didn't tell him." Quinn shrugged her shoulders as she accepted her new Mojito.

Yeah, there was that. Bree lifted her glass in a mock salute and took a big sip.

"Thank you for being there for me, you guys."

"Uh oh, we have officially reached the 'I love you, man' drunk portion of the evening," Cady snorted.

"Oh, I'm not there ... yet." Bree smiled and raised the wine to her lips again.

Setting her glass down, she made to scoot her chair back to go visit the ladies' room. The woman at the table behind her was practically backed up against her. Bree muttered an 'excuse me' and waited for the blonde to move closer enough to her own table so Bree could get out of her chair. Rolling her eyes, she frowned at the woman's back. Some people just had no concept of personal space!

•••

His mom had outdone herself. Okay, given that he hadn't been home to celebrate his birthday in—oh, his entire adult life—he figured she had every right to make a big deal. But the balloons and streamers? Ryan felt the flush creep across his face and down into the collar of his shirt to tickle his neck.

"Wow, Grandma, way cool!" Wesley pushed past his father, admiring the decorations that covered nearly every square inch of the house.

"Aw, Ma, you shouldn't have." *Really, she shouldn't have.*

"Nonsense. This is the first time my baby has been home to celebrate his birthday in way too many years to count." She gave him a look that brooked no argument. "Consider this my chance to play catch up for all the birthdays I didn't get to spend with you."

"My mom always says that birthdays are more of a celebration for the mother than the child. Whenever my brothers or I have a birthday, she insists we wish her a 'happy birthing day.'" Bree's grin was sheepish.

"Oooh, I like that! Happy birthing day. Remember that, Ryan." Anne patted his cheek and gave Bree a warm hug. "I am so glad you could come with the boys tonight, Bree."

"Thank you for inviting me. Is there anything I can do to help?"

"Beyond keeping everyone company while I finish fixing up dinner? Not a thing. You two go on in and visit with your father." Anne waved them toward the living room and headed back to her own domain.

Ryan slipped his hand into Bree's as they walked. They were leaving Wesley to spend the night with his grandparents. Bree was coming home with him tonight. It was all he could think about. Happy birthday, indeed!

His father sat up straighter in his hospital issued bed. The slackness in his jaw was not quite as pronounced. His fingers were able to grip the television remote, even if they were still a little shaky. With enough concentration and patience, Bo was making real strides with his recovery.

"Hey, Dad. You remember Bree, right? She single-handedly saved my ass from being kicked off the football team?"

Bo nodded, a welcoming smile turning up the edge of one side of his mouth. Bree leaned in and gave the older man a quick hug. She turned and laughed at Ryan.

"You know, just because you've been gone all these years, doesn't mean we all have. I walk past the hardware store nearly every day. I'd stop by and have a little chat with your dad a couple times a week."

"I never knew that." Ryan watched the camaraderie between the two with wonder. Had his father just managed a wink? Damned if the old guy wasn't doing a hell of a lot better than they'd all thought.

"He'd keep everyone informed on his hometown hero son. I think half his sales came from folks coming in to ask how you were doing." She'd perched on the edge of the mattress, grasping one of his father's hands in her own.

"Oh, for the love of Pete! I'm not a hometown hero. I'm just a schmuck who got lucky enough to be recruited by UCLA to play a little ball. And what was there to tell? I am an accountant. I sit at a desk and add up columns of numbers all day."

"And you live in Southern California, which is wildly exciting to the people of this town, when you figure most of them have never been outside of New England. You have an incredibly smart, well-read son. Shall I go on?" God, she was giving him a look to rival one of his mother's.

"Grandma says to help Gramps to the table for dinner." Wesley popped his head in just long enough to issue the announcement before disappearing again.

"You're just full of surprises tonight, aren't you, Dad? Joining us at the table for dinner. That's incredible!"

His father grumbled something unintelligible. Given that he'd been brushing off his own importance just moments before, he wouldn't be surprised if his father was doing the same thing. Like father, like son.

The man had been resting on top of his covers, so it wasn't as difficult to help him out of bed as Ryan would have thought. The arm around his shoulders was strong, gripping tightly. Ryan walked slowly, allowing his father to shuffle along at his own pace. The smile on his face was huge, and he didn't care how goofy he looked. His dad was walking again. In a matter of weeks, after being told he really ought to consider moving to an assisted care facility like Kittridge Manor, he was up and walking.

Apparently there was a "birthday chair," judging by the cluster of balloons attached to the seat that had been his since he was a boy. Ryan shook his head, embarrassed by the attention, and yet honored that his mom would go to such great lengths. He helped his father take his seat at the head of the table and waited until Wesley and Bree were in their own chairs before batting at the balloons bopping him in the back of the head as he sat down.

"Holy crap, Mom—you still have that old thing?"

Ryan referred to the deep fat fryer that his mother had used to make his favorite birthday meal every year from the time he was about twelve until he'd gone off to college.

"Watch your mouth, young man! You're supposed to be setting an example." She clucked, passing a plate of homemade French fries to Bree.

"Sorry." He exchanged a mischievous look with Wesley before grabbing the tongs and helping himself to a piece of juicy fried chicken.

His mother had pulled her own chair up close to his dad's. Ryan watched as she cut up a piece of chicken and a few fries into bite size pieces and fixed a plate for his father. It said a lot for the man that he was willing to be fed in front of his son, his grandson, and his son's new girlfriend.

Girlfriend. Ryan paused, a fry halfway to his mouth, as he rolled the term over in his mind. God knew it wasn't what he'd been looking for when he and Wesley came back to Scallop Shores. But things had a way of working themselves out. And he couldn't think of a better way to spend his birthday than surrounded by all the people he loved.

After dinner, his mom returned to the fridge for cake and ice cream. How long had it been since he'd had cake that was actually made from scratch? Truth of it was, he'd given up even bothering with store bought cake for his own birthday since Wesley was a little tyke. Birthdays were for kids, anyway.

But as he took a bite of the rich devil's food cake with decadent buttercream frosting, Ryan moaned. Yeah, he could definitely get used to this. Around the table, similar sounds of appreciation could be heard. His mother sat up a little straighter, pride glowing in her eyes.

"So what was your favorite part of your birthday, Dad?" Wesley asked, before digging a finger through the frosting left on his plate and popping it in his mouth.

The part that was coming up after he and Bree left for the evening. But since he couldn't say that out loud, "Getting to spend this time with my son, my parents, and my favorite girl."

"Is Bree your girlfriend?" Wesley tipped his head to the side, studying both his father and Bree.

Ryan looked up to see that Wesley wasn't the only one waiting on his response. He winked at his son and turned his attention to the woman in question. "Yep. My girlfriend. My sweetie. My better half." He loved how he was able to turn her cheeks a bright shade of pink.

"Good." Wesley's response only served to broaden his own smile and deepen the blush spreading all the way down Bree's neck.

Though he tried to insist he help out with the dishes once everyone was done eating and the table had been cleared, Bree pushed him out of the kitchen. Then she snagged Wesley to help with the drying.

It had been a fun evening and he had meant it when he said he'd really enjoyed spending time with his whole family, but Ryan was anxious to finally be alone with Bree. This was the start of a new life together, the life they should have had all along. They would be a family, together with Wesley. But tonight was just for them.

They would reacquaint themselves, remembering everything that had drawn them together all those years ago. And they would explore each other with new eyes, as adults instead of the lovestruck teens they had been. Ryan shifted uncomfortably, his hand reaching to check for the telltale bump of the condom stuffed in his back pocket.

It wasn't like he'd needed to bring it with him. He could have left it in his bedside drawer. But his dad had always taught him to be prepared. Great. Now visions of pulling off on a remote stretch of road to make love to Bree in his pickup truck had him squirming for an entirely different reason.

"Dishes are done." Wesley flopped down on the couch to watch the episode of *Jeopardy* that was playing on TV.

"Thank God!" Ryan ducked his head to avoid the startled looks he got. Probably shouldn't have said that quite so vehemently. Crap.

"Wesley, dear, why don't you wish your father a happy birthday and let him and Bree go off to celebrate the rest of his birthday like adults do."

"Jesus, Ma!" His mouth dropped open in horror.

"By staying up late, going to a movie and maybe out for drinks. What did you think I meant?" She looked genuinely puzzled.

His father, by this point, was laughing out loud. His mom looked from father to son, not understanding what she'd started with all this. Ryan stood up quickly, thankful that Bree hadn't been around to listen to the exchange. He pulled Wesley in for a hard hug and a tender kiss on the forehead.

He started to hug his father but the man pointed to his back pocket, a sign they'd invented back when Ryan had been in high school and his old man had wanted to ask if he was carrying a condom. When he nodded in affirmation, he was rewarded with a shaky thumbs up sign.

Jesus. It was time to go. He rounded up their coats and called for Bree, who was still puttering around the kitchen, wiping down counters. She seemed nervous, but just as anxious to start the rest of their evening as he was.

Not taking the time to heat the truck up beforehand, they shivered and shook as they climbed in. Ryan cranked the heater up to the highest setting, grabbing a handful of Bree's wool coat and hauling her nearly onto his lap before kissing her roughly.

"I need you so bad I feel like I'm going to explode."

"Well then, let's break some speed limits, Casanova." She shocked him by cupping him through his jeans and squeezing.

He was going to die. Slamming the truck into gear, he tore out of the driveway, imagining his father would have renewed his laughing fit as he heard the tires squealing in hasty retreat.

Less than five minutes later they roared up the short driveway to the duplex. Bree yelped when he hauled her across the bench to slide out of his side of the truck. Pressing her against the cold metal, he kissed her deeply, reaching under her coat for any skin he could get his hands on. Her fingers dug through his hair and her tongue thrust boldly into his mouth.

"Ahem. Hate to interrupt, but it's frickin' cold out here and I can't feel my toes anymore."

Ryan wheeled around in shock. He'd had no idea they weren't alone. Who the hell was standing on his porch? And was that a suitcase? "What the f—?"

"Happy birthday, Ryan. Miss me?"

Stepping out of the shadows to stand directly under the porch light was his ex-wife, Haley.

Ah, shit. This was not good.

Chapter 11

Bree smoothed down her hair, took a calming breath, put on her game face, and stepped into the old warehouse that had been rented out for the calendar photo shoot. This was a huge day and she could not afford to be distracted. They were near the water and her stomach rebelled at the briny fish smell.

On her way out the door, she'd filled her favorite travel mug, a bright pink one that her little brothers had given her for Christmas, with a strong, dark brew. Raising it to her lips now, she changed her mind at the last minute. She needed all the help she could get to keep her breakfast down, this morning.

After Ryan had gotten over his shock at having his ex-wife turn up on his porch, prepared to stay a while, he invited Haley inside. To his credit, he'd invited Bree too, but she'd hightailed it back to her own place. She'd needed to be alone. Not knowing exactly what happened after that was doing a number on her nerves. Had Haley attempted to seduce him? Where had she slept last night? Or more importantly, where had Ryan slept?

There was absolutely nothing to worry about, she told her strung-out brain. Her overactive imagination had kept her from getting any sleep the night before. Bree tried to keep in mind that she and Ryan had found each other again. They were in a committed relationship. They had been about to take the next step before Haley had interrupted. They were going to be one big happy family, her and Ryan and Wesley. They were starting over. It was their second chance. Everything was just dandy.

"You okay?" Bree stumbled to a stop as Foster laid a hand on her shoulder.

"Of course. A little nervous I admit, but—" Oh, crap. The way he was looking at her. Haley was here. At the warehouse. The woman had shown up at *her* photo shoot.

"What kind of game does Haley think she's playing?" Foster sneered.

"Who says it's a game? People come home all the time. Maybe she's just looking for a fresh start." Her jaw ached with the effort to look unaffected by the woman's presence.

Heading off in search of the photographer, Bree tried to ignore the dull throbbing that was sure to turn into a killer headache by lunchtime. She didn't have time for this, for any of this. Seriously, what was Haley even doing here? No one invited her. Had they?

Across the warehouse, the former head cheerleader held audience, laughing and tossing her hair back. One possessive arm snaked tightly around Ryan's bicep. To his credit, the man looked as though he would rather be anywhere else. Nope, she had no time for this. Insecurities be damned!

The large, empty room had been set up in sections, each one with various props and backdrops to set the scene. Bree and Damian, a talented photographer known throughout the Seacoast, had already come up with a preliminary list of which man would model for which month, with some basic background ideas. Being early February, outdoor location shots were not practical. She imagined the men she'd lined up for the winter months were grateful.

As each of her models arrived, Damian insisted they get "into costume," which basically meant they were to strip down to their pants. In some cases, less, in some a little more. Lucas had been asked to bring his turnout gear, and now wore the heavy pants with nothing but his strapping chest and wide shoulders, liberally dotted with ginger freckles to match his red hair, to hold up the suspenders. Bree nearly melted in a puddle when she caught a glimpse of the shy firefighter rubbing his neatly trimmed beard against a Dalmatian puppy.

Was it warm in here? She plucked at her blouse, trying to generate a little breeze, while making a concerted effort to maintain eye contact. This wasn't awkward at all. No siree! She stepped around Cady's brother, Chase, who was in the makeup chair, wearing his dress uniform. Well, most of it. Snorting, she wondered where he'd put his badge.

"Hey, Bree, this guy says I'm supposed to leave my jeans unzipped. Don't you think that's a bit much?" Burke approached her, his hands held protectively over his package.

"Humor him. It won't take but a second. Damian promised nothing lewd. You're safe for now." She paused to fix his hair, seeing he'd wrecked the job the hairdresser had done only moments before.

As Haley's bubbly laughter reached her ears Bree grit her teeth and hummed the theme song to *Jeopardy*, making her way over to the first area that was sectioned off. Just because the woman had invited herself here did not mean she had to acknowledge her presence. It didn't bother her at all that Ryan's ex-wife was hanging all over him. The poor guy probably felt so awkward. Bree looked up in time to see Ryan high-fiving one of his old teammates.

The pencil in her fist snapped with enough force to send both pieces flying in opposite directions. Bree laughed nervously, thankful that the only person who had noticed was someone in Damian's employ. She gave the young woman a helpless shrug and hoped she just looked like a ditz.

Focusing on the task at hand, she rifled through the notes she'd made on the January setting as she reached the lifelike backdrop of a roaring fire. They probably could have gotten the real thing, but it would have meant hauling Damian and his equipment to one of the local hotels or bed and breakfasts, gaining permission and a lot of added attention from curious bystanders. She nodded at the thick, cozy rug on the ground, and the thin-stemmed champagne flutes ready to be filled. Sam was her Mr. January. Pondering her promise to add something techy to his backdrop, she figured it would be simple enough to have him studying something on an iPad.

The red velvet couch that greeted her for the February backdrop was a bit garish, in Bree's opinion. Though she liked the smart black tux draped over the back. Nice touch. She and Damian had argued about the placement of the model on this one. She felt that Foster should be seated on the sofa, surrounded by roses, chocolates, and a Valentine's greeting card, almost like he was taking stock of what he'd need for his date that evening. Damian wanted him draped across the couch cushions with the card and a single red rose, having fallen asleep dreaming of his love. Grudgingly, she knew the photographer would get his way.

March was set up for Lucas and his little Dalmatian friend with a picture of a fire engine. April was a workbench with soil, assorted pots, and lots of fresh flowers they'd had to struggle to find in winter. While she had originally pictured Dean with a surfboard, she had to admit that Damian's placement was better. Dean approached, offering her a comfortable grin and a friendly wave. He wore a pair of tight, grubby jeans with holes in the knees, and a liberal dousing of potting soil. Though it killed her to leave it alone, she imagined the smudge of dirt across his left cheek was deliberate. Bree gripped her clipboard to keep from messing up the makeup artist's work and headed for May.

A bike rider, a picnic scene, and a hot summer day by the pool. Check, check, and check. Oh my! She'd told Doyle to plan on swim trunks for his portion of the photo shoot. The man wore Speedos and a smear of zinc oxide down the strip of his nose. Nothing else. She never would have guessed he had quite so many tattoos. She mumbled a quick "good morning" and moved on.

Using her clipboard for a fan now, she hurried to the August set just in time to hear Damian and Jonah arguing over how he should pose by the ladder.

"You have the ass for it. Just trust me on this. Place one foot on the first rung and let's see you strain those back muscles."

"Jesus, isn't it enough that I'm wearing my frickin' tool belt and barely anything else? Leave me a little dignity, will ya?"

Seeing the two men square off in what could turn into a nasty showdown, Bree was quick to step in and alleviate the building tension.

"Jonah, if your back is to the camera, you won't have to worry about your face even being in the shot. The women of Scallop Shores may not even realize that it's you." Who was she kidding? The great ass? The tool belt? Hands down, one of the tallest men in town? How could it be anyone else?

"I hadn't thought of it like that. You're right, Bree. Thanks.' He smiled gratefully and she fled before he could see she wasn't exactly being honest with him.

"This is just like old times, isn't it, Ry?" Bree overheard as Haley giggled and gave her ex a squeeze.

"Yep. A little too much like old times. I feel ridiculous." Ryan tried to shrug out of his ex-wife's reach.

Squaring her own shoulders, she marched in. Show time.

"Now, I've got to tell you, Ryan. Yours was the only shoot I didn't have control over. The board members wanted it just like this." Ignoring Haley altogether, Bree gave Ryan a sympathetic smile.

The backdrop was a football field, with a patch of Astroturf to match. Damian wanted his ex-quarterback sprawled on the grass, letterman's jacket hooked on one finger and draped over his shoulder. A come-hither look in his eyes. He wore a pair of tight white uniform pants and a Wildcats helmet had been placed beside him.

"Not blaming you. Just don't like it." His words were terse, his back muscles tense.

"Hi there. I'm Haley, Ryan's wife. Oops, I mean ex-wife. How silly of me!" Haley held out a hand in greeting.

Oh, no she didn't! Several of the models had been standing near enough to hear Haley's introduction. Now they all waited, with bated breath, to see how Bree would handle this. The woman wasn't stupid, she was calculating. But why pretend she didn't know Bree? What was her game?

"We've met." Bree wasn't going to indulge Haley by explaining any further.

"Oh, yes. I saw you last night. You're Ryan's neighbor."

Yeah, his neighbor. She'd seen them practically screwing against the side of his truck and that made her just ... his neighbor. Awesome.

"Haley, this is Bree. Remember Bree from school? You asked her to tutor me." Ryan, it appeared, was the only one who didn't see this slight for what it was.

"The mousy little bookworm? No way! You look so different now. Almost ... pretty." Haley tried to reach for Ryan again but he stepped up beside Bree.

The woman had gone too far. Ryan's friends had turned narrowed eyes on her and started mumbling amongst themselves. An apology in his eyes, he settled a hand on the small of Bree's back and tried to guide her away from Haley. But Bree stood her ground. If she didn't say anything now, she'd be labeled weak.

"Hey, easy mistake. I looked a lot different in high school. We all did, though, didn't we?" Let her take that one how she would.

"But I'm really liking the new look. Makes me feel sexy, you know?" She took a step closer to Haley. "And I hope you don't find it too awkward that Ryan's dating the mousy bookworm."

She settled her back against Ryan's wide chest and tried to pretend she wasn't about to hurl. Lucas, Doyle, and Chase were clearly enjoying the exchange. Ryan's heart beat rapidly enough for her to feel it through her shirt. He knew, as she did, that Haley was probably not done with her. She needed to show Ryan's ex that she was not intimidated.

"Oh, sweetie, I have the best idea! Since Haley is staying with you guys for the time being, why don't you let her and Wes have a little bonding time? I bet it's been ages since she's seen her own son. You'll be right next door if they need anything." Game. Set. Match.

By the nasty look in Haley's eyes, it was high time for a hasty retreat. This time Bree let him drag her to a quiet corner of the warehouse. Without a word, Ryan wrapped his arms around her, kissing the top of her head as he rubbed her back in wide circles. They were quiet for a moment before he finally nudged her chin up with a finger so they were eye to eye.

"I feel like I'm on some freakin' reality show. Tell me Haley is not back in my life."

"Wish I could, Ryan." She stepped up on tiptoes and brushed her lips against his.

"Then tell me you meant what you said about having her spend time with Wes tonight. We can pick up where we were so rudely interrupted."

"Are you sure? Do you trust her with him?" Selfishly speaking, it had sounded like a great idea at the time. But the more she thought about it, the more Bree began to have doubts.

"You mean, am I worried she'll run off with him? Hell no! She never wanted him in the first place. She won't know what to do with him tonight. But she doesn't really have a choice. He deserves to get to know his mother, the good and the bad. And he is old enough to pick up on vibes. He needs to understand."

Bree liked to think that even Haley wasn't so cruel as to pass up the opportunity to play the role of "fun mom" for an evening. If she didn't intend to have a permanent place in her son's life, she could at least entertain him with the grand adventures she'd been having while Ryan was being a stickler about homework and brushing teeth. She wouldn't have to break Wesley's heart.

"You'll be right next door if he needs you."

He rested his chin on top of her head and let out a gusty sigh.

"I haven't gotten the whole story out of her yet, but I'll figure out why she's here and how to get rid of her. She may be Wesley's mother, but there is no reason for Haley to have any role in *my* life, whatsoever." Ryan kissed her again and headed back to the September backdrop, where Damian was waving his arms madly.

What a crazy nightmare! But they were facing it together. Confident that the doubts her imagination had conjured overnight were unfounded, Bree smiled a genuine smile for the first time that day. Whistling to herself, she headed for the October set.

Ryan's friend and former teammate, Jamie, was a mountain of a man. Which made the kittens in the basket on his lap look all the more tiny. It was an adorable juxtaposition and one that would have the women of Scallop Shores sighing as they forked out their cash.

Note to self, she thought. Make sure the Dalmatian puppy does not see those kittens.

• • •

Because his mother raised him right, Ryan helped Haley out of her coat before tossing it in the closet along with his and storming into the living room. Thank God Wesley had spent the night with his grandparents. Haley settled comfortably into a corner of the couch, her high heels kicked off and her bare feet curled under her.

"Seven years. No contact in seven years. And just to clarify, I am not complaining, merely stating a fact. But *my* kid is due home from school in exactly half an hour and he'll be expecting some sort of explanation for your presence." She may have given birth to him, but seeing as she'd signed her rights away all those years ago, he was perfectly justified in reminding her that Wesley was his kid and his alone.

"Rowr. Easy, Tiger. You're awfully sexy when you're worked up." Haley watched him with playful eyes.

"Could you be serious for one minute? Why here? Why now? Your parents are just a few streets down. Why couldn't you stay with them?"

"You'd think that would be the obvious choice, wouldn't you?" She studied her red lacquered nails, avoiding eye contact.

"Are you in some kind of trouble? Wait, are you pregnant?" Ryan stopped pacing and whirled on his ex-wife.

"Oh, please! Do I look like a stupid sixteen year old? The one and only time I ever got pregnant, I did it for you."

Ah, yes, the selfless martyr. He rolled his eyes, waiting her out. Haley squirmed around on the couch.

"They wouldn't take me in. They're a little fed up with my *choices*." She made finger quotes as she spoke.

"You were going to be an actress. You'd done some modeling. I know it's a tough business to break into, but I thought you were getting somewhere."

"Headshots cost money. Agents cost money. Schmoozing and being seen in the right places. You get the picture, Ry."

"Your parents were footing the bill for all of it." Ryan groaned, kneading the muscles at the back of his neck, sore from a night spent on the couch.

"It wasn't like I didn't try to help out. I'm not completely selfish. But you never know when auditions will come up and it's really hard to get a boss to juggle your schedule at the last minute."

"You got fired." He began to pace again.

"The catalyst in a series of unfortunate events." Her delicate sigh held just enough drama to remind him of her true calling.

Ryan had to admit that Haley made a damned fine actress. Even if she'd considered herself too pretty to hang out with the drama club kids in high school. Relying on her looks to get her where she thought she needed to be, Haley turned her nose up at high school roles. Her sights were set much higher.

"What happened, Hal?" He used the nickname she'd barely tolerated when they first started dating.

Her eyes snapped to his and for the first time he could see the turmoil. She was frustrated, angry, and upset. That was understandable. Haley was used to getting her way. But she was also scared. And this was a side of his ex-wife that he'd never seen before.

"Let's just say I couldn't afford the lifestyle I'd chosen for myself." She hung her head, picking at the knee of her skintight leopard-print leggings.

"I'm assuming you were still waiting tables at that joint all the Hollywood muckety-mucks frequented near the studios?" He pressed his lips together when she merely shrugged. "So you were fired from your job, then you were kicked out of your upscale apartment because you could no longer pay the rent. Am I close?"

"I lost the Prius too," she pouted.

"My alimony checks are still getting cashed. You got a hell of a deal on that. What, exactly, am I paying for if you don't have an apartment or a car?"

"How do you think I could afford to fly back home? Thank you for that, by the way." She had the audacity to sound cheerful, like he had bought her a gift.

"And now you're here to mooch off me. Live rent free. Eat my food. Use my washing machine and shower. How did you even know I was back in town? Or did you try looking for us in Cali first?" It didn't matter. If she was desperate enough, it wouldn't have been hard to find him.

"It's not like that. Give me a little credit. Is our getting back together so far out of the realm of possibility that you can't even imagine it?" She stretched her long legs out on the couch in her classic "Come and get me, Tiger" pose. Years ago, that would have had him rock hard and salivating in seconds.

"I'm with Bree now, Hal." He could have added, "Like I should have been all along," but that would have been unnecessarily cruel. No sense kicking his ex while she was already down.

"And besides, I'm not stupid—or blind. I saw the way you were ogling every single guy at that calendar shoot today. Why did you even come with me to that, if not to hook up? Whose number did you score? Hmm?"

She had the good grace not to deny it.

"You need money. You need to pay your parents back for all the help they've given you. You need to get back on your own two feet and support yourself, and you need to give up the idea of your own talk show."

"Reality show. And I will make it someday. Jesus, you're worse than my parents! Where do you get off telling me I have to give up my life's dream? It's not like you're some huge NFL All-Star with your own bobble head and T-shirts."

"Classy. Yeah, throw that in my face, why don't you? That hasn't been my dream in a long time. As a matter of fact, it was more your dream than mine. I just wanted to play ball. You wanted me to be the big household name."

"You have to admit that would have been a helluva premise for a reality show. The Hollywood starlet and her big, hunky pro-football husband."

Nope. He didn't care for it any more now than he did back when she'd first suggested it in college. In fact, the idea made him throw up in his mouth just a little. It was on the tip of his tongue to tell his ex that this just wouldn't work, but she must have sensed that. Haley flew off the couch, gripping his forearms and fixing him with an award-winning look of pure desperation, complete with tears.

"I have nowhere else to go, Ry. My parents are through with me. My brothers and sisters won't answer my phone calls or emails. I burned too many bridges trying to get what I wanted. And now I have to face the consequences."

Haley's family was a great group of people. Patient and caring, he couldn't imagine what it would take to get any of them to give up on one of their own. She might think that being broke, with no place to live, was bad. But if she'd alienated people that Ryan honestly couldn't see turning their backs on anyone, then Haley had much bigger problems than she realized.

"Do you think I want to be here? It's humiliating, having to admit that I need help. But this could be a good thing, Baby. I can help you out with Wesley. He deserves to know his momma. We have years of catching up to do."

Ryan tried not to flinch at the feel of Haley's fingers wrapped tightly around his arms. He wasn't sure when, but at some point, a long time ago, lust had turned to disgust and he could barely stand being this close to the woman. But she had a point. Wesley was her son, too, and even though he could legally tell her to screw off, he just wasn't that kind of guy. This was the part of parenthood where he had to do what he should, even if it wasn't what he wanted.

"Bottom line, Haley: you want to stay here, then you get a job. You put twenty-five percent of your earnings aside to pay your parents back. The rest you save. I won't make you contribute to rent or food, but I need to know you're socking everything away. And this situation is temporary. As soon as you are making enough to support yourself, then you find your own apartment and you become the woman your parents know you can be."

"I'll be your live-in babysitter, but I refuse to be your maid, as well." She'd let go of him to fold her arms across her chest and thrust out her pointed chin.

"You abandoned Wesley once before, but he is your son by blood, and as long as you live under my roof you will treat him like one. You're the damned actress. Pull out those skills and pretend you know what the hell you're doing." He threw her a hard look that dared her to argue.

"I'm not a 'kid' person, but I'll try. I don't know what to say to him. What's he into? What if he hates me?"

She paused, racing for the suitcase she'd set up beside the couch when he'd told her that was where she was sleeping last night. Digging around, she pulled out a package of airline snack mix and a pair of airline-issue throw-away headphones. She held them up triumphantly.

"Here. I got him a gift. What do you think?"

I think you're giving him the crap you didn't want from the plane ride, he thought, snidely. But he gave her points for trying. She wrung her hands and sent panicked looks out the window, waiting for the bus to drop Wesley off at the end of the driveway. She quickly chewed her bright red lipstick off her lower lip. A part of him wanted to feel bad for her. A very tiny part.

"Bree was right. This will be good for you guys tonight. I'll be next door, but he's eight years old, Hal. Unless the apartment is burning down, I don't want to hear about it. I'll be your buffer through dinner, but then you're on your own."

"What do you see in her anyway? She's a geek. A librarian who loves her books and probably has at least ten cats. She's so far beneath you, Ryan." Haley stopped worrying over the bus's arrival to look over her shoulder with a sneer.

The guys had tried to tell him that Haley was cruel to Bree. That she was catty and vindictive. But he'd refused to see that side of her. And that had been in high school. They had all changed so much since then. All of them except Haley. It made him sad. Sad for her, sad for her parents that had, apparently, given up on their daughter who just couldn't be happy with her lot in life.

"Show the best fake-enthusiasm at finally getting to know your son or I swear to God you can spend the night on the street. I don't give a damn if it's below zero." He gritted his teeth and sent her a warning glare as the bus ground to a squeaky stop in front of the duplex.

And just as if she'd flipped a switch, Haley was suddenly beaming with happiness and excitement. Only the lipstick on her teeth gave evidence to her true feelings.

Wesley was a good kid, the best. Though Ryan didn't want Haley in his life any longer than necessary, his son deserved to know his mother and he hoped the boy could charm the woman into falling in love with him. But would it be enough for her to want to take an active role in raising him? Probably not.

At least Wesley had Bree to show him what a loving, supportive mother was like. Yeah, Ryan could totally see them as a family. And if Haley ended up having a small role in it? Well, every family was a little dysfunctional, right?

Chapter 12

"Are you sure they're all right together?" Bree accepted the glass of wine Ryan handed to her before he carried his own to the spot beside her on the couch.

"Do I think it will be intensely uncomfortable for both of them? Yes. Do I think Wes is in any danger from a mother who doesn't seem to have matured any since high school? Not at all. Don't worry about it." He squirmed into a corner of the sofa and gestured for her to rest her back against his chest.

"I just don't understand why she showed up now. And why you? Surely she could live somewhere else." She'd put work and the calendar project on hold, and damn the consequences, in order to help Haley find her own place in town, if that's what it took.

"She has no money. And she doesn't have the support of her family. Not that I blame them. But what kind of example would I be setting for Wes if I kick his own mother to the curb when she's completely down and out? Besides, I get the feeling she's in more trouble than she's letting on. I was married to the woman, remember? She can't handle her own finances on the best of days. I just want to help her get back on her feet."

The rumble of his voice vibrated through her back, strangely relaxing and titillating all at once. It was hard to stay focused on her nemesis. "Does she realize how lucky she is to have your help? She'd better appreciate it."

"I don't want to talk about Haley any more. Drink up. Next time I swear I'm bringing a bottle of Tequila, instead of wine, if it'll loosen you up faster." Ryan reached around and clinked his glass against hers, waiting until she'd taken a sip before drinking from his own.

He was right. She was obsessing. This was their makeup night and Haley was not going to ruin it for them again. Bree felt the wine slide all the way down to her stomach. She'd been too nervous to eat dinner, so the alcohol was bound to go straight to her head. Loosening up would not be an issue for long. She giggled. Oh dear.

As though he sensed she was past loose and close to sliding off the couch, Ryan plucked the stemware from her hand and put it on the coffee table. He tucked her more comfortably against him, resting his chin on top of her head for a moment. She could smell the wine on his breath. It was bold, just like him.

"I didn't do this right, last time. I showed you how I felt, but I never said the words." Ryan turned her around to face him.

"You didn't have to say anything. I knew." Bree laid a palm over his heart, gasping as he gripped her chin between thumb and forefinger and tipped her face up until she was staring straight into his eyes, his very soul bared for her to see.

"Just the same … I love you. I loved you then, but I feel like that was so childish, immature. What I feel for you now, it's grown. I never stopped loving you."

"I love you too, Ryan. Now … then … always."

For one long moment they remained still, their eyes locked. If she were an artist, she would draw his face, his expression, as it was right now. But she was not, so she settled for committing it to memory.

"Do you remember our first time?" he whispered. His words tickled their way past her ear, as he'd shifted his body so he could reach her neck and feast on her collarbone.

Only like it was yesterday. Her mom and stepdad had taken a weekend trip to Cape Cod. They'd trusted her alone in the house for the first time. Any other teenager her age would have done something wild and daring, like throw a party. But Bree had planned to spend the night reading under the stars. She had been setting up her little backyard retreat when Ryan slipped through the side gate.

"I was supposed to be at the bonfire, down at the pond. The last hurrah before all of us went off to college." His voice was gruff, words interspersed with warm, wet kisses that had her writhing until they were both lying down, with their bodies flush on the long couch.

He hadn't spoken a word as he'd approached her that night, merely strode across the lawn and kissed her like it was the single most important thing in the world. The only thought her brain had been capable of forming at that moment was "finally." Never mind that he was Haley's boyfriend. Forget that this was wrong and that things would go back to normal in the morning. For this one moment in time, Ryan Pettridge was hers.

"You looked so beautiful, standing there in the fading sunlight, your bare feet digging into the grass, that hideous gunny sack dress hiding the most scrumptious body underneath."

She would have laughed out loud, had he not chosen that moment to cup her breast in one large palm. He kneaded and squeezed, finding her stiffened nipple with his thumb and torturing it through the layers of her clothing. Unable to stand it, Bree pushed at his hands until she had a little breathing room, then she yanked her sweater off over her head.

"I have to say, your taste in clothes has greatly improved over the years." Ryan eyed the midnight blue satin of her bra appreciatively before dipping his head to taste her right through the fabric.

Closing her eyes, she drifted back in time. Ryan had lowered her to the blanket under the stars, and she remembered hoping the neighbors wouldn't hear her soft moans and come over to investigate.

"Not just a beautiful body, a beautiful soul." Back in the moment, Bree arched upward as he brushed the satin cup down, claiming her with his mouth, the suction she could feel all the way down to her toes.

"Ryan ... need you." Her hips straining to meet him, she gripped his ass with fingers like claws, pulling him against her.

"Uh uh. I refuse to rush this. I've waited far too long for this moment."

Their eyes met and his searing gaze heated her blood, prickled her skin.

"My Bree, my perfect Bree."

He'd said the same thing to her that night, so long ago now. She'd trusted him with her heart. She'd trusted him with her body. Staring into his eyes as he'd accepted her innocence, so gently. And refusing to give in to his own pleasure until he'd ensured she had hers.

Ryan had ruined her for other men. Really, who could measure up? And so she had remained celibate all this time. Thirteen long, frustrating years. But he was here, now, and her patience was at a breaking point.

Screw the candles waiting in the bedroom to be lit. Screw the rose petals she'd scattered across the top of the comforter. Screw the fact that he hadn't even discovered the thong that matched the bra, now damp with his saliva. She needed him now. Here.

"Baby, please." Her breathy plea ended on a harsh gasp as his roaming hands had lowered her zipper, his fingers dipping inside to stroke her over-sensitized folds.

Trying to wiggle out of her jeans, Bree yanked Ryan's shirt off over his head and threw it. The muffled clink of glass against wood gave them both pause and had him sitting up quickly.

"Fuck. I'm sorry. I'll clean it up."

"Later," she growled, using the fact that he'd sat up to her advantage, and yanking his jeans and underwear down to his knees. "Kick 'em off."

The look in his eyes was equal parts shock and pure lust. Clearly unwilling to mess with this woman on a mission, Ryan did as she said, scrambling through a pocket in his jeans for a condom before he kicked them over the side of the couch. He helped her discard everything on him from the waist down.

"I didn't intend to do this out here, on the couch, Bree." He tried to take her hand, as though he meant to lead her into the bedroom but she slapped his away.

"Now!" Boldly, she held out a hand for the condom, praying she looked like a wanton temptress and not a fumbling idiot as she sheathed him as quickly as possible

Spreading her legs wide, she offered him a saucy grin as she wrapped a hand around his swollen cock and guided it to her entrance. His eyes darkened. She felt him expand in her palm. They'd take it slow the next time. Or the time after that.

The intense look on his face was the only warning she had before he'd grabbed her wrists in one hand, raised them above her head and drove straight to the hilt. He knew she needed no time to adjust to his presence, his hips already grinding hard.

This wasn't sweet, tentative teenage sex. This was adult sex. And Bree decided very quickly that she enjoyed adult sex more. A lot more. Lifting herself off the couch, she strained to draw him in as far as she could. A knowing smirk on his face and barely a pause in his momentum, Ryan swept a large palm behind her thigh and draped her leg over his shoulder. What was this?

"Holy hell on a popsicle stick!" The hoarse scream was ripped out of her throat as this new angle took her to heights she'd never dreamed possible. She knew her eyeballs were now rolling back in their sockets. So deep! So blissfully, deliciously deep.

Ryan's chuckle was low, his smug grin stretching his mouth wide. "Honey, we need to work on your dirty talk."

The man could tease her as much as he liked as long as he kept this up. Right there. Yes. That spot. That was the spot.

They were slick with sweat, something Bree didn't remember from their first time, and that had been in the sticky heat of late August. Then again, she did not remember working quite so hard for an orgasm back then, either. She hadn't known any better. But now she did. And the new Bree went after what she wanted, with gusto!

With a throaty cry, she came in shuddering waves, hanging on to Ryan for dear life. He was right behind her on this ride, neck muscles suddenly going rigid as he let loose a rumbling groan that magnified her own orgasm vibrating through her own body.

Tangled on the couch, they panted and sighed, sweated and laughed. She felt wicked and she couldn't wait until they did it all over again.

"*That* was not like I remembered it." Ryan sounded exhausted but just as happy as she felt. "I don't know what you did with sweet, little Bree, but this new you ... Hell, you're gonna kill me."

"Ah, but what a way to go, huh?" Devilishly, she licked his salty nipple, reveling in the strangled moan that caught in his throat.

"I think my shirt got soaked in wine."

"Good thing you live right next door."

They were quiet for a moment and Bree thought Ryan had drifted off. His voice tickled her ear when he spoke, as she had her head pressed to his chest.

"Let's not wait so long before the next time we make love, okay?"

Well, if he really meant it. Bree decided to show him she was ready for the next time right now.

• • •

Word got around fast in a small town. Ryan's mom had come in, presumably to help him set up the displays of seed packets and the various supplies. But he knew she'd heard about Haley staying with him and Wesley. She wouldn't come out and ask. She'd wait for him to offer up the information on his own.

"Your father wants to come in for a bit soon. Not to run things, of course. He just wants to see his store again, know that everything is being taken care of." Anne kept her eyes focused on the seed packets she was sorting by variety.

"Dad? Wow. Do you think he can handle that? I don't want him to have any kind of setback."

It had been a couple of weeks and Ryan had yet to hear back from the real estate agent with any offers for the store. He'd hoped to use this time to try and put some distance between his parents and the store, just in case. Except that his mother had started dropping by more and more often. And now his dad wanted to visit? They were going to make things a lot harder when the time finally came.

"So, ignoring the Prada-wearing elephant in the room, how are things with you and Bree?"

Better than he could have ever imagined. Ryan felt his cheeks heat as he thought back to the night before. He'd wished like hell that he didn't have to leave, that he could have stayed with her wrapped in his arms all night long. Oh, to be able to wake up next to her each morning. To have Bree's face be the last thing he saw before drifting off to sleep each night. But that would mean staying in Scallop Shores. A weighty life decision that had been knocking around in his brain for the last week or so.

"Will you stay?" His mother continued her line of questioning and Ryan tried not to snap at her for climbing inside his head. It was downright spooky.

"If we end up selling the store, what would I do for work? I'd need a job."

"Do we need to sell the store? I know it isn't your dream job, sweetheart. But could you see yourself running it ... for your dad?"

Ah, the classic guilt trip. There wasn't a mother alive who couldn't pull it off flawlessly.

Well, two could play at that game.

"So, you'd see your only son settle for a job he was only doing to keep his father's dream alive in order to keep your family close by?" He batted his lashes, the picture of innocence.

"You learned from the best." She pursed her lips, like she was trying hard not to smile, but Ryan could see the crinkles deepen in the corners of her eyes.

"It's not like I couldn't picture it, Mom. If it meant being around you and Dad ... and Bree. The past is the past and I was an idiot for staying away so long. If the folks in town want to remember me as some kind of hero, that's their prerogative. I don't have to agree with it, but I don't have to hide from it either."

"There is another option." His mother's voice was barely above a mumble and she spoke slowly, deliberately.

"Why do I get the feeling this isn't a position that would utilize my accounting skills?"

Ryan finished putting together the cardboard display he was working on and turned to study his mother. What was she plotting now?

"Coach Danvers is retiring this June. They are looking for someone to replace him as the high school gym teacher ... and football coach. I was talking to him over at Dade's the other day and he said if you were to apply, he'd see what he could do to help you get the job."

Ryan started to scoff it off. He didn't have the required classes. Except that he kind of did. When he had been planning his course load for the first couple of years of college, his advisor had insisted he figure out a practical backup course of study. At the time he'd thought it a hoot to consider being a gym teacher. If he wasn't drafted, then he could still immerse himself in all things sports.

Sure, he'd have to get his teaching credentials, but that didn't mean he couldn't at least ask about the position.

After his injury, when he'd turned his back on his love of football and sports, he had switched majors and gone into business, with a focus on accounting. Surprised at how satisfying balancing numbers was to him, he'd never looked back.

A high school gym teacher. And the chance to coach his old team. For the first time since his career-ending, stupid-ass fall in the dorm showers, Ryan was able to contemplate a future that incorporated his first love. The familiar burn of shame and embarrassment was noticeably absent.

"And what happens if we can't sell the hardware store?" He plucked the box of seed packets from his mother's arms and began to stuff the pockets of the cardboard display.

"Then we hire someone to run it."

Not the most practical solution, from a cost standpoint, but doable. If they could find a college kid, someone looking for minimum wage to apply toward their tuition and rent on a crappy apartment. It wouldn't be cost effective to hire on anyone with a family to support. Would they have to offer medical and dental? He'd look into it. And the sooner he found someone, the sooner he could work on his own qualifications for the teaching position.

"Will she try to mess things up for the two of you, do you think?"

Ryan stuffed the last package of pumpkin seeds into the display, trying to catch up on this new thread. They had been discussing hiring someone to run the hardware store. Then she'd thrown in a question about Haley, out of the blue.

Haley!

"That's perfect! Mom, you're a genius. She needs a job. We need her out of our hair. If we give her the store to run, she can get her own place that much sooner and I can have my life back.

I'm not sure how long she plans to stay in town, but this will do for the time being."

"Now Ryan, I have never trusted that woman. What makes you think she won't skim off the till?"

"I'll be doing the books. I'll catch on quick. And she knows better than to steal from me. She's desperate, but she's not that desperate." He frowned, hoping like hell that his last statement wasn't going to come back to bite him in the ass.

"I just never understood—" His mother let her words trail off.

"Go ahead, lay it on me. You never understood why I married her? You never understood what I saw in her?"

"No, I was going to say that I never understood why you didn't end up with Bree in the first place."

Whoa. "Why would you say that?"

"Oh, sweetheart, it was plain to anyone who saw the two of you that you were in love." Anne placed her hand on her son's shoulder, patting lightly.

"We hid it." He rolled his eyes. "Okay, we thought we'd hidden it. We didn't want to hurt Haley. I'd been dating her for two years. In high school terms, that was a freaking lifetime."

Ryan thought back to all those times sitting at his parents' kitchen table. The stolen glances, the way one or the other of them would accidentally brush an arm or a leg up against the other. When he was with Bree, they were in their own little bubble. It was so easy to pretend the rest of the world didn't exist—and, therefore, that nobody else could see just how they felt about one another.

"You would have done Haley a favor if you'd told her the truth." Her voice was sad but matter-of-fact.

"But then *you* wouldn't have Wes." Take that!

"No, but I might have a whole passel of grandchildren to love and spoil, and a daughter-in-law I could truly admire."

A child with Bree. How perfect that would be. Deep in his own thoughts, Ryan gathered the empty boxes and started for the back room to toss them aside until later. The jingle of the bell above the door had him spinning on his heel.

"Hullo, Ryan! And Anne, perfect. I have some amazing news and it's good that you're both here for it." Toby Horace, the real estate agent, burst into the store, all smiles and waving arms.

"Can I get you a cup of coffee, Toby?" Always the gracious hostess, Anne was halfway to the office to fix it before he called her back.

"I'm afraid I have to be on the other side of town very shortly. But I wanted to stop by and tell you that you got an offer. My client understands your situation and has offered to buy the hardware store outright. You wouldn't even need to liquidate your merchandise. He plans to keep the store here, as is. Every town needs its hardware store, right?"

That did make things easier, but it seemed too good to be true. Mr. Horace handed him a piece of paper, detailing the offer made by this stranger from out-of-town. Shaking his head, he gave it a quick scan, blinking when he got to the numbers listed clearly in bold print. It wasn't anywhere near what they were asking. It was more. A lot more. Holy shit. His fingers so shaky they were flapping the paper around, he shoved it toward his mother.

Anne let out the first expletive Ryan had ever heard her utter. And that was saying a lot, given all the damage he'd caused around the house growing up. Her lips trembled and her eyes were filling with tears.

It would set them up for life. No worries. Ryan saw that as a very good thing. But it would mean letting go of a piece of family history, something that had been part of the Pettridges for four generations. For the first time since he'd come back to Scallop Shores, the enormity of what they'd be letting go finally set in.

"What's the catch? This guy isn't even from Scallop Shores. Why our store? Why our town?" It didn't make any sense.

"From what I gather, the gentleman has a daughter in town. He's trying to find a way to connect, to gain some sort of tie to Scallop Shores that she can't reject outright."

"How long do we have to think about this?" Just because it looked like a no-brainer didn't mean they would be able to part with the store.

"He's in no hurry. Take your time and come to a decision as a family. I know how important this is to you all. I've attached his business card. His name is Frank Wattley. While I'd rather you direct all questions and concerns to me, I figure it couldn't hurt to let you do a little research on the man who could potentially take over the family business."

Horace shook Ryan's hand, gave Anne a brief hug and waved goodbye. "Tell Bo hello for me. Hope he's well on his way to dancing the two-step."

Ryan watched the man leave just as quickly as he'd dropped by. His mother turned around to wipe at a tear that had snuck past her defenses. Well, if they had time to think about it, then that's exactly what they'd do. He was going to head to the apartment and tell Haley to get off her lazy butt because she had a job—and she started today.

Chapter 13

The scent reached her before she'd even opened the door. Sweet with just a little hint of spicy. Bree wasn't any good at picking out ingredients individually. She just knew that whatever her friend had taken from the oven smelled heavenly. Eagerly, she yanked on the handle and plunged into Cady's Dream.

"I'll have a coffee and two of whatever is causing my taste buds to sit up and beg." Waving to a few regulars, Bree took off her heavy coat and draped it over the back of one of the padded chairs at the counter.

"Gingersnap cookies. Good choice." Cady beamed. "Talk ya into a latte today?"

"Sure, why not. I'm in a spectacular mood." She stretched her arms out lazily over her head and winked at her friend.

"So the photo shoot went well? All those hot guys in next to nothing?"

Bree blinked. She'd almost forgotten how well the photo shoot had gone. They weren't finished, but they had gotten some great shots yesterday. Another day ought to do it.

"Yeah, it couldn't have gone better." She accepted the espresso drink that Cady slid across the counter, refusing to break eye contact until the woman figured out what she was trying to communicate without sharing it with the gossips seated at the counter alongside her.

Like they were playing a silent form of twenty questions, Cady nodded, obviously trying to figure out what her next move should be. Bree nearly chortled when she saw the light bulb go off in Cady's head.

"And then after … *That* went well?"

"The post photo shoot activities went *very* well." She didn't even bother to hide the grin that stretched her cheeks to the point of aching.

"Excellent!" Then, as though she'd forgotten something important, Cady's brow wrinkled in confusion. Distress? She lowered her voice as she leaned across the counter. "I've been hearing some talk about Ryan's ex popping back into the picture. Should we be worried?"

We. God love her. Bree took a sip of her latte before answering.

"She's staying with him, if you can believe it. Not my favorite scenario, but it sure didn't change things any. In fact, she makes a great babysitter." Twisting to the side just enough so the men at the counter couldn't see her profile, Bree wiggled her eyebrows up and down.

Message received. Cady flashed her a thumbs up.

"Am I gonna get grossed out over my brother's photo in this calendar?" she asked, changing the subject before Old Man Feeney and his cronies caught wind of what they'd really been discussing.

"Truth? His was one of my favorites. You'll probably hate it. Though I highly doubt any other woman in town will commiserate with you—except maybe your mom and Auntie.

"Oh, and Burke? Cady, he was a natural. The camera loves him."

"He came home so embarrassed. It was hard not to tease him about it. He wore a T-shirt to bed for the first time since I've known him." Both of them laughed at this.

The bell over the door ushered in a new customer and Cady looked up, frowning. Bree turned around. Wonderful. Haley was busy looking around the coffee shop and hadn't spotted her yet.

"I've seen her before." Cady tapped a finger to her lips.

"Yeah, that's Haley. Ryan's ex."

"No, I mean ... where did I see her? It was just recently too." She sucked her bottom lip into her mouth and worked at it.

"Oh! At Smitty's. She was sitting right behind you."

Bree's eyes widened as she thought back to that night, remembering the blonde who had so rudely invaded her personal space. She'd never caught a glimpse of the woman's face, but now she realized that had been intentional. The woman hadn't wanted her to know who she was.

They came to the horrible realization at the same time. Ryan's ex had overheard Bree's confession about the miscarriage. The sneaky snoop!

"You want me to kick her out? I can do that. It's my place." Cady put her hands on her hips, battle face on.

"Thanks, you're a doll. But I've got the advantage here. She doesn't realize I know. She's not going to threaten me with something I fully intended to tell him about anyway." Eventually. Someday. When the time was right. Crap.

Aware that she'd unintentionally drawn the attention of Mr Feeney and his peanut gallery, Bree sighed, gathered her coat and purse and moved to a table in the corner. By the time she got back for her latte and plate of cookies, Haley was standing at the counter, perusing the menu.

"Hey there! Let me buy you a cup of coffee, Haley. I got us a table over there."

"Okay ... A tall, skinny macchiato. Extra foam."

"You should try one of Cady's pastries. They are just to die for."

"I don't eat sweets." Ryan's stick-figure-of-an-ex grimaced. Glancing around the shop, she added, "The last time I was in town, this place was a Chinese restaurant. Tealeaves, I think it was called."

"Yep, it's changed hands a lot over the years. But it's all mine now," Cady offered proudly.

Haley shrugged, like it didn't matter to her either way. Cady turned to fire up her espresso machine and Bree felt just a moment's panic as she tried to decide if she should wait at the counter with

Haley or return to the table. When the other woman made no effort to acknowledge her presence, she gritted her teeth, ignored the heat flooding her cheeks and tried to walk, not run, back to her seat.

Her days of intimidating me are in the past. She can't bother me anymore. They were mature women who didn't need to pigeonhole themselves with labels like they'd done in high school. Sure, she was still a bookworm, but she was a sexy, confident bookworm. Bree tried to gobble down her cookies before Haley could see them and comment on the added calories she was consuming.

She'd come so far. She felt really good about herself now. Her life was exactly the way she wanted it. Except that the one person who had the ability to make her feel like a scared little ugly duckling was back in her life. Well, it was up to Bree not to give Haley the ammunition to tear down her newly built confidence.

"Thanks for the coffee." Haley set her drink down, pulled out a chair and perched on it.

"Um, you're welcome." Maybe Haley really had changed and the mean girl tendencies were a thing of the past. "How did things go with Wes, the other night? He's a great kid, huh?"

"Oh, we had so much fun. I was surprised to see how much we had in common."

"Really?"

"Of course not!" Haley barked out a cruel laugh. "My little boy spent the entire evening singing your praises. 'Bree this.' And 'Bree that.' It was nauseating." She rolled her eyes before returning her attention to her coffee drink.

Trying to keep from grinning at this revelation, despite the venom in the other woman's voice, she simply watched her. Haley could disguise her words to look as though she'd been bored, but Bree knew better. She was jealous of Wesley's relationship with Bree. And if she could get jealous, then there had to be a heart in there somewhere.

"So really, what *does* he see in you anyway? I mean, when I chose you for his tutor, I thought I'd found the homeliest, dullest creature in our graduating class. That's always been a mystery to me." Haley narrowed her eyes as she watched to see how deeply that barb would embed itself. And just like that, she was back, folks!

Bree sighed at the not-so-subtle turn of conversation from Wesley to Ryan. Mentally brushing off the hateful insult, she shrugged.

"I don't think it matters really. As I heard it, you left him ... and Wes. What's the deal? After all these years you've decided you want to be Donna Reed?" Might as well put all her cards on the table. If Haley had her sights on Ryan, she wanted to know now, rather than later.

"Why, do I make you nervous? You should be. Honey, I won him last time and I could easily do it again. Your type," Haley paused to flick a skinny, perfectly manicured finger at her, "can never keep a man's attention. They need a real woman."

Last time. So she had overheard what was meant to be a very private conversation.

"Why does it bother you so much that he loves me? I mean, you guys were over a long time ago." *Even before you got married, if truth be told.* Bree lifted her heavy stoneware mug, leaned back and watched Haley as she took a sip. The old Bree would have been terrified to reveal such a truth to anyone, let alone the one woman she feared could take it all away from her. But the new Bree was more direct.

"Oh, please, you think he loves you? How cute! He knows about your little puppy dog obsession with him and he took advantage of an easy target. All he wanted was to get in your pants. Honestly, you really make it too easy for him."

"I'm sorry you see things that way."

And she was. She felt sorry for Haley. The woman had spent a lifetime using her looks to get what she wanted from men. It was no wonder that she saw their motives differently than other women might

"Clearly you're going to make me say it." Haley's lips twitched in a smirk. She amped up the tension by taking a sip of her coffee, licking the foam from her lip with a delicate swipe of her tongue.

Bree waited. Here it came. Haley wasn't going to be happy when she realized she no longer had the power to cow her competition into submission. Bree calmly took a sip of her latte, her arched brow the only indication she had any interest in this big threat.

"Ryan and I share a history. We share a child." The sneer on Haley's face left no mistake that she twisted the knife intentionally. "Your feeble little attempt to force him to stay with you failed. Just back off. He chose me last time and he'll choose me again."

"What the hell are you talking about?" Bree's voice came out louder than she'd meant, and she looked up guiltily.

Cady looked like she was ready to haul out a baseball bat and chase Haley to the next county. Old Man Feeney and the rest of the men at the counter had swiveled in their seats to see what the commotion was about. Bree shot them a "mind-your-own-business" glare and turned her focus back to the serpent sitting across from her.

"Yes, I know all about your miscarriage. Boo hoo. How sad you must have been when that little bun in the oven didn't turn into a ring on your finger.

"And because you failed, you kept it from Ryan. So now I've got a lovely little secret. Stay away and I won't spill. Everyone's happy. You might even get to keep him as a friend. Wouldn't that be nice?"

"And if I tell him the truth first? Hmm, who do you suppose he'd choose? The woman who loves him and his son and would do absolutely anything for them? Or the woman who left him once already for fame and fortune—neither of which she got, as it happens."

Haley's face had turned a sickening shade of purple and she looked as though her head was going to explode. Nope, she hadn't anticipated any fight from Bree whatsoever. If the subject had been anything but the most painful time in her life, she would have almost enjoyed herself. But having it tossed in her face this way, it was an all-time low—even for Haley.

Immersed in their intense discussion, they didn't notice Ryan until he loomed tall over their table. Had he heard any of that? They both eyed him, mouths slightly open.

"Not the pair I would have expected to see enjoying a cup of coffee together, but stranger things have happened." His smile was friendly and devoid of censure, so Bree let out as shallow a sigh as she could manage, without him noticing.

"Hey, Hal, I looked for you at the apartment. I found you a job. Finish up your coffee and we can go."

"Now? Today?"

"Yeah, you need the money. I need you out of my apartment. Win-win." He winked at Bree. "Come on, drink up."

"What kind of job? Where?" She looked at him in horror.

"You're going to run the hardware store."

"The family business? Really?" Her calculating gaze turned to Bree.

"Yeah, sure."

"I'm not thirsty anymore. Let's go, sweetheart." Haley stood up from the table, put on her coat and tangled her arm in Ryan's.

"Wish me lots of luck today, babe." He leaned down and gave Bree a breath-stealing kiss before leaving with the duplicitous woman intent on making her life a living hell.

Was she worried that Haley really would steal Ryan back? No. But she had forced Bree's hand. She'd have to tell him about the baby now. And when she did, she had to believe that he'd understand her reasoning for not mentioning it much sooner.

She had wasted far too many years of her life dwelling on the heartbreaking loss of their baby. Now that things were finally on the right track between her and Ryan, she felt an even stronger compulsion to protect him from the pain she'd lived with for so long. It was a lie by omission and bringing the truth to light could draw them closer together or it could tear them apart for good.

But he deserved to know what had happened. And if he was unforgivably angry for her having kept it from him, then that was a consequence she'd have to accept. Haley no longer had the power to hurt her. Ryan did.

• • •

Pleading a headache, his mother had left the hardware store fifteen minutes after he'd arrived, Haley in tow. Ryan envied her. He pressed his lips together and looked heavenward as Haley cooed over all the cute gadgets, the pink handled tool sets and the flowered gardening boots.

He left her rearranging the seed packets he'd just spent the morning setting up, by color. Customers would be more attracted to the rainbow spectrum, she'd insisted. Yep, sure. Either they were in there to buy seeds or they weren't. But it had kept her busy and out of his hair, so whatever made her happy.

There was a gaping hole where Jonah Goodwin had bought out all the fluorescent light bulbs he'd had on the shelf. Ryan had suggested he head to the nearest Sam's Club, where it was cheaper to buy in bulk. But Jonah told him their company only bought local. Good guy. Nice policy. Heading into the storage room, Ryan prowled through the endless stacks of boxes looking for more.

While he searched, he let his mind wander. He ought to be thinking about the offer on the store. Instead, his mother's words came back to him. She and his dad had known he and Bree had feelings for each other. Doyle and Luke had said roughly the same thing. But they'd been so careful, neither of them acknowledging it for fear of hurting Haley. Surely if she'd known, she would never have married him. Right? Because who would voluntarily play second fiddle to another woman? Unless they had an ulterior motive?

He left the doors to the storage room propped open in case Haley needed to call for him. So he made little sound as he wheeled the dolly loaded with boxes out to the main aisle of the store. Haley was no longer puttering in front of the seed display. He checked behind the counter and still came up empty.

His mother had been worried about Haley stealing from the register. Could she have skipped that and gone straight to the safe? Ryan left the dolly in the middle of the store and headed for the office. Haley sat in his father's old office chair, eyes glued to the offer on the store. She looked up when he coughed from the doorway, eyes bright with excitement.

"This is freaking amazing! You guys are set for life."

"If we take it." Ryan strode forward, snatching the paper off the desk and shoving it in a drawer with a slam, before turning a glare on his ex-wife. "I'll kindly thank you not to poke your nose into things that are none of your concern." He nodded toward the door, wordlessly telling her to get her butt back to work.

Squeezing the bridge of his nose, he followed after her. He looked back once, wondering if he ought to move the buyer's offer from the drawer in his dad's desk. The man had very little in the way of security. In fact, the deed to the friggin' store was in the same drawer. Later. He'd deal with it later.

It had seemed like such a good idea, earlier that morning. Hire Haley to run the hardware store. If she were earning a salary, she could pay back her parents, her creditors, anyone who might be in line to get back a little of what she owed them. Then, eventually, she could get her own place. Now he wasn't so sure. Doubt reached up to trace its icy fingers along the back of his neck. Ryan ran a finger inside his shirt collar.

"God, why wouldn't you? It's not like you want to run the family hardware store for the rest of your life. You've got a condo back in California, don't you? You've got a job waiting for you."

He didn't quite know where she was going with this line of questioning, but he didn't like it. He hauled a box off the dolly and carried it down the center aisle, turning left when he reached the aisle where light bulbs were shelved.

"Why do you care what I'm leaving behind in California, Hal? I'm here now. I had figured it for a temporary thing, but now I'm thinking of staying. And you're flat broke, or so you would lead me to believe. So that means you're here for the duration too. Right?"

When she didn't respond immediately, Ryan looked over his shoulder. Haley looked longingly back at the office. She had no plans to stay in town and earn an honest living. She was still looking for a way to become that next reality TV star. He closed his eyes and shook his head.

Haley was expecting him to go back to his old place in So Cal. She was counting on the fact that, because she was Wesley's mom, somehow that earned her the right to tag along. Free room and board here in Scallop Shores was not what she was after, ultimately. She needed to be back where the action was. Oh, the poor deluded woman.

"I need you to grab the rest of the boxes off the dolly, then you can wheel it back out to the storage room. It's taking up too much room out here."

"You want me to lift boxes? They're humongous! I could—"

"Chip a nail? Yeah, ain't gonna lie. It could happen. But they're light bulbs. The boxes are a lot lighter than they look. Thanks, babe. You're a doll." Ryan pasted on a fake grin and nodded toward the cart.

She did as he asked, surprisingly. But just before she turned to wheel the dolly to the back room she tried again.

"So you're considering it. Selling the store?"

"It's a hell of a deal. We'd be crazy not to at least think about it. But, Hal, you need to understand something. Whether the sale of the store goes through or not, Wes and I are staying here. I'm giving up the condo. I'm not going back to California."

Wow. It was the first time he'd actually said the words out loud. But it didn't make them less true. If he couldn't get the teaching position, he'd find something else. If they sold the hardware store to this mystery buyer, that just gave him a little breathing room to find a job he'd be happy with.

Haley didn't say anything, but he could tell by the way her lips were pursed that she was working something out in her head. He was probably going to regret asking, but if he was going to trust her enough to run this store in his absence, however temporarily, he had to know what he was getting himself into.

Stocking the shelf as quickly as he could, Ryan broke down the cardboard boxes and carried them to the back room to dispose of later. Haley was sitting on the empty cart, staring off into space. Keeping an ear out for the bell above the door, he sat down beside her on the cart.

"What is it you're looking for, Hal? You don't want me. You don't want Wes. What would make you happy? What would fulfill your dream?"

She looked away.

"You'll laugh at me."

"I'd never laugh at you. I want to support you. You need money? Is that it? You want to go back to So Cal and make it as an actress? But what if it never happens, Haley? At what point do you decide 'enough is enough' and just do what makes you happy?"

"That does make me happy! I'm a good actress. It's what I know."

"Then get yourself financially stable so you can get back out there and grab your dream. Make those producers fight over you."

"Easier said than done, I'm afraid." She still refused to make eye contact.

"No one said it would be easy, babe. We're talking sacrifices here. No more mani/pedis. No more living beyond your means. Scrimp and save. You're a smart woman. You can do it."

"Why are you being so nice to me?" Haley finally looked at him, suspicion narrowing her eyes to slits.

"Because I made a lot of mistakes and still I learned that it wasn't too late to find love and start my life over. I believe the same can happen for you."

"What could you possibly have in common with a nerdy bookworm?" She stuck out her bottom lip.

One would think she'd hate to keep being beaten over the head with the fact that he'd found love with someone else. But if she was going to ask it again, he would tell her again.

"More than I could have ever realized. And finding new ones every day."

"I believe I just found my motivation to get back out to LA as soon as I can." Haley rolled her eyes and made sounds as though she were about to hack up a hairball.

"You're welcome."

He should have gone easy on her. After all, she was having a harder time connecting with Wesley than he was. Haley had no clue that Harry Potter (and the multitude of other characters Wesley brought up at every opportunity) was part of a book. She thought Wesley was talking about his little friends at school. Which caused the boy an endless fit of giggles. And the fact that the mix-up was bringing father and son closer together—major bonus.

Ryan laughed as Haley stood up in a huff, her ridiculously high heels clacking on the cement floor as she hurried back toward the front of the store. He had a soft spot for his stubborn-as-hell ex-wife. The woman insisted on learning life's lessons the hard way.

Chapter 14

"So letting her live rent-free in your apartment with you and Wes wasn't enough, you had to hire her on to work with you all day, too?" Bree bit the side of her cheek, frustration causing her to speak her mind.

She wanted to take back the words as soon as she'd uttered them. Now she sounded like a shrew. It wasn't as if she didn't trust Ryan not to fall for whatever tricks Haley hid up her sleeves. It was his ex she didn't trust.

They were supposed to be enjoying some quiet alone time but Bree was so consumed with guilt after her talk with Haley, and that was turning her into a real bitch. She had to tell him about the baby. And now was as good a time as any. Ryan pushed himself off the couch.

"No, that's not it at all. I hired her to work the store *for* me, not with me." He palmed the top of his head as he turned in a circle, coming to rest in front of her, a sheepish grin making him look like the boy she'd fallen in love with back in high school.

"Geez, guess you haven't developed the ability to read minds yet, huh? I'm sorry. There's been so much going on that I forgot I haven't told you all of it."

He sat back down beside her, pulling her hands into his lap and squeezing them excitedly. She stared at him blankly.

"We got an offer on the store. A big one. Wait. That came after. It's been a hell of a day! I have so much to catch you up on. First, there's a position open at the high school."

His words were tripping off his tongue so fast that Bree found herself leaning in to catch it all. She felt like they were playing some sort of game, only he'd never explained the rules.

"You want to be a teacher? Since when?" Confusing, but she could work with that. The part that seemed to be leaching through was that he wanted to stay in Scallop Shores.

"Not just a teacher, a Phys Ed teacher. And football coach. Coach Danvers is retiring this year. They're looking for a replacement. My mom heard."

God bless Anne Pettridge!

"Do you have the credits? Don't you have to be certified to teach in Maine?"

"That's what I intend to do while Haley is running the hardware store."

"And the offer on the store? Where does that come in?"

"Oh yeah. So I put it on the market just to see, you know? We weren't sure if it would generate any interest. I don't even know if I can get Dad to agree to a sale. It's his baby, you understand.

"But my Realtor comes in yesterday with this crazy-ass offer for the entire store—everything, as is. Says the guy fully intends to leave it as a hardware store. This kind of money … my parents would want for nothing, Bree."

"So the job you hired Haley for might only be temporary?"

"Well, he could keep her on for as long as she needed the job, potentially. But, ultimately, it would be temporary. She doesn't plan on staying in Scallop Shores."

Thank the Lord!

"When does she leave?"

Dammit! She just couldn't keep the bitchy to herself tonight. But instead of calling her out on her royal cattiness, Ryan chuckled. He pulled her into a hug and kissed her gently.

"Hey, thanks for going out of your way to be nice to her. I know it can't be easy."

You can say that again!

"So, you said you had something you wanted to talk to me about?" he prompted.

"Hmm?" Had she actually started this conversation? No, she wasn't ready.

Tugging her hands from Ryan before he could notice the sweaty palms, Bree swallowed nervously. Now or never. He deserved to know. She had to have faith that he'd see her "lie of omission" as a way of protecting him. Gripping her thighs to give her hands something to do, she looked him in the eye and began.

"There is something you don't know about that night we spent together, that summer."

Her nerves were already so fried that the hesitant knock sounding on the front door nearly unseated her. She was pretty sure she'd squealed. Ryan gave her a funny look and stood up to answer the door. Bree was right behind him.

Wesley stood on the doormat, head down, shuffling from one foot to the other.

"I know I wasn't supposed to bother you unless it was an emergency, but I kinda had no choice."

"Buddy, what's wrong? Are you hurt? Is your mom hurt?" Ryan pulled his son through the door, stepping out to look toward his own apartment.

"Dad, she's clueless. Please tell me that woman is not really my mother. My mother would be smarter, more like ... Bree." Wesley gave her a shy smile as he pushed his glasses up.

Pressing her fingers to her lips, Bree blinked rapidly. Her heart felt like it filled her entire chest cavity. God how she loved this kid!

"What happened, Wes? Where is your mother?"

"She went out. Said she had to meet a friend. Dad, she told me to go to my room and get my copy of *Goodnight Moon* and bring it over here, to see if you or Bree would read it to me. *Goodnight Moon*, Dad!" Wesley threw up his arms in disgust and pushed past them to flop down on the living room couch.

"I've got to say, I'm impressed she even knew that title. I bet if she hadn't taken off so quickly, she might even have been able to read it to you herself." With the look of adoration Wesley was currently giving her, Bree refused to wipe the smartass smile from her face.

"She was supposed to be babysitting." Ryan shook his head in consternation. "I mean, she was spending time with you. What was so important that she had to leave?"

"I dunno. I was telling her about the different houses at Hogwarts. I thought we could try to figure out which one she would have been sorted into. But she was busy putting makeup on and she kept changing out of a black dress and putting a red one on and then switching back again. It was really weird."

Haley was going on a date? So much for her empty threats to steal Ryan back for herself. Things just got interesting.

"She had no right to leave you like that! I'm going to call her, tell her to get her butt back here." Ryan's features were set in a hard line as he reached in his back pocket for his cell phone.

Bree rested a hand on his arm. She didn't say a word, just waited for him to look at her. Haley was a grown woman. She'd do whatever she pleased. Ryan sighed, nodding slightly before leaning in to kiss her on the forehead.

"I vote we pretend that freak lady is not my mother and she does not live with us." Sensing that his mom was clearly in trouble, Wesley was pushing his boundaries.

"And what would Harry Potter have to say about that? The Dursleys were his family and look how they treated him? I think it's always best to treat family with kindness and respect, don't you?" Bree merely lifted a brow but by the way the smile fell off the boy's face, she knew her message had been received loud and clear.

"Hey, bud, what do you say you sort Bree and I into our houses?" Ryan joined his son on the couch, rubbing his knuckles on the top of his blond head. Wesley giggled, trying to duck away from his dad's reach.

"We need a sorting hat."

"Oh! I've got one!" She really did. Bree had found it on eBay a couple of years ago and brought it to the library whenever she set up a Harry Potter event—which was at least twice a year.

"Of course you do," Ryan teased as she raced off to get it.

She returned to find them in a tickle match on the couch, Wesley's skinny arms and legs flopping around as he howled in laughter and then gasped for air.

"You better not make him pee on my couch," she jokingly admonished.

"Yeah, Dad. Don't pee on her couch." Wesley dug his way under Ryan's armpit and really got him good.

Hugging the Sorting Hat to her chest, Bree watched father and son playing. She felt happy. Haley gave this up, not once but twice. Bree didn't know what could be more important than the love of family.

"Hey, this calls for some popcorn. I'll be right back." She ducked into the kitchen to fix a late-evening snack.

Humming the theme song to *Jeopardy*, Bree moved from cupboard to microwave to cupboard. She gathered supplies, started the popcorn going and located a bowl big enough for sharing. She debated mixing up a pitcher of lemonade and let out a squawk when Ryan's big arms wrapped around her from behind.

"Sorry the evening didn't end up going like we'd planned." He nudged a lock of hair away from the side of her neck with his nose and kissed her once, twice, three times.

"S'ok. Really." Had the popping started? She was finding it hard to concentrate.

"We'll talk about that night another time, all right?"

That night? Oh! Right.

"You really looked like you had something you wanted to get off your chest and I'm all about honesty and talking things out."

Thank God he couldn't see her face the way he was holding her from behind. The guilt and shame she felt for not telling him about the miscarriage was surely on display for the world to see.

"Soon, Ryan. We'll talk soon."

• • •

Dade's Grocery was a Scallop Shores landmark, and hadn't changed a bit in the years that Ryan had been gone. He waved to Mable Sweeney, the head cashier. The woman had been there his entire life.

"Well, if it isn't our hometown hero," she gushed.

He smiled, even while gritting his teeth. The urge to argue the title was becoming less and less of a compulsion.

"You know Haley was in not too long ago. Funniest thing. She bought a whole bunch of those scratch tickets. Scratched 'em all off right at the next counter too."

"Yeah? She win big?" Ryan rolled his eyes. Leave it to his ex-wife to waste her money on lotto tickets when she was supposed to be working on saving it.

"No, actually. And darned if she wasn't upset about it. Asked me if I could spot her another twenty. Figured she'd just waste it on more tickets so I told her I didn't have any cash on me. She stormed out."

"She's been a little stressed out lately, Mrs. Sweeney. Sorry about that."

Okay, so she was probably looking for easy cash. The stubborn woman did not understand the concept of earning an honest living. And he really didn't understand where this had all come from. It wasn't like Haley's parents had spoiled her terribly. They were simple folks. She'd been one of four kids, so money was more of a struggle than a surplus in their household.

Ryan had always enjoyed visiting Haley's house. Her mom stayed home to take care of the kids. Her father was a mechanic for the school, making sure the buses were kept in perfect condition. When they'd been dating, he had told her he'd hoped to have a large family like hers someday. At the time she'd agreed. Looking back, he realized she probably would have said anything if she thought it was what he wanted to hear.

Snatching up a plastic basket, Ryan headed for the cereal aisle. He'd left Haley alone at the hardware store for the first time and he didn't want to be gone too long. His dad had a little fridge in his office, so he could pick up some milk while he was here, too. They were running a special on granola bars, so he threw some in the basket to pack in Wesley's lunches for school.

The store was largely empty on a Wednesday morning. Ryan passed a mother and toddler with a tiny "shopper in training" cart. He remembered Wesley at that age. Sighing, he wondered why he was in such a melancholy mood. He was worse than a woman, seeming to have babies on the brain now. Scrubbing a hand over his face, he headed for the beer aisle. He needed to pick up some manly refreshments.

"Hey, Ry, what are you doing here?" His friend, Doyle, paused halfway down the aisle, like he'd been caught doing something he wasn't supposed to.

"Um, shopping. Isn't that what most people come to Dade's for?" He shook his head and made a beeline for the middle cooler.

Ryan's stomach clenched as he recalled an unpleasant memory from childhood. They were maybe ten years old. Doyle and another kid, Kenny, had tried to talk him into stealing from Dade's. They told him he could join their club if he'd shoplift. Could have been anything. They weren't picky. But they could keep their stupid club. His dad and Mr. Dade were good friends and there was no way Ryan was stealing anything from anyone, especially a friend of the family. Fortunately, ring-leader Kenny moved away shortly thereafter and Doyle quit being such a dick.

"You aren't pissed about last night, are you? She said you'd understand."

Aha. Doyle was the reason Haley couldn't decide between the red dress and the black one. Huh. She'd hooked up with one of his football buddies. He ought to feel bad for the guy. But it wasn't like Haley was back in town to stay. Still, it didn't explain why his friend was acting so odd.

"It's not your fault. But she was supposed to be spending time with Wes, you know? It's been a long time and they have a long way to go in order to rebuild their relationship. I didn't expect her to just up and leave."

"Hey, man, I'm sorry. She called and said she needed to get out. Asked if I'd swing by and pick her up."

"Well, I hope all the fuss she made over her appearance was worth it." Ryan started to chuckle, then stopped when he saw the guilty look on Doyle's face.

"Come on, dude! It's not like I care. We haven't been married for years. I've moved on. I'm with Bree now. Relax, you're welcome to Haley and all of the high maintenance that goes with her."

All right, so giving his friend permission to boink his ex-wife was a little on the bizarre side. And in the beer aisle at Dade's Grocery, no less. Ryan looked around to make sure no one was a party to their conversation.

"I never meant ... I thought ... Shit." Doyle opened his mouth and closed it several times. He swiped a palm over his face that was ... sweating. What the hell?

Ryan set his basket of groceries on the floor and clapped a hand on Doyle's arm. This had officially gone well beyond weird. He shouldn't feel the need to reassure the man, but Doyle looked so damned upset.

"You understand she's only staying with me to get back on her feet, right? It's not like we're getting back together. Is that what she's telling you?" Ryan narrowed his eyes.

"No! Actually I was talking about before. I meant to tell you I've always meant to tell you."

A sick twisting in his gut told Ryan that now would be a good time to cover his ears and walk in the opposite direction. Whatever had Doyle looking so miserable could not be pleasant. And he'd be just fine with his old friend choosing to keep this little confession to himself.

"I don't know what you think you need to tell me, but I'm sure it can wait. We'll have drinks sometime over at Smitty's. I'll kick your ass at darts." He realized his poor choice of words when Doyle visibly winced. Jesus.

"No, this is something I should have done a long time ago. It's just that I thought, we all did, that you and Bree were in love with each other."

There it was again.

"We figured it was only a matter of time before you hooked up. That you were finally going to break things off with Haley and be with the one you were meant to be with."

So the entire football team seemed to realize Bree was his destiny a good friggin' thirteen years before he'd wised up and figured it out for himself. But if everyone had known, how had he managed to keep his true feelings from Haley? She should have gone ape shit on him.

"Then that night of the bonfire at the pond? When you didn't show up, we all figured you'd finally made your move." And they'd nailed it. Dead on.

"What's your point, Doyle?" Neither confirm nor deny.

"I figured if you hadn't broken up with her yet, you would be by morning. You know? I assumed she was fair game."

"Wait. Haley?" Ryan whipped his head around, lowering his voice to a hiss before leaning toward the other man. "You slept with Haley the night of the bonfire?"

Doyle's nod was brief and barely discernible, but his hangdog expression told Ryan all he wanted—or didn't want—to know.

"I guess you made up or something. I never understood why you ended up staying with her, let alone marrying her. She never told you, did she?"

"Were you hoping to marry her yourself?" The giant elephant sitting on his chest made it hard for him breathe, let alone get the words out.

"God no! You're right—too high maintenance for me. I mean, she's a great time, but—" Doyle seemed to realize he was digging himself in deeper, the more he continued to talk. He snapped his lips shut.

"She never said a word. I guess Haley had herself an agenda and I was just part of her big plans. Christ Almighty, I am such a schmuck!"

"Or you could choose to look at it this way, that it might have taken a little longer than you'd planned, but you ended up with the right girl. Right?" Doyle's eyes darted nervously, like he was plotting a quick exit.

"Yeah, you're right. Bree would never lie to me about anything so important." If he'd only known about Haley and Doyle, his life would have been a lot different.

"I should take off. I just thought you should finally know." Doyle shrugged, snagging a twelve-pack of Bud out of the cooler and turning back to him, almost as an afterthought.

"She told me something last night. Well, she asked me for a loan first. When I told her I couldn't come up with the money she kinda freaked out. Said she owes some money to some guy back in LA and she's running out of time before it's due. You know anything about this?"

What did you get yourself into now, Haley? Ryan spit out a handful of curses as he glared at the floor.

"Nope. News to me. Which would be our normal pattern, I guess."

Doyle gave a half wave and hurried to the cash register to pay. Ryan grabbed his own twelve-pack, picked up his basket of groceries and headed in the opposite direction, intending to take his time while he waited for Doyle to check out and leave.

He thought he was being so noble, doing the honorable thing and staying with a girlfriend he'd betrayed because he'd mistakenly figured she was in love with him. Joke was on him. Haley used him as her "get out of Scallop Shores" card.

All those wasted years he could have been with Bree. The woman he'd never stopped loving. The woman who deserved better than the jerk who'd taken her virginity and left with no explanation.

Chapter 15

Her first hint that something was wrong came when she knocked on Ryan's door and he didn't answer—but Haley did. The smug smile on the woman's face was all Bree needed to be certain that she was missing some key information. Information she sure wasn't going to get from Ryan's ex-wife.

"He's not here. Ryan left to drop Wesley off at school. Something about needing to speak to his teacher."

"Why? What's wrong?" Bree reached out a hand and tried to push the door open further. Wrong move.

"Excuse me! What goes on in our son's life is none of your business. Go back to stacking library books. I need to get ready to join Ryan at our store." Haley looked down her surgically sculpted nose and wiggled her fingers to indicate Bree should back up so she could close the door.

Fine. She'd worry about Wesley later. She turned around, skirted the icy spots on the porch and descended the stairs, heading for her car. If something were wrong, Ryan would tell her. Then again, if something were good, he'd tell her. Wouldn't he?

Buckling in and cranking the heater, Bree frowned as she poked at the radio presets. Every channel always seemed to play their block of commercials at the same time. She backed out of the driveway and headed to the warehouse on the waterfront where they'd met a few days before for the initial shoot.

What concerned her most was that he'd forgotten he was supposed to join her for the rest of the calendar photo shoot. Damian didn't need him for the whole thing, but Ryan had planned to be there just the same. So if this thing with Wesley was more urgent than she realized, that would definitely distract him. She was sure he'd be along as soon as he could.

Three hours later, Bree had to admit Ryan wasn't coming. Only a handful of the models were here today. Jamie needed her help wrangling escapee kittens who wouldn't stay in their little orange basket. It was like herding … cats.

Riley groused about posing next to a skyscraper of a Christmas tree when it was clear he wouldn't have been the one to decorate the upper half. Taking a step back, Bree tapped her chin. He had a point. The entire juxtaposition of the shot was just too funky. Riley sat stiffly in his chair. His jaw was clenched and she knew he was seconds away from losing his temper.

Rather than figure out a whole new December layout, they could switch Riley with Sam. Sam had finished his shoot the first day, but had come back with Riley today. She asked Damian if they could set up the backdrop for January again, this time with Riley lying on the rug. Everyone thought he would have looked more natural, sitting in his wheelchair beside the fake fireplace, but he'd insisted on lying down. It took the three of them to get the stubborn man out of his chair and positioned on the floor where he looked comfortable and "come hither," not like he'd fallen out of his wheelchair and waited for someone to rescue him. But this really worked. Riley's idea was a lot better than the layout that he'd originally been assigned.

Sam stepped up, shrugging out of his sweatshirt and tossing it to Bree before heading for the holiday tree-decorating scene. Damian took a few shots of Sam placing the star on the top of the tree. He handed Sam a wrapped gift and told him to hold it in his lap, like he was hiding the real gift underneath. Good Lord! Bree knew her photographer was having just a little too much fun posing his models for this calendar.

They took a break and she called Ryan again. Damian had complained about the football helmet causing a bit of glare in Ryan's photos and wanted to take some more. His phone went straight to voicemail. Oh, come on! It was one thing to have to drop Wesley off at school and forget that they were driving in together this morning. It was something else entirely to blow off the whole shoot.

Doyle had come in to retake his photos. Apparently he didn't look sweaty enough for a summer day at the beach. If anyone were to ask her, she'd say a certain photographer liked the look of the many tattoos that covered Doyle's arms and back. Bree hoped he'd decided to wear board shorts instead of his Speedos today. Nope. Oh, lucky her!

A stinging awareness had her flexing her hand, where she noticed a long scratch across the top. She really hoped Damian was happy with the October shots today because she'd rather not see those kittens again. Rubbing in a little saliva to wash away the blood, she crossed over to where Doyle waited for the photographer.

"Hey, you haven't heard from Ryan today, have you? He was supposed to be here this morning and I think he forgot." Her smile bright, she refused to look any lower than the man's chin.

"Ryan? Why would I have talked to him today?" Doyle's eyes darted this way and that, refusing to connect with hers. Odd.

"Bree darling, be a love and oil up our Mr. July, would you?"

"I beg your pardon?" She swung around, hands on her hips and fixed Damian with an incredulous stare.

"My assistant couldn't make it in today. Some stomach bug going around. The baby oil is on that chair over there."

"I think Doyle can figure out how to slick himself up. And, really? Is that necessary?"

"Doyle needs his hands dry in order to hold the beach ball. And it was my understanding that you hired me for my artistic vision. If you would like to hire someone else, I can take my things and go."

Wonderful. She'd pissed off the prima donna. Sucking in a deep breath, Bree plastered on a kiss-ass smile and swallowed all the things she wanted to say. The words swam in her stomach, causing a bellyache and making her wish this day was already done. Damian smirked and turned on his heel, heading back to take some more shots of Sam in front of the Christmas tree.

"Just his upper torso is fine—front and back—if you please." Damian threw the words over his shoulder as he left.

"*If you please*," she mimicked, glancing over at Doyle to see if she could coax a laugh out of him. He wasn't paying any attention to her.

"Don't worry, I promise Ryan won't get upset over our little intimate moment." She giggled, trying to lighten the mood.

Instead, Doyle groaned, looking even more miserable than he had before. What was his problem today?

Bree grabbed the baby oil off the beach chair and dribbled some in her palm. Doyle turned his head to the side, refusing to look at her, so she started with his back. Nope, not awkward at all. She tried to concentrate on the designs sketched on his back. They were symbols that she didn't recognize. Tracing one made Doyle flinch and she realized she was probably making things worse.

"Everything okay today? Besides … this?"

"Whatever he said … I feel awful, you know? I just hope you know I didn't mean to hurt anyone. I thought it was all cool."

She paused a moment to try to make sense of that, then shook her head, admitting defeat. Walking around until she was face to chest with one of the best fullbacks Scallop Shores had ever seen, Bree tried to hurry the process along. Doyle hissed when she slathered the oil across his lower stomach. Oh, god, was he ticklish? This was just getting worse and worse.

"Bree, I'm so sorry. I was distracted with some things this morning and I completely forgot we were supposed to come here together. I got your messages. Somehow my phone got turned off—"

Ryan had come into the warehouse at a run and spotted her right away. She glanced over her shoulder when his breathless excuse abruptly cut off. He was glaring daggers at Doyle, hands clenching into fists at his sides. Anxious to finish up so she could wash her hands and put some distance between her and this awkward altercation, Bree stepped up on tiptoes to apply oil to his inked shoulders.

"So one of my women wasn't enough? You needed to have the other one too?"

"The other one?" Bree turned around, her shrill tone carrying throughout the warehouse. Heads started popping out of other sections. She didn't care.

"I'm one of two, now? Is that it? You have a pair of girlfriends? That's a bit excessive, don't you think?"

"I meant Haley *was* mine. Now she's not. You are. Or you were." He spoke to her, but his eyes never left Doyle.

Ryan's nostrils flared and Bree got the feeling the only thing keeping him from throwing a punch was the fact that she stood in between the two men.

"I had nothing to do with this. That creepy photographer told her to put this oily shit on me for the pictures."

"And you didn't enjoy it one bit!" Ryan ground out.

"Ryan, lay off him! Doyle has been miserable about something all day. I haven't been able to get it out of him but it doesn't take a rocket scientist to figure out that you're at the root of it."

"If you knew what he did, you wouldn't be taking his side."

"Pretty little models, we're getting along well, yes?" Damian swept in from the other side of the warehouse, hands on his hips.

"I think they'd get along better if they each stayed in their own section." Bree grabbed a towel and wiped her hands, staring at the man who was acting like a stranger today.

"I should go. I can come back—"

"We finish this calendar shoot today. No one leaves until their part is done. Get into your costume and find your backdrop." Damian clapped his hands twice and left them just as quickly as he'd swooped in.

"Ryan, we need to talk." Bree reached for his hand to walk with him toward the September set.

He shrugged her off, looking from her to Doyle and back again. His shoulders were hunched, but he no longer looked angry, just sad.

"Not right now. I need to be by myself for a bit." Starting to head for the other side of the warehouse, he spun and gave her a mournful stare. "I'm sorry I flaked on this morning."

Okay. That he was sorry about. How about being sorry for almost coming to blows with one of his oldest friends? Or being sorry for assuming that Doyle was making the moves on her? Or for not taking a quick minute or two to explain what the hell was going on? When would he be sorry for that?

Ryan's sneakers scuffed across the cement floor of the old warehouse. He didn't say another word. Just kept walking.

Damn it!

• • •

Ryan wasn't hiding. He just happened to have a craving for his mother's cooking. What was the point of finally living in the same town as his parents again if he couldn't drop by for a home-cooked meal once in a while?

Sure, he'd left written instructions on closing the store for Haley to follow, rather than go over it in person. And yeah, he may have ducked out of the photo shoot before remembering to say goodbye to Bree. But he hadn't heard any complaints from Wesley when he'd swung by the apartment and told the kid to pack an overnight bag in case they didn't make it home tonight.

He just needed time to think, to sort out what was what. It was impossible to do that at his place. Standing in the living room doorway for a moment, he watched Wesley and his dad playing a game of chess. His father's hand was still very unsteady, so when it was his turn, Wesley would steady his grandfather's arm so that the man could move only the piece he wanted to, not knock over everything in his path.

Wandering down the hallway, Ryan paused to study the photos his mother had put up over the years. Family vacations, Little League, birthday parties. He sneered at a picture of the entire football team just after they'd won the state championship. There he was, sitting on Doyle's and Foster's shoulders. Then a picture of him with Haley, senior prom. God, he had the urge to take a swing at that frame, smash the glass to bits, and rip the photograph to shreds.

He'd wanted to ask Bree to prom. She would have looked so beautiful. But he had his stupid status to maintain. And she didn't go. Not even stag. A childhood memory she would have gotten to experience, had it not been for his stupid ego.

The pictures trailed off after that. A wedding photo of him and Haley. A few scattered ones of Wesley that he'd sent over the years. But nothing as consistent as his own documented childhood. Nothing like it would have been, had he moved back to Scallop Shores to raise his son after his divorce.

Pity party for one, please! Ryan sighed in disgust, flopping down on the futon shoved in the corner of his old bedroom. Wesley had left his backpack open and several library books were spilling out on top of the bed. An ever-present copy of *Harry Potter and the Goblet of Fire*, which Ryan had recently learned was Wesley's all-time favorite book, lay on top. It reminded him of Bree, and he shoved it back inside the book bag and zipped it up.

He flung an arm over his eyes and groaned. Things were going so well. They finally had a shot at happiness. Now one stupid conversation with Doyle had him rethinking everything. Bree deserved better than him. She deserved a man who would make the right choice the first time. A man who would fight for the honor to be with her.

Instead, he'd chosen the girl who had apparently been honing her acting skills on him all along. He wondered if Haley ever loved him. God knew he'd stayed with her in order to protect his reputation, his status. She could have just as easily been dating him because she looked best on *his* arm. But staying with him after high school? Marrying him? It was all some giant game to Haley. But it was his life she'd toyed with.

"We're not having anything fancy tonight. Just spaghetti and meatballs. But you're welcome to call Bree and invite her over. That is, if you aren't avoiding her." His mom leaned a hip against the doorframe, wiping her hands on a dish towel with apples embroidered on the edges.

"I'm not—" Ryan frowned when her raised eyebrow challenged him to finish that sentence. He knew better than to lie to his mother's face. She might be smaller than him, but she could still bring him to his knees with one disapproving glare.

"I want to go back in time, Ma. I want to choose Bree, like I should have. I want to have never married Haley." He finished on a groan, grinding his back teeth together.

"Nonsense! You wouldn't be the person you are today if you didn't make the stupid mistakes you were meant to make in your youth."

"But we could have been together all these years."

"Or not. Maybe you would have been together for a while, but whatever issues you needed to work on within yourself would still have come up and then you would have ended up divorced from Bree instead of Haley.

"You are together now because now is when you are *meant* to be together. Don't overanalyze it. Don't go wishing for do-overs.

Accept that things happen for a reason and be happy. Just be happy, Ryan."

"She deserves better than me."

"You are who she wants. And I think Bree Adams has waited a long time for her happy ever after, wouldn't you agree? Haley managed to pull you two apart once already. Don't let her get away with it again."

"I have so many regrets, Ma."

"We all do, baby. But don't let this be one of them. Grab your chance at happiness and hang on tight. Bree loves you and she loves Wes. Anyone can see that. You two need her."

He definitely couldn't argue with that.

"Maybe I'll bring her home some leftovers. I'm not quite through with my super funk."

"Fine. But I'm not fixing a plate for Haley."

"Jesus, I wish I'd never taken her in. Would I be an evil prick if I kicked her out?"

"Watch your mouth. What if your son heard you talking like that?"

"So I should just suck it up and let her stay?"

"I didn't say that. I just said make sure Wes doesn't hear you talking about her. If her poor parents no longer acknowledge her, take your cues from them. Boot her ass to the curb!" Anne winked at her son.

Twisting the dish towel in her hands, she snapped it at his foot.

"Take your super funk out to the kitchen and fix a salad while I'm finishing up dinner. There are a few dressing choices in the fridge."

Scrambling up from the futon, he scooted through the doorway, trying to avoid another towel snapping. He heard it whistle past his butt just as he pulled an evasive maneuver the likes of which he hadn't used since his days at UCLA. They were both laughing by the time they arrived in the kitchen.

"We need to discuss that offer on the store," Ryan reminded his parents once everyone was seated and the bread basket had finished making its rounds.

"No!" His father's fist came down hard on the table, rattling the plates and silverware.

Okay, this could mean that no, he did not wish to discuss the offer. Or no, he did not want to accept the offer. But the man had just spoken his first word since the stroke and, while he stared vehemently at his son, everyone else at the table wore broad grins. This was good. This was very good.

"Tell me how you really feel, Dad." Ryan winked.

The man waggled his finger threateningly at him, but the sparkle in his eyes ruined its full effect.

"Tell your father about the position at the high school," his mother prompted.

"Wait, Dad, you want to be a teacher?" Wesley asked.

"Not just a teacher, pal. A gym teacher. And the football coach. What do you think of that?"

"You mean we could stay? In Scallop Shores? Like, forever?" Hope shone on Wesley's face. If only it would always be this easy to make his son happy.

"That's the plan."

"I have an idea. Let's move out of our apartment and find a bigger place." Wesley swiped at his mouth with a napkin and pushed his glasses up the bridge of his nose.

Uh oh. Thinking Wesley meant that their apartment was cramped now that Haley was staying with them, Ryan realized he probably ought to explain that she'd be leaving soon. Was it possible that mother and son had managed to bond during the time she'd lived there?

"You know your mom and I aren't getting back together, right bud?"

"Duh! I meant a bigger place for you, me, and Bree. If we're staying, that means you're going to marry her, right?"

All eyes were now on him. Marry Bree. Ryan felt his smile stretch wider and wider. He liked the way this kid thought.

"Would you like that?"

"Yesh!" His dad's fist came down on the table for the second time that evening, spittle flying from his lips.

Looks like it was unanimous. They were not going to sell the store and they were, no, *he was* marrying Bree. If she'd have his stubborn ass.

Chapter 16

Bree didn't know if this new persona was better or worse than the shy one she'd hidden behind in high school. The new Bree certainly seemed a glutton for punishment. Take the other night for example. Ryan had left the photo shoot, that afternoon, before they even had a chance to talk. Old Bree would have taken that for the hint it was and slunk off to her apartment to read. New Bree banged on his door that evening until it was answered by Haley, wearing nothing but a tiny silk robe and sipping on a glass of wine.

If she were less sure of herself, Bree would have assumed that Haley was planning to throw herself at Ryan once he got home and Wesley was safely tucked in for the night. The funny thing was, by the time Haley finally got to the door, Bree had already discovered Ryan's missing truck and figured out he was probably hiding from the both of them. So the smug look on Haley's face really did nothing to cow her like it did all those years ago.

Whatever makes you feel better about yourself, you sad little witch.

But New Bree wasn't going to slink away and admit defeat. Ryan may have needed some time to hide out from his women problems but enough was enough. They'd danced around each other for a few days, managing to avoid being alone together but that wasn't solving anything. Get over it already. They could discuss their relationship another time.

Today she had the final proofs for the calendar she wanted to show him. Damian had been working overtime to finish up her project to get back to the one he'd set aside. She was proud of how it had turned out and she wasn't going to wait for Ryan to feel comfortable enough to come to her. She was going to him.

And because she was just that amazing, she stopped by Cady's Dream that morning and picked up coffee for Ryan, herself, and even Haley. Someone, somewhere, better be keeping a tally of brownie points for stuff like this, 'cause she'd earned it. Holding the drink carrier in one hand, she reached out to pull open the door to Pettridge Hardware when Ryan suddenly loomed in the spotless glass.

Bree squealed, stepping back suddenly as he pushed the door open and held it for her to get through with the drinks and her laptop bag.

"Great timing. This concerns you and I think it's only fair that you're here for this." He flipped the store sign to Closed and locked the door with a decisive click.

What on Earth had she walked in on?

"I brought coffee." Uncomfortable with the palpable current of tension, Bree straightened her spine and made a beeline for the counter, where she set down the drink carrier.

"Ooh, you shouldn't have!" Haley purred as she reached for the drink with her name on it. "Wait, did your little friend at the coffee shop spit in it?" She looked down her nose at Bree.

"Probably." She smiled brightly as she reached for her own double shot mocha and took a sip before turning to see what sort of bug Ryan had up his butt today.

"Thanks for the coffee. I don't deserve it, and neither does she." He pointed to Haley. "Really."

Bree's heart started to pound and she wrapped a second hand around her drink to keep from spilling it. Oh God. The short robe. The wine. The other night. Wait. Was this why he'd still been avoiding her? He was going to admit to being seduced by his ex-wife, wasn't he? Like a boa constrictor was slowly wrapping her in its clutches, her breath came out in quick little pants.

"What did I do now, Mr. Uppity? Are you still pissed that I left Wesley alone that time? I told him to run over and knock on the door."

Ryan paced the front of the store, turning repeatedly to stare out the window. He seemed uncomfortable about having this conversation anywhere the townsfolk might overhear and eventually headed deeper into the store, back toward the office. Haley rolled her eyes toward the ceiling like he was being melodramatic. Bree followed quietly, declining the only chair in the room even when he gestured for her to sit down. She remained in the doorway, ready to run once she heard the awful news. Haley, unconcerned, sashayed into the room and dropped into Bo's office chair, spinning around a few times for good measure.

"This might come off a tad hypocritical, but I had a very enlightening conversation with Doyle the other day. In the grocery store, of all places." Ryan leaned against the far corner, folding his arms across his chest.

"Okay, so I went out with him once or twice. Nothing wrong with that. We're both single and not looking for anything serious. Big deal. You aren't my keeper." She sounded like a petulant teenager who'd been caught sneaking out after curfew.

Bree wondered when the woman planned to grow up and take on adult responsibilities. Goodness knew she hadn't taken any steps in that direction yet. But the tone of the conversation began to ease the tight band constricting her own breathing.

"I don't give a damn what you do now. It's what you did a long time ago that has me wanting to wrap my fingers around your skinny little neck and squeeze ... hard."

Looking from one to the other, Bree tried to catch up on what wasn't being said. Because there was a huge part of the equation she was missing. She wasn't sure how this had anything to do with her. Haley's eyes widened before she turned her attention to the paper cup in her hands, refusing to make eye contact with her ex-husband.

"Admit it, Haley!" He kicked backwards at the wall so hard that the frame holding the store permit fell to the ground and shattered.

"What do you want me to say? I screwed Doyle at the party you flaked on? Because I was lonely. Because you were in town getting some from your nerdy tutor? So what!" She set the coffee down hard enough for some to spill out, staining the papers on the top of the desk.

"You think that's the part that bothers me? That you slept with Doyle? You two are welcome to each other. You deserve each other."

He raked his hands through his hair, shooting a quick glance Bree's way. He looked so sad, so guilty. Bree wanted to go to him, take him in her arms and tell him he did nothing wrong. But she sensed there was more to this story and fear rooted her to the spot.

"You knew all along. You knew I loved Bree. You knew I'd been with her. You knew I was with you only out of a twisted, stupid sense of guilt and shame. You knew I didn't love you.

"You convinced me that you loved me. That you wouldn't be happy unless we were together. You had our lives planned out. I went along with it because I thought I was doing the right thing, for you and for Bree. I thought I had betrayed you.

"You acted so fragile when we first got to college. You refused to leave my side. You never actually came out and said it, but you implied that you'd hurt yourself if I ever left you. I figured if you found out about that night, you'd do something drastic. And now I realize that was just an elaborate hoax. Congratulations, it was your best role yet." Ryan clapped his hands together, his eyes empty and cold.

"Yes, thank you. I was quite proud. But had I known how things would turn out, I wouldn't have bothered. You were going places. We were going places. Until you ruined your career. Brilliant move, by the way. Slipping in the shower? Who does that? I can't believe I wasted the best years of my life on you. You really could have been something."

Bree gasped. The woman had no shame!

"That's it, I'm done. Get out of my store. Get out of my apartment. Pack up your crap and get the hell out of my life." Ryan sneered, taking a threatening step toward his ex-wife.

"You can't do that! Where will I go? You wouldn't let the mother of your child live on the street, would you?" Haley was onstage now, in her element.

"Watch me."

"Ryan, sweetheart, I have the perfect solution." Now Haley was backpedaling. "Never want to see me again? Sell the store to that buyer offering the butt load of money. Give me enough to pay off my creditors and float me for a few months in LA, just until I get back on my feet. I'll get out of your hair. I'll disappear."

"I'm not selling the store, Haley."

"You're not?" This from both women, who stared at him puzzled. It was an incredible offer with the ability to set him and his parents up for life. He'd be crazy not to take it.

"Look, it's not my store to sell. It's Dad's. And he doesn't want to sell. Bottom line. I'll run it myself. It'll work out." Again, he was looking at her and not Haley.

If that's what made him happy. She just wanted him to be happy.

"Fine. I'll stay with Doyle. He's the only person in this podunk town who appreciates me." Haley stood up with a flourish, brushing past Bree, still standing in the doorway.

They both turned to watch her go. She got about halfway through the store before she spun around, fixing Bree with a calculating glare.

"But since we're all spilling our nasty little secrets, you ought to know that sweet, innocent Bree has the juiciest one."

No! She said she'd tell him. It wasn't Haley's place.

"This isn't your business, Haley. I already explained that I'd tell him. Not you."

"You've had thirteen years to tell him. I think that's plenty long enough, don't you?"

Haley looked her up and down, sneering. The cold, flinty look in her eyes chilled Bree to the bone. Ryan turned to her. She could see him out of the corner of her eye but she was too ashamed to face him.

"What's she talking about, Bree?"

Please don't hate me. I love you, Ryan.

"You know that amazing night you spent with Bree? The night you cheated on me? Did you remember to wear a condom, by any chance?"

Haley let that sink in before she continued.

"Our darling Wesley wasn't your first child, Ryan. You and Bree made a baby too. But she wouldn't keep it. So sad." Haley's pout was a mockery of all the pain Bree had experienced.

"That's a lie! I lost the baby! I didn't abort it. Ryan, I had a miscarriage. I swear to God!" Tears filled her eyes and panic drilled through her gut. She was going to throw up or pass out, she wasn't sure which yet.

"Get out! Get the hell out of here!" Ryan pushed past her, grabbing Haley by the upper arm and hauling her to the front door where he unlocked it with one hand, opened it and shoved her onto the sidewalk.

Turning around, he began to walk back toward the office, eyes unfocused and hands trembling.

"Ryan, she's lying. I didn't have an abortion. The doctor didn't know what went wrong. He said these things just happen. That it was probably for the best. Twelve weeks. Our baby lived for twelve weeks inside me. I'm so sorry I couldn't bring it to term." The words were tumbling from her lips, mixed with the salt from her tears.

"Haley's lied to me all along. There is no possible way I could believe her now." However, he refused to look at her. "I need to be alone, Bree. Please just let me deal with this my own way."

He didn't say another word as he slumped into the desk chair, banged his elbows down on top of the desk and dropped his face into his open palms. His shoulders were quaking and Bree wasn't sure if he was crying or just really, really close. She waited a moment and when he still didn't acknowledge her, she slipped quietly out of the store.

That was it then. It could have gone one way or the other. At least now she knew. Whether he harbored any doubts over her version of the loss of their baby versus Haley's, or whether he was upset because she'd kept her miscarriage from him didn't really matter. It was too much. They were through.

• • •

Crack! The brightly colored billiard balls spun crazily toward the far end of the table. Ryan sunk two of the striped ones on the break, earning a high five from Luke. After he missed the next shot, he propped his cue stick against the wall and retrieved his beer mug. No bottles for him tonight. He was drinking from a pitcher.

At first he felt guilty for asking his mom if Wesley could spend another night there, especially since it was a school night. But she'd gushed about all the time they had to make up for, that she was just so grateful to finally have her grandson living in the same town that she *could* take him for sleepovers. She told Ryan they'd make their own pizzas from scratch and probably a batch or two of cookies. Then she'd insisted he take all the time he needed with Bree. Damn it. She thought he was with Bree.

Guzzling down another few swallows, he didn't notice Luke had finished his turn until his friend was waving a hand in front of his face. Ryan nodded, grabbed the cue stick and circled the table. He lined up a shot but gave the ball a little too much momentum and it spun right back out of the pocket.

Of course he didn't believe Haley. Bree would never get rid of a baby, whether they were together or not. She valued life too much. But the alternative was just as gut-wrenching to consider, if not worse. She'd suffered a miscarriage, lost a child. And she'd faced it alone. He'd as good as abandoned her, so why should she feel she could come to him with the news? Sure, Bree could have gone to his parents for an address if she really wanted to find him. But he didn't blame her one bit for keeping the news to herself. He didn't deserve to know.

He wondered how Haley, of all people, had found out about what was probably the most tragic event in Bree's life, next to the loss of her father and then stepfather. But knowing his sneaky, manipulative ex, he was better off in the dark on this one.

Studying the table, he realized Luke was kicking his ass now. When had that happened? He could have been cheating for all the attention Ryan was putting into this game. Lining up another shot, he sunk the eight ball, swore a blue streak and stalked back to the tall table that held his precious beer. Time for another round.

"Hey, I know it's considered girly to talk things out, but I won't tell anyone if you won't. See? We're drinking manly beer, so it's okay." Luke punched him lightly on the shoulder as he sat down, holding up his own mug before taking a drink.

"I found out some shit that would have caused me to make some very different decisions back in my stupid-ass college years."

"Everyone makes dumb choices in college. We were still kids. We didn't know any better."

"Yeah? What was your dumb choice in college?" Ryan peered over the top of his glass.

"I was desperate to lose my virginity, you know?" An embarrassed flush crept up past Luke's beard line, rivaling the red of his hair. "I found out afterward that she was the Dean's daughter. Almost got myself kicked out of school in the first semester."

"But did you get her pregnant?"

"What? Hell no! Wait ... Is *that* why you married Haley?" Luke's forehead was wrinkled, like he was trying to do the math and it just wasn't adding up.

"No. Catch up. I got Bree pregnant."

"When were you with Bree?" Luke looked even more confused now, frowning into the bottom of his beer mug.

Ryan scoffed. Could there have been someone at the big party at the pond who didn't know where he'd been instead?

"The night of the big sendoff, before we all went away to college. At the pond? I didn't go. I went to see Bree instead."

"That's right. You weren't there." The color had returned to his friend's cheeks as realization dawned. "Haley came alone." Luke's voice trailed off and he had the good grace to look away.

"But she didn't leave alone, did she?" Ryan's laughter was bitter.

"So go back to the Bree thing. She has a kid? Your kid?"

"She lost it. She lost our baby and dealt with it all on her own."

"That makes more sense then," Luke mused, while stroking his bearded chin. "I mean, I'm shy. I get shy. But Bree took her quiet to a whole new level. She always had this haunted look, like she was dealing with some deep shit."

Yeah, this wasn't making him feel any better. All the hurt she'd gone through ... alone. The agony of losing a child. She probably wanted to die herself. He'd felt like his own heart had been ripped from his chest when he'd heard the news today. God, his poor Bree.

Ryan held up two fingers and waved down the perky brunette waiting tables in their section of Smitty's. He ordered another pitcher and ignored the teasing flirtatiousness in her eyes. She didn't seem to notice and pulled a card from the deep cleavage of her blouse, sliding it across the table toward him. "Call me," she mouthed before heading off to fill their drink order. Disgusted, Ryan picked up the card and flipped it toward Luke.

Like a broken record, he explained why he'd stayed with Haley. Why he'd ended up marrying the deceitful witch. Luke looked miserable on his behalf. More beer had come and he refilled his glass and swallowed deep.

Trying to remember that things weren't always bad, Ryan closed his eyes and thought about the good times with Haley. She'd been so supportive of his dreams. He'd come home from practice and she was right there, ready to massage away the aches and listen to his day. Whenever they lost a game, she cheered him up and reminded him that he'd played his best. She'd even memorized his plays, knew which ones had been pulled off flawlessly and which needed work. He'd loved that she could talk football.

After the accident and the subsequent surgery, she'd been his nursemaid without complaint. She'd driven him to physical therapy. She'd pushed him to do his exercises at home. And when he'd longed for a baby, his last ditch effort to save a marriage doomed from the start, she'd given in. Even though he knew she was terrified that losing her figure due to a pregnancy might cost her the chance to become a successful actress.

Now he realized that the only reason she stayed was because she had nowhere else to go. The first director to give her a shot at a paying gig also turned out to be her next sugar daddy. He would have liked to hope that she hadn't slept her way into the arrangement, but when she signed over her rights to Wesley with no fight, it certainly had him wondering.

And the woman had no qualms about telling him exactly what his shortcomings were then. Ryan thought back to the day she'd left. Any other man might have been heartbroken, if not for himself, for the child she was leaving behind. But he still remembered the profound relief that had quieted his soul for the first time in years.

"Still, Haley's not all bad. I've seen her visiting her grandpa up at Kittredge Manor a few times since she's been home. She reads to him." Luke's words interrupted his thoughts.

"Really?"

"I overheard her talking to him one day. She sounded really scared. Something about needing a lot of money, that she'd gotten herself into trouble and had no one left to turn to."

Tipping back his mug to guzzle down those last sips, Ryan spied Doyle standing awkwardly at the door of the bar. He set the empty mug down with a clunk and waved his old friend over. The man walked like a prisoner toward the gallows.

When Luke saw who Ryan had been gesturing to, his eyes widened. Did he really think there would be some kind of showdown? Aw shit. He didn't want a fight. He'd had enough of fighting.

"Pull up a chair. We can get another glass." Ryan motioned to one of the empty tables.

"Nah, it's okay. I was just gonna have a quick beer and head out." Doyle's features were tense, his eyes scared.

"Oh, for crying out loud! I'm not going to hurt you. I apologize for being a dick the other day at the warehouse. If anything, I feel sorry for you." He shook his head, rolling his eyes in disgust.

"Wait, why?"

"For getting saddled with Haley? When I kicked her out today, she whined about having nowhere to stay, and I figured since you two had gotten cozy again, she'd end up crashing at your place."

"No, man. She left town. I saw her earlier. Told me she'd gotten the cash she needed in order to start over. Said she was headed back to LA."

"But she's broke. Where would she get ... Fuck!"

His friends were staring at him. With sudden clarity, Ryan knew where his ex-wife could get her hands on a large chunk of money.

"I need to get home, fast! I think Haley might have stolen the offer for the hardware store."

Chapter 17

The library board members were seated around the long conference table in the meeting room. Bree had the floor, presenting the final version of the calendar. Martha fanned a hand over her face, but her giant smile showed just how pleased she was with the results. Harold looked uncomfortable as he nodded and mumbled his own acquiescence.

However, the more the female members of the board voiced their appreciation, the more Harold seemed to realize the money they were likely to make with this project. He sat up straighter, rubbing his meaty hands together. She swore she could see dollar signs dancing in his eyes.

"Young lady, if this goes as well as I think it will, you just may be looking at a raise."

It wasn't a promise, by any means, but it was far more than she'd expected. The board was pleased with her efforts. Harold was heaping praises on her and had already started discussing ideas for upcoming library fundraising projects he'd like her to be in charge of. Bree should have felt proud ... elated even. She was getting the recognition she never realized she craved until this moment.

But her heart wasn't in it. Not this morning. Her heart hadn't been into much of anything since she'd left the hardware store the day before. The look on Ryan's face when Haley blurted out that bold-faced lie. It was like he'd been stabbed through the heart. And not by his ex-wife, but by the woman he professed to love.

She wasn't going to let this go without sitting down with Ryan and explaining what really happened. And why she hadn't told him. God knew there were a million times she could have told him in the months he'd been back. But he needed time to process what he'd learned, skewed as it was.

Yeah, *Ryan* needed time. That was it. Bree yanked the laptop cord from the outlet on the wall and wrapped it neatly before snapping the computer shut. She knew once she sat down and had a heart to heart with the man, that things would officially be over.

One woman's lies had already altered his life. Though her own lie was technically one of omission, it was still something she should have owned up to long before now. One deceitful woman in his life was more than enough. Bree completely understood if he never wanted to speak to her again.

The board members filed out of the meeting room, Bree trailing a few steps behind them. She was struggling with the zipper on her laptop bag and didn't notice the small grouping of people milling around the circulation desk. However, the stage-whispered "Pettridge's Hardware" got her attention fast. Head snapping up she strode forward, pushing her way to the front of the cluster.

"What's going on? What about Pettridge's?" Her heart raced as an active imagination conjured up pictures of the hardware store on fire, broken into by thieves, or destroyed by hoodlums.

"Oh, we figured you already knew. Aren't you dating Ryan now?" Alice, one of the older librarians, eyed her curiously.

Bree wasn't about to give them any more grist for the gossip mill.

"I haven't seen Ryan since yesterday morning. Has something happened? Is his father all right?" she pressed on.

"It's that ex-wife of his. Haley. She stole the store." Alice and several library patrons watched her closely for a reaction.

Now that was just ridiculous! Bree rolled her eyes and started to walk away from the desk. Small-town living. You knew nothing had happened of import in a while when someone had to come up with a whopper like this.

"And I suppose she just dropped it in her Gucci handbag and strolled away, did she?" Bree threw over her shoulder as she tried to put some distance between herself and the gossipmongers.

"In a manner of speaking. She got her hands on the offer for the store, contacted the buyer herself, and said she'd cut him a deal if he paid cash." Bree knew the woman spoke the truth when she turned back around to stare and was met with Alice's know-it-all grin.

"But that's impossible. Surely she couldn't … "

"Apparently the buyer is not from around here. She still has Ryan's last name. She told the guy she was his wife. Gave the man a discount if he'd pay in cash. Up front."

Was Haley really clever enough to conjure up a scam of this magnitude? Bree couldn't imagine the woman involved in anything that required the least amount of effort. She had to be incredibly greedy … or desperate.

"I need to talk to Ryan. Where is he?"

"The police were called to the hardware store this morning. Toby Horace is over there too. Everyone is trying to figure out how to find Haley. Seems she's skipped town."

Well, duh! You don't steal hundreds of thousands of dollars and then stick around to rub it in everyone's noses.

"Alice, can you cover story time in an hour? I've already got the books and supplies set up upstairs. I'll ask Martha to watch the desk for you."

Making arrangements to duck out for the remainder of the day, Bree hurried to the hardware store. She wasn't sure whether he'd push her away or not, but she had to try. Ryan needed as many people on his side as he could get. God, if she could wring that horrible woman's neck right now, she would!

The closed sign was still up at Pettridge's but all the lights were on and Bree could see several people milling around. She knocked softly at the door and Anne hurried to let her in. She gave the woman a comforting hug.

"I came as soon as I heard. I am so sorry. Is there anything I can do?"

"Just be here for him. He feels so responsible. I've never seen him so beaten down before." Anne squeezed her hand and kissed her cheek.

Bree followed the woman's gaze to Ryan, who stood in the crowded back office with his father, Chase Eaton, Chief Hanson, Toby Horace, and a tall man she didn't recognize. Ryan looked terrible. Even from this distance, she could tell he hadn't slept all night.

"How could this happen, Anne? Seriously, Haley isn't smart enough to pull off something like this." Bree shook her head in disgust.

"Until last night, I would have agreed with you." The older woman rubbed her eyes with her knuckles.

Arms wrapped around each other's shoulders, they walked up the center aisle of the store until they were standing in the doorway of the office. Now that she could see him up close, her heart contracted painfully. Ryan's eyes were bloodshot. His hair stuck out at all angles. A couple of days' worth of beard lent him a dangerous air. His father sat in his chair, Ryan's hand clamped protectively over his shoulder.

"It shouldn't have been this easy," Ryan snarled.

"I didn't do my research well enough. It was my fault. I knew yours was a family-run business. When she called and told me she was your wife, I didn't think anything of it. She told me about your kid and the life-saving surgery he needed and I reacted on a gut level." Grim-faced, the man shook his head while studying the ground at his feet.

"I have a daughter of my own that I would do absolutely anything for. But I should have called Horace before signing the contract." He finally looked up, glancing quickly at the faces all turned to him.

Ryan hooted.

"Oh, that's rich. Our kid is one hundred percent healthy, and even if he did need a life-saving surgery, you can be damned sure Haley would not be the one fighting for it." His lip peeled upward in an angry sneer.

"It's my own damned fault. I left the offer letter just sitting on my desk at home. She'd already pounced on it once at the store. I should have locked it away. I handed her the stupid keys to the store, where she somehow knew to find the deed. Jesus, I may as well have signed off on the whole thing!"

"Haley played everyone, Ryan. And it wasn't your fault. Bo's stroke threw the whole store out of whack. And you can't blame that on anything but bad luck." Chief Hanson shrugged, giving Bo a sort of half-grin. Bree remembered hearing that the two men had been friends since their grade school days.

"The store deed should have been locked up in a safe deposit box at the bank," frowned the real estate agent, holding up his hands in surrender when everyone in the room turned to glare daggers at him. "Hindsight ... I know."

"Look, I'll drop the whole thing if I can be assured I'll get my money back. I can see that you weren't planning to sell," the Tall Guy offered congenially.

"I'll track her down if it's the last damned thing I do." Ryan pushed his way through the crowd, his eyes widening when he finally registered Bree standing in the way of his dramatic retreat.

She stood her ground, holding her breath as she waited to see if he'd throw her out of the store or accept her being there as a gesture of support. They locked eyes for a long moment before he grabbed her by the hand and pulled her down the back aisle of the store.

"You shouldn't be here. Now's not a good time." He spoke softly, his mouth close to her ear.

"Now is the perfect time. You need me, Ryan. You all do." She placed her hand on his chest, and drew comfort from the fact that he seemed to lean into the touch.

He looked back toward the office.

"I have to find her. I have to make this right."

"We'll find her together, Ryan."

"No, you don't get it. I did this. I fell for her lies all over again. And this time I didn't just ruin my own future. I ruined my parents'. I ruined yours—again. Fuck. I've got to go." He started to turn toward the door and Bree held on fast.

"Ryan, stop. Let Chief Hanson do his job. Trust Chase and the rest of the police force. This is what they do, sweetheart. You take care of your parents. Your mom is so worried about you. Take care of her. Take care of your dad. This has to be so hard for him. We need to make sure he doesn't relapse." Her steady gaze held his as she tried to wrap him in love and support with just a look.

"And take care of you. Ry, you look like death warmed over. This is all on Haley. You are beating yourself up over something that you didn't do."

"Why are you here, Bree?" He pulled her into his arms, his voice cracking under the strain. "I don't—" He didn't finish his sentence, just crushed her close, pressing his mouth hard against the top of her head.

I don't want you here. I don't deserve your support. It could have been either. But it didn't matter. She was here. And she wasn't going anywhere.

"I'm so sorry." He whispered against her hair, his arms quaking around her body. He didn't elaborate and she didn't ask.

Again, his words could have had a thousand different meanings and right now things were so chaotic that she wasn't sure how to interpret them. Instead, she just held him close, rubbing his back through the thick denim of his shirt.

"I've got this. I promise not to go all vigilante. Really. I'll talk to you soon." Ryan stepped back enough to rest his forehead against hers.

She was being dismissed. Okay, well, at least she could say she tried.

"Call me if you need anything." She cupped his scruffy cheek in her palm and placed a gentle kiss on his lips. Her heart shattered when he pushed her away just as gently.

Blinking hard to keep the tears at bay just long enough to make it outside, Bree put one foot in front of the other and concentrated on reaching the front door.

"Bree, I ... "

"Yes?"

"I was just going to say that, yeah, I'll call you if we need anything." Ryan swiped a hand over his face and turned to rejoin the men in the office.

Regardless of the ambiguity of his earlier words, Bree knew a brush off when she heard one. Despite her efforts, a single tear tracked down her cheek as she slipped out the door and hurried to her car. Knowing she'd never be able to hide her heartache behind a cheerful enough facade to fool a group of four year olds, Bree went back to her apartment for a good cry.

• • •

Ryan watched Bree leave. He bit his tongue to keep from calling her back. He'd started to tell her he loved her. But that would have done nothing more than give her false hope. He'd had a lot of time to think last night and the only solution that made any sense was to move his parents back to California with him. Thankfully, he hadn't burned any bridges there yet, and still had a job and a condo to go back to. It might not come to that. But he'd severely underestimated his ex-wife and now he had to scramble to clean up this nightmare if it turned out that they couldn't find her.

"Hey, we're gonna get out of here. If we learn anything, we'll let you know. I'm really sorry, bud." Chase slapped him on the shoulder as he nodded to Ryan and his parents just before following the chief outside.

Toby spoke in hushed tones with Anne and Bo, hugging them both before seeing himself out.

"You're welcome to stay as long as you'd like," Mr. Wattley said. "I stand by my word. If your ex-wife is caught and my money is returned, the hardware store is yours. I'll be staying at the Scallop Shores Inn for the next few days. Just in case. If the authorities cannot find her by then, I'll make arrangements to get the keys back from you." The man gave him an awkward handshake and hunched into his coat against the driving rain that had just come in from shore.

Ryan started to lock the door, scoffed at himself for bothering and turned back toward the eerily silent store. No background music. No more crowded office. His mother sat behind the cash register, wringing her hands. He knew she was dangerously close to losing it and he wasn't sure how he'd handle that when it happened. His father struggled to his feet with the aid of his new walker and shuffled slowly down the aisles that were as much a part of him as his own limbs.

He thought they'd had time. After all, he'd only just kicked Haley out yesterday. If only they had found her before she met with Wattley, before she filed the paperwork. But her treachery ran deeper than any of them knew. Ryan had assumed that it was yesterday's debacle that had caused her to steal the offer and the store deed. In reality, she had started this ball rolling a full week before and it was too late for him to do anything but wait and see if the police could track down Haley. Doyle said she was in LA already. But how did one search for a woman paying for everything with cash? And what if she'd been lying to him too?

"So much for being a town hero, huh? More like town moron." Using his arms, he hefted himself to the counter and swung around to face his mother.

He could tell she wanted to say something but refused to indulge him in his wallowing. She watched him steadily, her eyes dry for now.

"I wanted to secure your future, yours and Dad's. I didn't want you to have to worry about money."

"It's not your responsibility, Ryan. Your father and I set up a retirement account before you were even born. True, his stroke was not something we had planned on, but it isn't something that is going to break us, either. We'll be all right." She gripped his hand and squeezed.

"He needs private nurses. Therapy. He has no money coming in. I want you to come home with me to California. You can stay with Wes and me at our condo until we find a place for you both to live comfortably."

"Right. An old folks' home. Shame on you!"

"No, Ma! Assisted living. Not like Kittredge Manor. You and Dad would have your own place. You could still cook and clean to your heart's content. The only difference is that they have medical personnel on staff and he could get all the help he needed." Ryan slapped a palm on the slick surface of the counter.

"Listen, Ma, I still have my job waiting. This is what I came out here to do. Once I sold the store, I was to go back. Not many places would offer a deal like that. Now would be the perfect time to count our blessings and be thankful I still have a source of income to go back to."

"And what about Bree? Are we just going to ask her to pack up her life and move in with all of us? One big, happy family?" she asked in a warbling voice.

He'd found his mother's tipping point. Damn it. Her lip trembled as she stared with red-rimmed eyes. She hadn't been angry about his part in the store being sold out from under them. But when it came to Bree Adams? Now she was pissed.

"There are things you don't know, Ma. I thought it would work with us. I wanted it to. I really did. But this is just too big for any of us."

"Do you love her?" She swiped at her eyes with the sleeve of the ratty brown sweater he'd swear she had owned since he was a little kid and fixed him with a baleful glare.

"Yes, Ma. I love her. But I want her to be happy. She deserves happy. Bree has had a lot of hurt in her life. And—"

"And you're the one who hurt her. Yadda yadda, boo hoo. You want to be a hero, Ryan? Stay and fight. Stay and face the town gossips who are going to make your life a living hell for the next few months. Stay and be the one that brings Bree some joy for once.

"Show her how much you love her instead of running from her, running from your feelings. Quit your precious job in California. Sell your fancy condo in the suburbs. Put down roots in Scallop Shores and fight for *something*, for once in your life." Anne rose from her stool and skirted the counter, hurrying toward the restroom at the back corner of the store.

Feeling like the biggest jerk in the world, Ryan swiveled around to find his father standing a few feet away. He'd heard the whole conversation. The older man worked his jaw a few times, his mouth slightly open. Ryan could see his tongue moving but nothing came out. Heaving a frustrated sigh, his dad merely nodded. Message received.

He'd straighten out things with Bree just as soon as he found Haley and made her return the money she'd stolen. Snatching up a pen and a notepad beside the register, Ryan began to write down every place he could think of in Los Angeles where his ex-wife might be hiding. He added in a list of mutual acquaintances that the police could contact to see if she'd been in touch.

His mind racing, he felt better than he had in hours. He was being proactive. He was going to help them find Haley and bring her to justice. Then he was going to find Bree and ask her to forgive him for not being there when she lost their baby. They had a lot of time to make up for and he'd be damned if he wasted any more of it trying to run away from confrontation. His mother was right. It was time to stand up and fight.

Chapter 18

This wasn't the time to feel sorry for herself. Ryan could try to push her away all he wanted, but he needed to know she was there for him. No matter what. Bree threw off her handmade afghan, picked up her mug of tea that had long gone cold and stared disgustedly at the pile of wadded up tissues scattered on the floor. She scuffed to the kitchen in her fuzzy pink bedroom slippers to rinse out her cup, pausing to dash a little cold water on her eyes at the sink.

A timid knocking at the door had her grabbing for a dish towel to blot her eyes. Good. He'd come to his senses and was ready to accept her help. Pulling the towel quickly through a drawer handle, she ran to open the door. She blinked when she realized it wasn't Ryan.

Wesley hurled himself through the door, throwing his tiny arms about her waist and crying as though his whole world was coming to an end. He was soaked to the bone and his teeth chattered uncontrollably. Bree peeled off his coat, removed his sneakers and lifted his slightly unwieldy eight-year old body to carry him toward the couch. He wrapped his skinny arms tight about her neck, his breath hitching as he snuggled close.

Covering him in the afghan she'd just abandoned, she set him on the couch and left to make him a cup of cocoa. She debated whether or not to call Ryan as she hurried to fix his son a hot drink. But there was a reason Wesley had come to her and not his father. She owed it to him to at least explain himself before she brought Ryan in on this.

She fixed a tray with the hot chocolate, a plate of Girl Scout Thin Mints she'd just gotten the day before, a bag of mini marshmallows, and a spoon. Adding a stack of napkins she carried it out to Wesley, who sat scrunched up in one corner of the couch. Bree set the tray across his lap and sat down on the coffee table to watch as he doctored his drink with the marshmallows.

She waited for him to speak first. But now that he'd stopped crying, Wesley seemed to be trying to figure out whether he was in big trouble or not. He kept his gaze focused on the tray on his lap, twisting at a napkin with one hand and breaking a Thin Mint into little crumbs with the other.

"I might be mistaken, but I could swear school doesn't let out for a few more hours." She canted her head to try to catch his eye.

"And you're supposed to be at the library. I looked for you there first." Wesley finally looked up, thrusting out his jaw stubbornly.

Touché. Bree sighed.

"So what was so important that you needed to come find me before school let out for the day?"

"The big kids on the playground were being really mean. They were saying that my mom stole my grandfather's hardware store. Then they were making fun of my dad, calling him a dork for just letting her get away with it. My dad is not a dork!" He looked miserably down at the tray.

"When we were supposed to line up for recess, I snuck out the back. And you know what? They were wrong! I went to the store and it's there. It's still there. Why would they say that?" Cupping his hands around the huge mug, he brought it to his mouth and took a few sips.

"Was your dad still at the store, Wes? Did he see you? I'm sure the school has reported you missing and no doubt he's worried sick."

"I didn't think about that." He frowned.

"Why don't I call him and tell him you're here? You don't have to see him just yet, if you aren't ready." She made to pull her phone out of the pocket of her pleated khakis but Wesley put up his hand in a gesture that bordered on desperate.

"Wait! I saw him. But you're right, he didn't see me. I heard him talking to Grandma. Bree, it's real bad. He wants Grandma and Grandpa to come live with us—in our condo in California."

The poor child was confused. He'd walked in on a conversation already in progress and he wasn't getting the whole story.

"He said we *had* to go back. But I don't want to go. I don't want to leave you." Had the tray not been sitting firmly across his legs, Bree was sure he would have launched himself into her arms again. Poor child.

"Okay, well then he feels he doesn't have a choice, sweetheart. He wouldn't do this unless he couldn't think of any other way." Her heart ached for all of them, herself included.

How did one explain to an eight year old that his mother had sold the family business right out from under his dad and grandparents and then stolen the money? In little Wesley's world bad guys were more recognizable, like Voldemort. Bree didn't have the heart to tell him that his own mother was the evildoer in this case.

"Maybe if we could just ask my mom to take back what she did? Make it all right again?" Wesley looked up hopefully.

"That would be great, Wes. It's just that your mom isn't in Scallop Shores anymore. She bought a plane ticket to Los Angeles and that's a really big city. There is no telling where she is right now."

"She's not in Los Angeles. She's in New Hampshire." Wesley looked just as confused as she felt.

"What makes you think she's in New Hampshire?" Everyone knew she wanted to go back to her career, back to the chance for fame and fortune in Hollywood. And New Hampshire was only one state away. If she was looking to hide, wouldn't it be smarter to give herself a bit more space?

"I heard her on the phone one night. Dad was over here. She was talking to a friend that she used to go to school with. Um ...

Willow?" He rubbed at his forehead as he searched for the right name.

"Willow Fox? They were on the cheerleading squad together." Maybe if they could track down Willow they might have a shot at finding Haley.

"Yeah, that's the one. My mom said she needed a place to lie low until things died down. Is she not feeling well?"

"You think Willow is living in New Hampshire and that's where your mom went?" But would Willow still have the same last name? Did they have enough information to track down her address? Maybe her parents were still in town. No, they'd sold their lobster pound and moved to Santa Barbara ages ago.

"I know that's where she went. 94281 Badger Falls Road, Chester, New Hampshire," he recited.

Bree's jaw dropped. She stared at the boy. How on Earth?

"Wesley?"

"I know. Weird, huh? I've noticed that happening more and more lately. I hear something once and it just stays there, in my head. It sticks." He grinned broadly. "Comes in real handy at school though."

Wesley had a photographic memory. Holy crap!

"Kiddo, I think you may have just saved the day."

If she hurried, she could get to Haley first, convince her to return the money. Ryan would see that she was willing to do anything to help him, help his family. Then maybe he'd forgive her for not telling him about the baby. He and Wesley would stay, right? They could still have a chance at making things right.

"Wes, put on your shoes and coat. I'm going to drop you off at the hardware store, assuming your dad is still there."

"But you're going to get my mom, aren't you? I want to help."

And his father would kill her for driving his child to another state, possibly putting the boy in danger if Haley was feeling cornered.

"Buddy, you're in deep enough as it is. Don't forget there are already going to be consequences for leaving school property without telling a teacher."

"Oh yeah." Wesley hung his head, pushing at the glasses that started to slide downward.

"Come on. I've got a long drive ahead of me." Bree lifted the tray so Wesley could scoot out from underneath it.

"And Wes? Your dad needs to know where I've gone. But he doesn't need to know right away. Do you understand what I mean? If you could give me a head start, I'd appreciate it. I think your mom would much rather talk to me than the police, don't you agree?"

The boy nodded gravely and ran to the hallway to put his things back on.

Bree grabbed her purse, checked to see that her phone was charged and shrugged into a raincoat. At the last minute she realized she was still wearing her fuzzy pink slippers. A heroine off to save the day she was not!

• • •

Ryan's hands shook so badly, he dropped his cell phone. This wasn't happening. His nightmare of a day had taken a horribly sick turn for the worst when the school called to inform him that Wesley was missing.

"What do you mean, missing? Where would he go?"

"That's what we were hoping you could tell us. He did not return to his classroom with the rest of the students and a search of the building and the school grounds came up empty."

Wesley would never leave school on his own without telling anyone. He was a good kid. The only alternative that came to mind chilled his blood. What if Haley kidnapped Wesley to use as leverage so that he wouldn't press charges? She'd give him his son back if he let her take the money and walk away?

"My ex-wife. Maybe she … I don't know … " He couldn't even voice his fears. Saying it out loud lent credence to the fact that it could actually be true.

"Mr. Pettridge, I am sending a police officer to your house right now."

"The store. Please send him to the hardware store. That's where I am," Ryan corrected the school principal.

Given everything Haley had put him through, he knew she was capable of this and more. She was probably realizing just now that she hadn't thought through her escape. If he had his way, Haley would be on the run for the rest of her life. If he couldn't see her behind bars, then he would make damned certain her life was a living hell.

Swiping all the phone parts off the floor and snapping them back into place, Ryan let out a sigh of relief when he found it still worked. Now he just had to sit around and wait for Haley to call him. She'd want to hand him off and be done with this sooner rather than later, right?

Choking back a sob, Ryan clenched his fists and wore a trail from the front of the store to the office and back. Taking shallow breaths to keep from losing it altogether, he whispered prayers to a God he hadn't ever taken the time to acknowledge before.

He ought to call someone. His parents—no. They had just left the store not too long ago and he knew his father would be resting. The man had been under far too much stress for his overtaxed body. Bree. Yanking his phone from his pocket, Ryan dialed Bree's number and cursed a blue streak when she didn't answer. And why should she? He'd given her the bum's rush earlier. She probably thought he hated her. Truth was, he needed her now more than ever.

The front door rattled and the telltale bell overhead rang out as someone entered. Hopefully Chief Hanson had sent Chase back. If he had to deal with the police twice in one day, he wanted it to be someone he could count on. Ryan spun on his heel and hurried back to the front of the store. But instead of Scallop Shores' finest, Wesley stood just inside the door, looking tiny, wet, and thoroughly bedraggled.

"Oh, thank God! You're okay!" Ryan ran forward, dropped to his knees and pulled his son into his arms. He let the tears course, unchecked, down his cheeks.

"Did she hurt you? Did she threaten you in any way?" He studied the boy's face for cuts and bruising, checking his clothing for rips and tears.

"Nobody hurt me, Dad. I don't know what you're talking about."

"Your mom. How did you get away?"

Wesley's answer was muffled against the fabric of his shirt as Ryan had already wrapped him in another Papa Bear hug. It didn't matter anyway. He was home. He was safe.

Chase chose that moment to walk in. He stood quietly to the side while he waited for Ryan to pull himself together. The relief on his friend's face was an expression only another dad would have. Chase got it. He'd be bawling like a baby too if his kid had been taken.

"Does this mean she's still in town? We can still catch her." Clearly, the officer had come to the same conclusion as Ryan.

"Dad, I wasn't kidnapped." Wesley pushed himself out of Ryan's arms, refusing to look at either man as he studied the toes of his soggy sneakers.

"But the school called. They reported you missing."

"Am I going to be arrested?" Wesley looked up at him with huge eyes. His whole body was shaking.

"Of course not! Kiddo, we're just so happy that you're safe." Ryan was starting to realize what his son was trying to explain to him. "Wait, Wes, did you leave school on your own?"

His answer was a slow, guilty nod.

"Oh my God, you scared the hell out of me! Why would you do that?" Backing up to give the kid some space, Ryan raked his hands through his hair.

"The older kids at recess were picking on me, saying Mom stole from the hardware store and making fun of you for letting her do it." Wesley's small voice was filled with righteous indignation.

"Hey, I'm gonna get out of here, let you two have some privacy." Chase ruffled the boy's wet hair, nodded at Ryan and left the store.

Ryan scooped Wesley up and set him on the counter by the cash register. He ought to be mad as hell that his kid had scared twenty years off him. But he was just so relieved Wesley had made it to him in one piece.

"Why did it take you so long to get here? The school called ages ago."

Again with the guilty look. "I was here ... earlier. I slipped in while you were talking to Grandma. I heard you saying we were moving back to California. I got mad at you. I don't wanna go!" He let out a wail, the likes of which Ryan hadn't heard out of him since his terrible twos.

And he deserved it. He'd pushed Bree away and then he'd sent his kid running off, God knew where. Ryan braced his hands on either side of Wesley and leaned forward until they were touching foreheads.

"If you'd stayed a bit longer, you would have heard your grandmother chew me out for that decision."

"Yeah? *You* got in trouble?" Wesley sniffled, scooching forward to wrap his arms around Ryan's waist and rest his cheek against his father's chest.

"Kinda. It's been a long day, kiddo. What do you say we go home and I run you a hot bath?"

"Big boys don't take baths."

"Big boys that don't want to catch pneumonia take baths."

"Fine. You win." Wesley hung on tight as Ryan hooked his hands under the boy's arms and swung him off the countertop.

They shut down the store and got settled in the car. Ryan drove through town, wipers slapping at the rain that seemed determined to stick out the day. There was a reason why New Englanders called spring "mud season." It was going to coat everything.

"Dad, why were you so worried that Mom had taken me? She's my mother. She would never hurt me, right?"

Ryan always prided himself on being honest with Wesley. Well, with a little leeway when it came to Santa Claus, the Tooth Fairy, and all his imaginary friends. He hated to badmouth the kid's own mother, but it was high time he tell him the straight-up truth.

"Your mom made some bad choices, bud. You know how you felt when Officer Eaton came in? Probably kinda scared and like you wanted to run and keep running until you knew you were safe?"

Ryan kept one eye on the road but watched for his son's reaction in the rearview mirror. He looked thoughtful, a little worried. His nod was quick, jerky.

"Well, you didn't do anything wrong. Now imagine your mom, who knows she has done something that can put her in jail. She must be feeling incredibly desperate. And desperate people do dangerous things. They can't help it, bud. They're scared out of their wits and they just lash out."

"So, she could hurt someone that might be trying to help her?"

The tone of Wesley's voice, more so than the actual question, had Ryan yanking the truck to the side of the road. He turned in his seat to find that Wesley had gone ghost-white. His eyes were wide and he trembled, shaking his head from side to side.

"Wes, what's going on? You need to tell me so I can help. Please." He tried to keep from shouting but his nerves were about to snap. His whole body told him this was bad. This was worse than Haley stealing the money from the sale of the store bad.

"We were trying to help you. Bree said if she could talk to Mom, she could convince her to give the money back. You could buy back the store and we could stay in Scallop Shores.

"I didn't know she could get hurt. Dad, we have to save her!"

Sweet Jesus, Wesley had gone to Bree! Ryan closed his eyes, feeling as though a thousand shards of ice stabbed through his skin. Heart pounding viciously in his ears, he gave Wesley what he hoped was a reassuring smile.

"You know where your mom is, then?"

A small nod.

"And Bree is already on her way there?"

"I was supposed to give her a head start," he muttered shamefully.

Pulling into the nearest driveway he came to, Ryan turned the truck around and headed for his parents' house to drop off Wesley. If Haley touched a hair on Bree's head he was going to strangle her with his bare hands.

Chapter 19

Bree remained in her car, eyes fixed on the one-story brownstone for a full fifteen minutes after she'd arrived at the address Wesley had committed to memory. Her GPS got her there roughly ten minutes later than predicted, but at least the rain had stopped about halfway through New Hampshire. She blew on her icy fingers. She'd turned off the engine as soon as she'd pulled up to the curb, afraid that the exhaust plumes would draw unwanted attention.

The fact that she had rushed off to confront Haley without any kind of solid plan was now starting to filter in. Bree couldn't be sure Ryan's ex was even alone in the house. Willow might be there. Or worse yet, Willow could have a husband, a big brute of a man. With the lies that Haley was sure to have told them, he would be more than happy to rush to the defense of one of his wife's oldest and dearest friends.

But it was too late. She was here now and she had to do something. It was barely two in the afternoon, so chances were pretty good that Willow and her imaginary, muscle-bound husband would be at work. Haley could be hanging out on their living room sofa, counting her ill-gotten cash and watching daytime television.

Bree peered through the windshield. She could detect no movement at the windows. A light was on at the back of the house, in deference to the lack of sunlight that day. Someone was home. With any luck, just the one particular someone she sought.

Now or never. She tapped nervously on the steering wheel and dug down deep for the courage to face this cornered lion. Seriously, it wasn't like Haley would be packing a weapon. If she could just stay clear of the woman's meticulously lacquered talons, she ought to be safe. Right?

Just talk sense into her. Bree opened her car door and stepped out, shutting it as silently as she could. *Convince her that prison orange would not be a good look on her.* Heart beating so hard she worried she might pass out, Bree ducked down when she passed the front windows and slipped stealthily up onto the porch. *Appeal to her sense of right and wrong and the kind of legacy she wanted to leave her child.*

There, that ought to do it. She had a plan. Sort of. Bree blew out a breath and knocked on the door, stepping to the side so there was no way Haley could peer out and see who was there.

When the door opened a crack and Bree saw that it was Haley, she bravely stuck her foot inside and prayed that she could push her way in before Haley removed her foot from her body with a body slam to the door.

"You!" Haley snarled but made no attempt to push her bodily out the door. She leaned out to see if Bree was alone. When she saw that the librarian hadn't brought the cavalry with her she threw up her hands in disgust, turned and walked down a long hall that opened into a small kitchen.

Accepting this as the only invitation she was likely to receive, Bree hurried through the door and down the hall. She worried that Haley might have an escape route in mind with an exit out the back of the house. Though once she reached the doorway to the kitchen, she paused, perplexed. Haley merely settled at a worn kitchen table, wrapping her hands around a mug of tea and stared into its brown depths.

"How did you find me?" Haley didn't sound angry or maniacal. She didn't act desperate or cornered. She just looked exhausted.

"Wes overheard you talking on the phone a few nights ago."

"So where's Ryan then?" Haley kept her eyes focused on the teacup.

For a moment, Bree worried that she had given up her element of surprise. Haley was acting calm now, but that was her shtick, wasn't it? Acting. Bree couldn't let herself fall for anything that might put her in danger.

"He's on his way. I thought maybe we could talk, just the two of us, first."

"Oh, and then we could do each other's nails and braid each other's hair! It will be so much fun!" Without warning, Haley shoved the tea off the table, where it sailed a good two feet before smashing against the tiled kitchen floor.

Bree jumped but remained where she stood, not willing to let Haley know how badly she wished to run back to the safety of her car and hightail it back to Scallop Shores. She watched the other woman with mounting concern. Haley's eyes darted back and forth, like she was looking for the next breakable item to destroy. Maybe this one would be aimed at Bree's head.

"It was always you. He always wanted you. Even my kid likes you better. What is it about you that makes everyone go out of their way to worship at your feet?" The chair legs scraped against the floor as Haley turned to fix Bree with a lethal glare.

"You had no life in high school. You have no life now. And no one seems to mind. They love you anyway.

"I was the best cheerleader in high school. The prettiest girl in our class. I was the one who got that role in the shampoo commercial when I was only six years old! I was born to be an actress. I have everything it takes. Yet no one wants me. Why is that?" Haley's voice had risen to a shrill scream, spittle flying past her thinning lips.

Bree knew she had to defuse the situation. Sidling into the room, she cautiously took a seat across from Haley at the table. Unless the woman chose to pick up her chair and throw it at her, she had no ready weapons with which to harm her.

"You're still the prettiest. I think you're going to make an amazing actress. Those producers are fools for not giving you a chance."

"You think I don't realize you're just placating me? You don't really believe that."

"Oh, yes I do! Haley, you fooled us all. You used your acting ability to con a wealthy businessman into handing you hundreds of thousands of dollars. No one saw it coming. It was flawless."

"Except that you found me." Haley hung her head and Bree was reminded of Wesley in that exact moment.

"The planning and the execution were flawless. The follow-through needed a little work."

"You're going to ask me to return the money but I have to tell you not to bother. And before you go thinking that it's from some selfish attempt to buy my way into Hollywood, it isn't. I am not that shallow, despite what everyone thinks of me."

Bree leaned across the table even as Haley became more distraught. She watched the upset woman's hands clench into fists, then curl into claws before her fingers stretched out rigidly and trembled. She was frightened.

"Tell me the truth, Haley. For once in your life, tell me exactly why you stole the money."

"Ha! And then you'll leave and just let me be?" Haley looked at her, wildly.

A calculating gleam in her eyes had the little hairs on Bree's arms sticking straight up.

"Does Ryan really know you're here?" She reached out and grabbed Bree's fingers in an icy grip. "If I tell you the truth, you would see that I had no choice. You wouldn't have to let him know you'd even seen me. Just go back home to your perfect life, with your perfect man and the perfect child that I was too self-absorbed to hang on to." Her voice cracked.

Heart breaking for the woman who had once had it all, Bree wasn't sure what to say. If she lied and said Ryan didn't know, she could talk a confession out of Haley. If she admitted that he really was on his way, she wouldn't learn anything. But something told her that Haley not only wanted to talk to someone, she needed to. And despite all the hateful things Ryan's ex-wife had done to her over the years, Bree wanted to help.

"What is the money for, Haley?" She put as much empathy and compassion into the smile she slid across the table. *Please let this work.*

"I made a mistake," Haley began, letting go of Bree's hands to stand and pace near the counter by the sink.

Bree followed with her eyes, scanning the counter for knives or scissors, anything that a desperate fugitive might make a grab for if things turned ugly.

"I needed money. God, I always needed money. Like I told Ryan, head shots are expensive. And I had to be seen at all the right restaurants and nightclubs, you know? You can't valet park a Honda Civic, so I had to have the best wheels too. It was so expensive. And I just wasn't making enough to cover it. My parents stopped bailing me out. I think they hate me now. I can't say that I blame them." Haley braced her hands on the counter, her attention focused on the backyard and the houses on the next street over.

"You borrowed money from a loan shark? Someone who wouldn't take no for an answer when you told them you couldn't pay them back?"

"See? You've always been so smart. If I'd been half as smart as you, I wouldn't be in this nightmare right now."

"How much do you owe them, Haley?"

"About fifty thousand, give or take." She shrugged her shoulders, keeping her back to Bree.

"Look, I tried not to do it this way. I really did. I couldn't get a loan from anyone. I even spent my last twenty bucks on lottery tickets. Couldn't even win a damned dollar back. I swear someone's got it in for me or something."

"I'm not entirely aware of how much that gentleman was willing to pay for the hardware store, but I am guessing that whatever he paid you was significantly more than fifty thousand dollars." Bree sighed, standing up from the table and crossing to the sink, where she propped a hip against the counter and forced Haley to meet her eyes.

"This guy, he wants it delivered in person. I only have until March 15th. I was going to wait until things died down a little, pay for a train ticket with cash. Then I could send the rest to Ryan once I'm in Los Angeles." Haley's words were coming out faster and faster the closer she got to the end of her spiel.

Bree just looked at her and waited.

"Okay, so I thought maybe the rest could help me get back on my feet, and then I wouldn't have to ask anyone for help again. I need it, Bree! Please just let me do this. Let me be as successful in my life as you are in yours.

"You have everything. You won. All right? Is that what you want to hear? You won. You're better than me and I admit it. Now please just go back to Scallop Shores and you and Wes make a pact never to speak of this with anyone."

Again, Bree just looked at her. She'd spent almost her entire life feeling inferior and intimidated by Haley. But to see her now, begging and pleading. She was a pitiful shell of the vivacious girl she'd been when they had both fallen in love with Ryan.

"Did you ever love him? Even just a little?" Bree was morbidly curious enough to ask.

"He's a good guy. He deserved more than me. Yeah, I loved him as much as I can love anyone, I suppose. I'm sorry. I took away so many years of your lives together."

"No." Bree shook her head. "We did that to ourselves. You just made it a little easier."

A loud pounding rattled the front door in its frame. Haley squealed, grabbing Bree for comfort.

"Haley Pettridge, this is the police. We have the house surrounded. Come out with your hands up."

Bree reached for Haley's hand and gave it a squeeze. Her heart ached for the woman whose body shook from head to toe. It was time to face the music. Together they walked toward the front hall, hand in hand, hip to hip.

"Bree Adams, are you in the house?" The same deep voice reverberated through the door.

Oh, God, would she be considered an accessory to a crime?

"Yes?" she called back, a bit timidly.

"We're gonna get you out of there, ma'am. Hang tight and we'll get you to safety soon."

"They think I'm dangerous." Haley's whispered giggle held a touch of awe.

"If it's any comfort to you at this point, I came into the house fearing for my life."

"No kidding? Wow, I'm a better actress than even I realized."

Stunning Bree, Haley wrapped her in a tight hug. She could feel the other woman's racing heartbeat and she knew that her real nightmare lay just beyond that closed door. With true compassion, Bree hugged her back, admiring her for the courage it took to hold herself together in what must have been the most terrifying moment of her life. Stepping back, Haley reached for the doorknob, took a giant breath and slowly turned the handle.

• • •

With a beep and the blink of a green light, Ryan swiped the key card and stepped back to let Bree enter the hotel room. It wasn't particularly late and they could easily have made the drive back to Scallop Shores that night, but he was shook up and the thought of not being able to hold her for the entire hour it took to drive back home was pure torture. Besides, they were long overdue for a talk. After all the horrible things he'd imagined Haley doing to her during his panicked ride across the state of New Hampshire, he needed some dedicated alone time with his love.

Ryan had ended up hitching a ride with Chase, once he'd gathered enough wits to involve the police in Bree's recklessly independent investigation. Chief Hanson had called on ahead and alerted the Chester police department of the warrant out for Haley's arrest. So they'd been notified when the police picked up Haley and suggested that Bree follow along and wait for Ryan at the station.

She looked nervous when he showed up, perhaps afraid of how he'd react. She'd just charged into the lion's den and she was worried about what *he'd* think? He crushed her in his arms and kissed every surface of her face, hair, anything he could reach. If he could glue this woman to his side, he'd do it in a heartbeat.

Knowing that his parents were waiting for a call, Ryan whipped out his cell phone and assured them that Bree was safe and Haley had been arrested.

Then Wesley got on the phone, apologizing again for putting Bree, the woman they both loved, in danger. He asked to speak to her, telling his dad he needed to hear her voice to know that she was all right. She was so calm and gracious as she spoke to his son.

"Yes, I am one hundred percent okay, sweetheart. No, your mother didn't try to hurt me." This was said with an arched brow and a steady gaze leveled straight at Ryan. "Listen, you stop apologizing, young man. You saved the day. Your dad is not going to punish you." Another pointed stare. "You take good care of your grandparents and we will be by first thing in the morning to pick you up. I love you, Wes."

Her words gripped his heart, squeezing tight. Tears sprang to his eyes and for the millionth time that day, Ryan wondered what he would have done if Bree had been hurt, or worse. She and Wesley were his world, his tiny, more than self-sufficient world. And she was a rock. The woman had put herself in harm's way—on purpose—and acted as though she'd merely taken a little road trip.

Before they could be on their way, he had to admit to calling her mother in a panic and alerting her to Bree's vigilante mission. Her only reaction was to roll her eyes and sigh as she dug her own cell phone out to reassure her mother that she was just fine. As she spoke to her mom, her eyes never left Ryan. She looked ... amused. He sure as hell didn't get what could be funny about this situation.

"I'm not ready to share you with anyone," Ryan admitted as they returned to Bree's car, parked in the visitor lot at the police station.

"We could get some dinner." She dug her keys from her purse and dropped them in his palm.

"I was thinking more along the lines of getting a hotel for the night." He prayed she wouldn't see this as him taking advantage of the situation.

"Perfect. We need to talk." Her smile was tentative, shy.

They'd swung through a fast food joint on the way to the hotel, but neither of them was very hungry and they threw most of their burger and fries away.

Tossing the key card onto the nearest night table, Ryan wiped his sweaty palms on his jeans. There were only a few times that he'd been this nervous. The championship game against Gorham for the state title. When he knowingly married a woman he did not love. And the day Wesley was born—from the moment Haley went into labor until the time he got to hold his son in his arms and know that he was healthy and perfect in every way. So yeah, it'd been a while.

"Hmm, no mini bar." He drummed his fingers against his thigh as he took a quick look around the room.

"Being alone with me makes you want to consume large quantities of alcohol?" The amused grin returned to her lips.

"Okay, seriously? You aren't just a tad uncomfortable? I mean, I thought we came here to discuss the baby? Our baby." Ryan sat on the edge of the bed, stood up just as quickly and stalked to the loveseat by the window.

"I'm sorry. I don't mean to joke. It's just that I've had a lot more time to process this." Bree slid onto the cushion next to him and reached for his hand, her floral perfume swirling around them both.

"How did you even live?" He turned to her, his grief so close to the surface that he was afraid it would choke him.

She watched him closely, her eyes narrowed, whether in anger or speculation, he couldn't be certain.

"Just so I'm clear, which version are we going with? Mine or Haley's? Because I swear I would never end a life, especially one conceived in love, like our baby was."

"I told you I couldn't believe her. I meant that. It was just a lot of shit to take in and I handled it badly. I should never have tried to process it alone."

"I can tell you, from experience, that is definitely not a healthy thing," she agreed.

"It killed me to think of you having to deal with it all on your own. To know you didn't feel you had a choice in coming to me about the miscarriage. But when I came back to town, couldn't you have told me then?"

Summoning the courage to look up, his heart broke. Gone was the mischievous smile from earlier, replaced with hurt. Her eyes were lined with pain and he could see her revisiting the stinging memories in her head like it had happened yesterday.

"This. This is why." Bree reached up to cup his cheek, her fingers soft and warm against his skin. "How you look right now. Knowing what you must feel." Her hand moved to his chest, right above his rapidly beating heart.

"I tried to protect you from the truth. I *knew* how it felt. I knew how it shaped my entire life and I didn't want that for you. But I was wrong to make that decision for you. You deserved to know the truth. I was working up the courage to tell you. Haley just beat me to it. Well ... sort of."

"About that. How the hell did she ever find out?"

Bree groaned, raising her eyes to the ceiling for a moment before responding.

"I knew I needed to tell you. But you have to understand that this is something I've kept to myself all my life. Even my mother doesn't know."

Whoa. She really *had* been alone in this.

"So I stepped out of my comfort zone and met Cady and Quinn at Smitty's for drinks. I figured if I could practice opening up, telling someone, then I could tell you."

"It wasn't me, though ... that made the opening up part hard?" He hated sounding so unsure, but he had to know.

"You made it, um, distracting." She looked down through her lashes at their hands that had linked together again in her lap.

"I love you. And I love our little angel in Heaven. And because I've been doing a piss-poor job of showing it, I want you to understand right now that I intend to spend the rest of my life showing you just how much you are loved and cherished."

"You're trying so hard and I appreciate that," Bree said but her slight frown told him he was still being unclear.

Ryan smacked a hand to his forehead. He was still doing it. There was only one way to make things perfectly clear. It was time.

He shifted off the couch and knelt before Bree. He dug around in his pants pocket, felt a moment of panic then the butterflies subsided as his fingers wrapped around his grandmother's engagement ring.

"Bree Adams, I can't erase the last thirteen years, nor I am told should I want to. But if you'll have me, I will make the next fifty or sixty the best years of your life. Will you marry me?"

"Is this what Wesley wants too?" Tears rolled down her cheeks as she waited for his answer before she gave him one of her own.

"Wes, my mom, my dad, and probably everyone in Scallop Shores, as well." He beamed.

"Then, yes, of course I'll marry you." Bree pulled him back up onto the couch and kissed the socks off him.

Ryan debated calling their families again, but decided it would be more fun seeing their reactions in person the following morning. Again he lamented the fact that there was no mini bar in their room, though this time because they had no champagne with which to celebrate, not to soothe his nerves.

"You and that danged mini bar. There are other ways to celebrate, you know."

Bree stood up from the couch, crossed to the window where she pulled the drapes shut and slowly made her way to the bed, discarding clothing as she went. Stretching out in the middle of the comforter, she blew him a kiss and crooked a finger, beckoning him to join her. Forget champagne! He liked this idea better. A whole lot better!

EPILOGUE

The Men of Scallop Shores calendar was back from the printer and officially on sale to the public! Bree arranged a party at the library, refusing to allow Cady to cater it because her best friend deserved to be a guest and not the hired help for this special evening. Besides, this night called for champagne, and Cady wasn't licensed to serve alcohol. The stack of calendars on the circulation desk grew smaller and smaller as the night wore on. It looked like her first foray into fundraising was a success.

Dressed in a little black sheath that she'd bought just for the occasion and heels that emphasized her toned calves, Bree was feeling confident and proud. She'd pulled it off. She had put herself out there and the world had not come to an end.

She'd had the models from the calendar form a receiving line as guests first began to enter the library. Now that the party was in full swing, everyone was mingling. The guys were under no obligation to dress up for the party, but she was pleased to see that each one had worn a suit and tie. Later in the evening, they would adjourn to the conference room, where space had been set up for the gentlemen to sign calendars, should they be asked. And by the looks they were receiving already, Bree knew they would most definitely be asked.

"You throw a hell of a party, sweetheart." Ryan flagged a passing caterer and relieved him of two flutes of bubbly, handing one to Bree.

"I'm glad you think so, because we have an amazing wedding to plan." Her smile was as brilliant as the ring she'd worn for a few weeks now.

"I am up for absolutely anything—as long as I get to keep my shirt on." He winked.

"Are you sure? Because I was thinking a beach-themed wedding. You and all the ushers in Speedos?" She couldn't hold back the giggles as Ryan quickly paled.

"Hey, did you tell your beautiful fiancée the good news yet?" Mr. Stevens, the principal at Scallop Shores High, approached the couple, holding hands with his wife.

"He did indeed. He's been acting like an excited school boy since yesterday." Bree smiled warmly at the principal.

Since Ryan didn't have the necessary credentials to qualify as a Phys Ed teacher, the school had given that job to someone else. However, they couldn't deny that he was the best candidate to coach the football team. So they had split the position into two and hired Ryan to take the Wildcats all the way to State.

Now that Pettridge's Hardware Store was back in family hands, Ryan seemed more than happy to take over running it. His mom would spot him during practices and their customers would just have to wait until Ryan and his muscles got back if they wanted something heavy lifted.

Bree smiled to herself as she recalled that for the last few weeks, Bo had insisted on visiting the store on a daily basis. He'd sit in his chair, in the office, working on getting his grip back by picking up the items on his desk. And sometimes he'd just snooze. Hey, it was his store. He could do what he pleased.

Wesley split his time after school between the hardware store and the library. If it was his day at the hardware store, Bree would have dinner waiting when they got home. If he was at the library, it was Ryan's turn to cook. They cleaned up as a family, because it got the job done faster and they just plain enjoyed being together. Bree overheard Ryan speaking to Wesley one night as he tucked the boy in.

"I need you to understand something, Wes. The hardware store is your legacy. It will be yours someday. But it shouldn't define what you choose to do with your life. You are a smart kid, and I know you're going to do incredible things. Find what you love the most and go after it with everything you've got."

"But, Dad, you're running the hardware store and you said you don't love it."

"The store doesn't define me, son. It's only one small part of who I am. I love football. I pursued that dream to the best of my ability. I love Bree and I love you. I'm making us a family and that is everything I need to make my life whole."

The day he let the accounting firm know he would not be back, the family celebrated. And when he'd put his condo on the market, they took Wesley out for ice cream. It was like waking up to Christmas morning every day, and that was something Bree could really get used to.

Slipping away from Ryan, Bree took a small sip of champagne and then gazed around the room. All these people were here to support her fundraising efforts. She'd come a long way in a short few months and each person that had a part in her transformation was in the library tonight. She was a lucky woman.

A few members of the board had taken up position in front of the stairs leading to the children's library. Harold held a plate full of hors d'oeuvres, noshing on a flaky wrapped pastry as Bree approached. She was greeted with broad smiles and pats on the back and shoulder. Yep, she was one lucky woman.

"Well, if it isn't the head of our fundraising department!" Harold said in a booming voice.

"We don't have a fundraising department," she pointed out.

"The board voted on it just this evening, as a matter of fact. Well, most of the board. It would have been a conflict of interest to have you vote on your new position, wouldn't you say?"

"Well, that would be one of her new positions," Martha laughed.

"Yes, yes. Head of the fundraising department and newest member of the library board. Congratulations, you're going to be a very busy woman, Ms. Adams." Harold puffed out his chest, jostling the rest of the food on his plate.

Bree blinked, looking from one face to another, trying to see if she was being pranked. Aside from looking very pleased, no one appeared to be joking around.

"First order of business, if you don't mind my bringing up business during a party ... ?" Harold paused.

She nodded, waiting to see where this was leading.

"We need to replace the computers at each station. They are going the way of the dinosaur, and it's better to get new ones before they just plain go kaput."

"And, naturally, it isn't in the budget to buy new ones this year," Bree finished for him.

"Naturally. So what would you suggest as a fundraising strategy to get the library its much needed new computers?"

Bree smiled mischievously. Her eyes darted about the room, and the makings of a terrific idea began to form.

"Well, the calendar was a great idea. But what if we could top that? What if we did a bachelor auction?"

She may have snagged one of the hottest single guys in Scallop Shores, but there were plenty more left. Tapping her chin, she spotted Foster in the corner of the room. Not too far from him, shy Lucas and artfully tattooed Doyle spoke with a group of senior women from Kittredge Manor. Ah, and there was Riley, her prickly veteran who was more of a teddy bear than he cared to admit. Yes, she could definitely have fun with this new project. The Bachelors of Scallop Shores. Someone for everyone. Bree swallowed the rest of her champagne and went in search of another glass. After all, it *was* her party.

"I'll tell ya what's worse than them stupid geese dressed up in people clothes—" Old Man Feeney jabbed a gnarled finger in the air, waggling it around for effect. "Those plywood cutouts Margie Nixon stuck in her yard of the ladies bent over showing off their bloomers. Downright scandalous!"

Gritting her teeth and glancing around the bakery, Cady did a quick inventory to make sure her customers didn't need an immediate refill of their coffee. She reached under the counter and withdrew an empty jar, setting it on the Formica with a thunk. That garnered a couple of bored looks from several of her elderly customers but they quickly went back to their discussion.

She rummaged through a basket under the cash register and came up with a marker and some Scotch tape. Smiling, she neatly wrote: Cady's NY Dream Fund. Taping the label to the jar, she slid the container toward her regulars sitting at the counter. "There you go, boys. Tip jar. Fill 'er up." She winked at Old Man Feeney.

"Ayuh. Good luck with that, Little Miss Fancy-Britches. I think all your tippers are already in New York City." Feeney and his cronies chortled.

Cady blew out a sigh and rolled her eyes. They were probably right. The people of Scallop Shores were stuck in their ways. They were stubborn. They didn't like change. They didn't do fancy. They cringed at exciting.

She'd been trying to get the morning regulars at Logan's Bakery to try something besides regular drip coffee for almost a year. Mr. Logan had refused to approve the expense of a new espresso machine so she'd gone out and bought one with her own money. Needless to say, it had not been the wisest investment.

Earl Duffy tossed back the last of his caffeine and held the ceramic mug out for more. Like an assembly line, empty coffee mugs were pushed out toward her side of the counter. Dutifully, Cady filled them all and then headed for the display case of pastries. They'd be asking for their second helping of morning sugar now.

"Cady, be a doll and get me another bear claw?"

"I could do with another cheese Danish while you're at it."

Down the line she went, refilling coffee and topping off bellies. It was the same thing every day. Nothing ever changed in this town. So dull. So predictable. Crouching, Cady opened a new box of sweetener packets so she could refill the containers on the counter. The tinkling of the bell over the door signaled a new customer. Deciding to have a little fun with her theory that the town was indeed predictable, Cady called out from her spot on the floor to the woman who came in at this time every morning.

"Good morning, Gladys. Be right with you. How's that hip this morning? I made your favorite today, raisin bran muffins."

The long pause was enough to wipe the smug smile from her face. The snickers from the old men lining the counter had her cringing. Then the deliciously deep voice that told her "I love raisin bran muffins" made Cady want to sink beneath the surface of the old cracked linoleum. Her cheeks hot with embarrassment, she rose on shaky legs and faced her unexpected customer.

"I'm so sorry. I thought you were someone else."

"Clearly."

Once she got a good look at the source of her mortification, she decided it had been well worth it. This man had *city* written all over him. In a room full of flannel and denim, his gray slacks, wool blazer, and perfectly crisp white shirt were a welcome sight. His neatly clipped dark hair and baby-smooth cheeks were a direct contrast to all the buzzards turned to him, their own visages long due for a trim and a shave.

"What can I get you?" Cady asked breathlessly.

"I'd like a soy latte—and one of those raisin bran muffins." He winked. Her heart skipped a beat.

"Look at that, would ya, boys? Someone who's willing to try one of my fancy coffee drinks." Cady smirked at the men who made no effort to hide their curious stares.

"Enjoy it while you can. Who knows when you'll make another?" said one of the regulars.

"Actually," the stranger interrupted, "if it's good, I'll order one every day." He spoke to the men at the counter but kept his eyes on Cady. Mesmerizing green eyes.

Shaking her head to get herself back on task, Cady rushed to fill his order. Her fingers lightly caressed the espresso machine as she poured, packed, and pushed buttons. Working this fancy coffeemaker, inhaling the heady scent of the beans, and listening to the loud whirs and chuffs as it transformed raw ingredients into a delicious hot treat made her happier than she thought possible. Would it kill the rest of the town to give something different a try? Just once in a while?

Her hand trembled slightly as she set the paper cup on the counter. She shook open a tiny paper bag, snagged a muffin out of the case with a pair of plastic tongs, and slipped it into the bag. Folding the top over, she handed it to the gentleman. He reached out, covering Cady's fingers with his own. Truth be told, she'd been expecting the touch, but not the jolt that traveled all the way up to tickle her behind the ears. He held her gaze even after he released her hand. Flustered, she broke eye contact.

"Cady's NY Dream Fund," he read aloud, gesturing toward the pathetically empty tip jar.

She nodded, irritated with the way her body was reacting as she felt her cheeks signaling a second blush-fest. *Stop acting like a ninny. He's just a man.* A gorgeous man who looked like he'd just stepped from the pages of a fashion magazine—or straight out of her fantasies.

Cady's eyes widened as he stuffed the change she'd handed him into the tip jar. He'd just bought a twenty-dollar muffin and latte! A smile crinkling the corners of his eyes, he gave her another wink and turned to go.

"Gentlemen." He called the farewell over his shoulder, the bell tinkling overhead once more.

"Them tourists sure are getting here earlier and earlier every year." Old Man Feeney slowly shook his head.

"No." Cady narrowed her eyes and tapped her finger to her lips, her gaze focused outside on the man stepping into his fancy foreign car. "This one's not a tourist. I'm not sure what his story is, but I'll find out."

• • •

The computerized voice belonging to his GPS chirped that he had arrived at his destination. Burke frowned. He wasn't a "roughing it" kind of guy. Yeah, he wrote for one of the country's leading travel magazines, but he left the sleeping-on-the-ground, no-indoor-plumbing assignments to the more adventurous writers. Give him a five-star hotel any day.

He'd been picturing a cheerfully painted little bungalow. A cute white picket fence surrounding the property. Bright contrasting shutters at the windows and immaculate landscaping. And a shoreline. Or the hint of a shoreline. Where the hell was the Atlantic Ocean?

Slumping down in his seat, Burke made no attempt to leave the comfort of his Lexus GS. He took a sip of the latte cooling in the console. So far it was the only thing the small town of Scallop Shores had working in its favor—a decent soy latte. Okay, that wasn't fair. His mind wandered to the perky townie behind the counter.

It was hard to judge her age, given that her honey-blond hair had been pulled up in a high ponytail. She wore no makeup, which had made her rosy pink blushes even more evident. A slow smile spread across Burke's face. He'd enjoyed putting that blush on her cheeks. The barista, bakery worker, whatever her title, was nothing like the women who normally caught his eye. But he doubted he was going to find sophisticated, polished women who spent hours at the salon in Scallop Shores. So, when in Rome—

Snatching up the white paper bag from Logan's, Burke pushed open the door and unfurled himself from the car. A sickening squelch had him squeezing his eyes shut and muttering a few curses. Not a paved driveway, or even a gravel one. No, his cottage-by-the-sea came with a mud driveway. Charming. Well, he could kiss his leather loafers goodbye.

The magazine was putting him up for the summer. Financially speaking, it wasn't cost effective for him to stay in a fancy hotel for months on end. If there were even such a thing as a fancy hotel in Scallop Shores. He said he'd make do with one of the numerous B&Bs. His editor told him he'd take the cottage and be grateful. Oh, the glamorous life of a travel writer.

Leaving his bags in the trunk for the time being, Burke stepped away from the Lexus and turned in a slow circle. Taking a deep breath, he filled his lungs with clean, fresh air. Pine mixed with the salty tang of the sea. It seemed an odd combination but it worked. It was so quiet out here. Surely that would change, once tourist season was in full swing. But for now, if he listened closely, he could almost hear the trees whispering for him to slow down, take it easy. He shook his head, wondering where this fancifulness came from.

He'd come to Scallop Shores as a favor to his editor. His assignments normally focused on the more metropolitan areas of the world. Meredith had promised he could go anywhere his heart desired if he'd spend tourist season in this little dot on the map she'd discovered a few years back, and had finally convinced the magazine to do a series on. Much as he adored the woman, he'd been fully prepared to hate the town.

There was one street light that he'd counted. Not a single Starbucks, Barnes & Noble, McDonalds, or any other sign of civilization. He knew that going in, having read that the town was zoned as a historical landmark and would not allow any chains to build inside city limits. The reality of it was no less of a shock to his system. If it were possible to go into withdrawal over these modern conveniences, Burke was sure he was experiencing it.

Fumbling for the key that he'd picked up from the realtor in the town-proper, he headed for the weathered front door. He paused to scrape the mud from his shoes before entering the cottage. He'd been expecting a musty, closed-in smell, so he was pleasantly relieved to see the windows cracked open and crisp curtains rippling in the slight breeze. He detected a whiff of lemon—furniture polish, perhaps.

The front door opened directly into the kitchen with a hallway to the right that led to the rest of the house. Burke's tour was over quickly, as there were only three other rooms to explore. The living room was on the other side of the hall. A quick glance out the large bay window revealed tall pines obscuring his view of his neighbor. He shrugged. This was probably a good thing.

One bedroom and a small bathroom were at the back of the cottage. Burke peered into the bedroom, ready to find fault with the tiny room. He arched a brow, nodding his approval at the sight awaiting him from this vantage point. Now, there was the ocean. Sure, it was farther away than he would have liked, but he imagined sunrises and sunsets were spectacular. There was no writing desk in the bedroom and he began to mentally calculate whether or not the beat-up table in the kitchen would fit down the hall and through the narrow doorway. This was where he wanted to write.

And as it did, more often than not of late, thinking of writing brought that niggling sensation of dissatisfaction. Burke wanted to write. He loved putting his thoughts on paper. But travel writing? Working for the magazine? It wasn't his passion. He wanted to write novels.

Not just any old novels, but horror novels. Grinning at the irony, Burke wondered if Maine was big enough for two horror authors. Hopefully his schedule would allow for a weekend sojourn to Bangor to visit the home of master storyteller Stephen King. The man was a legend. Burke would make the time.

Sparing one more glance at the inspirational view of the Atlantic, Burke headed back outside to get his things. It wasn't the Ritz-Carlton, but this was his home for the next few months. Recalling that at least one writer on the magazine's payroll would be sleeping on the cold, hard ground tonight put his own situation in perspective. Provided he could get a latte every morning, and a little time with Blondie Ponytail, it might not be so bad.

Also by Jennifer DeCuir:

Five of Hearts

Praise for Five of Hearts:

" . . a light romance with enough tension to entertain readers."—
Anna Fitzgerald, *InD Tale Magazine*

Drawn to Jonah

Praise for *Drawn to Jonah*:

"The characters in DeCuir's book have drawn me in, enveloped
me in a hug, served me something warm and gooey to eat, and
invited me to be part of their family. Heartwarming, sexy, and a
dash of magical realism makes this book a must buy."—Brooke
Moss, author of *Baby Bump*

"Jennifer DeCuir's writing is as warm and cozy as snuggling up
to a crackling fire on a cold winter's day!"—Laura Marie Altom,
author of *The SEAL's Christmas Twins*

"This book was absolutely amazing . . . I loved the ending and I
highly recommend this book to anyone who wants to read about
love, taking chances and family."—Night Owl Romance

In the mood for more Crimson Romance?
Check out *The Gift of Love*
by Peggy Bird at *CrimsonRomance.com*.